ADAM CRESCENT

AND
THE RISE OF THE RAZORWOLF

ADRIAN EVES

DEDICATION

To Casey, who listened.
To Kendal, who read.
And for BeBe, because you know.
This one's for you.

CONTENTS

CHAPTER ONE

THE PRICE OF FREEDOM

The day was absolutely scorching. Normally, as the day progressed, the heat in the sleepy kingdom of Roddington dwindled to a low intensity; on this particular day, however, the warmth was unnaturally oppressive. At an inactive street corner, the small blacksmith's shop had not managed to escape the savage summer air. The overpowering stench of burning iron kept the few passersby at bay, and in the workshop, an already cluttered heap of metal caused additional discomfort. All sorts of machinery and elaborate contraptions like peculiar spinning racks crowded the small space, and one would have to be relatively nimble to avoid a bump on the head.

Gregor the mastersmith was out on business. Even though the streets were quiet, someone still had to watch the shop. Even in such a sleepy land as Roddington, someone had to be skilled enough to work with metal. Gregor needed to place his trust in someone who could take care of the shop during his leave. Luckily, he had a reliable apprentice.

CHAPTER ONE

Fourteen-year-old Adam Crescent had lived around the blacksmith's shop with the kind mastersmith for as long as he could remember. His personality was in short supply of both awkwardness and angst, for he frequently walked about the shop whistling many a pleasant tune. He knew that Gregor had adopted him, as their features were extremely different. Adam had brown hair, pale skin, and, as he had been told, sparkling sapphire eyes. He was tall and skinny, but he always managed to stand with good posture. Gregor had a stockier build, and his eyes were green and wise. Adam rarely asked any questions about his real parents, because Gregor had answered them long ago.

On this particular day, when he was left alone to tend the shop, there were no new orders for swords. Not even a wayside wanderer came by to peer into the shop. He detested watching the shop whenever Gregor went out on business trips because it was terribly boring. The refinery remained lifeless, and Adam sat on the floor, dozing comfortably against the stone wall of the fireplace. The room was silent, and time in Roddington seemed to trickle by.

At that moment, three loud knocks resounded from the large oak doors at the north end of the shop. Adam nearly fell over in surprise, and then he quickly rose to receive his mysterious visitor. In a couple of wide, excited strides, he dodged the overhead chains and made his way across the room and over to the door, which was protected by a rather large, complex lock. His heart fluttered at the prospect of company.

For a brief moment, Adam fumbled with the apparatus designed by Gregor himself. "Fourteen years and I still have trouble with these blasted things," Adam muttered irritably as he fumbled with rusty cranks and squeaky levers. At last, the elaborate contraption clicked loudly, and the door squealed as it opened slowly.

Another boy of the same age stood before Adam, yet he was taller and much stockier. Adam looked at his guest's angular face, which was covered by long, dirty-blond hair. A pair of hazel eyes stared back into his.

"Well hey, Tyrule," Adam said casually and leaned against the doorframe.

A smile formed on the other boy's face. "Busy day, Adam?"

Adam forced a laugh. "I wish. So what brings you here?"

"Well, I thought I'd drop by and visit. No harm in that, is there?" Tyrule replied sarcastically.

"That's what they say. I'm surprised you aren't being tailed by the normal crowd. Being popular sounds pretty tough."

"It's definitely harder than it looks."

"I don't know. It seemed pretty easy when you were flirting with the gypsies in the market the other day," Adam laughed.

"Oh, don't remind me," Tyrule muttered.

"For the record, I stayed out of the way only to avoid putting you to shame."

"Oh, sure. Just let me in."

Adam pushed the door open even further and backed away to admit his friend. Tyrule put his hands together and offered a mock bow, and then he proceeded to enter the workshop.

As Adam made his way back to the fireplace, Tyrule eyed the shelves with interest. Adam watched with an amused grin, knowing that he could barely contain his amazement. Tyrule looked at a large rack of beautifully crafted swords in awe.

"Hey, Adam," he said, "can I hold one of the swords?"

"I guess," Adam said with a shrug as he took a seat in his familiar spot by the fireplace.

"How great would it be if we actually got to use them one day? Talk about exciting!" Tyrule exclaimed.

"Come on, warrior prince. Now's probably not the best time to go out and raise an army," Adam remarked sarcastically.

Tyrule laughed and said, "Warrior prince? Oh, I'll show you warrior prince."

"I'm trembling with fear."

Tyrule narrowed his eyes. "Mock me all you want, but it all boils down to skill." He removed a sword from the wide rack overhead.

Adam's wide smile quickly disappeared. Tyrule, who took no notice of Adam, swung the shining sword back and forth and felt its weight in his hand. After a couple of labored twists, he pointed the blade at Adam, who merely stood beside him, unimpressed.

"Come on. Just this once," he begged.

Adam looked up and saw Tyrule with the sword in his hand. Challenges had always been his weakness. Adam rolled his eyes and walked over to the sword rack nonchalantly. Making eye contact with Tyrule, he removed a sword from the rack without giving it much attention. He flourished the sword with the speed of an accomplished swordsman and then pointed his blade at Tyrule, who stepped back cautiously. Adam smiled wryly, and his eyes narrowed in the spirit of competition.

"I hope you can keep up with me," Tyrule said in a poor attempt at self assurance.

Adam smirked. "Tyrule, you forget that I've lived with these my entire life. It's you who should be worried." And with that, Adam slid his own blade across Tyrule's.

"We'll see." Tyrule sneered and lunged forward.

Adam countered the strike with unfailing vigilance. Faster than the blink of an eye, he whirled around and swiped at his opponent's feet. Tyrule barely had time to process the attack, and he faltered as he struggled to regain his footing, cursing under his breath.

"Poor form," Adam jeered.

"I'm only getting started," Tyrule retorted hotly and leapt to his feet.

They sparred all over the workshop, ducking under shelves and dodging the hanging sword racks, and their blades resembled silver streaks as they slashed through the air. Adam clearly had the upper hand as he drove Tyrule into a corner.

There was no real object to their duel, so after a time both Adam and Tyrule began to sling their swords around lazily. The sport quickly turned into mere amusement.

"Adam, I have to say that this is the most fun I've had in a long time!" Tyrule laughed as he dodged several stray swipes.

"That's interesting, because I didn't know losing could be so much fun."

Tyrule gaped at Adam indignantly. Seizing the opportunity, he sent a series of thrusts in Tyrule's general direction, who nearly toppled over while trying to block the attacks. While it was clear who the better swordsman was, Tyrule was no amateur: several times, he managed to put Adam on the defensive.

He delivered a wild swing, which missed Adam by an embarrassingly wide margin and came down upon a loose chain. The chain was attached to one of the sword racks, and when Tyrule's blade cleaved it neatly in two, the rack began to spin out of control. The collection of swords fell out of the erratically rotating rack. Adam had little time to attend to this, because he was fending off Tyrule's frenzied attacks.

Tyrule, realizing his advantage, grabbed an end of the broken chain and sailed up into the air as one of the overhead racks came crashing to the floor. He gripped the chain tightly and vanished behind a wide pillar. Adam cried out in surprise when Tyrule suddenly flew out of nowhere and delivered a heavy kick to his chest. Adam stumbled backwards and tripped over one of the many swords that littered the floor.

Breathless, Adam sat upright and raised a hand in the air. "All right, Tyrule, you've won—but only because you're stronger," he remarked irritably.

Tyrule, who landed gracefully after releasing the chain, walked over to Adam. "Well, I suppose," he said, out of breath, "but I still think I'm the better swordsman."

Adam forced a laugh. "Not a chance. Besides, if it were strictly a matter of skill, I'd be the one bragging right now."

Tyrule scoffed in reply and extended a hand toward his friend. Adam reluctantly accepted the gesture, and Tyrule pulled him to his feet with relative ease. Adam dusted all of the rubbish off of his clothes.

"That was fun," Tyrule said.

"Yeah, if you call cheating—"

Suddenly, there was a loud bang, and the two boys whirled around to face the front door. The tall figure of Gregor, clad in black, stormed into the room. His long black hair lay slicked back on his head, and his intense green eyes were fixed on Adam.

"Adam, Adam! Come quick!" he exclaimed.

Adam and Tyrule nearly dropped their swords in surprise.

"What is it?" Adam asked.

"One of the king's men! He'll be here any minute, and—what have you done?" Gregor shouted.

"It was an accident, I swear!" Adam said quickly.

"Accident or not, clean it up fast! Tyrule, what are you doing here? And why are you two carrying swords?"

Tyrule opened his mouth to speak, but he could not put the right words together.

"He was only visiting me," Adam answered.

Gregor regarded the pair with a dubious expression. "A visit?" he said as he bent down to pick up some of the fallen swords.

"Wait, you said one of the king's men was coming. Are we in trouble?" Adam asked.

"No, no. I received a letter a few days ago."

"Well, you made it sound like there was going to be trouble."

"There certainly will be if you don't help me fix this," Gregor warned.

"Can I help?" Tyrule asked.

"Oh, he speaks," Adam remarked.

Tyrule elbowed him in reply.

"Actually, Tyrule, you should probably head home," Gregor said. "Try the back way."

Both boys nodded and walked to the rear of the shop in silence. As Tyrule reached out his hand to clutch the tiny doorknob that opened up to the backroads, Adam stopped him.

"He wasn't supposed to be home this early," he whispered.

Tyrule paused for a moment. "You've got the worst luck," he said crossly.

"I know, I know."

"I hope he doesn't stay angry with me," Tyrule said apologetically.

"You know he won't. Besides, what's the worst he could do?" Adam asked with an innocent shrug.

"Tell my father," Tyrule answered seriously.

"Oh. Right," Adam said and scratched his head. "I forgot about that."

Tyrule nodded. "Well, I'll see you soon. In the meantime, stay out of trouble!"

"You might want to try the same!"

"You know what I mean."

"You have my word," Adam said and placed his hand over his heart.

Rolling his eyes, Tyrule pulled the door open and disappeared outside. The door squeaked as Adam pulled it closed. He slowly walked back into the open shop and spotted Gregor hanging up the racks. From this distance, Adam could not help but admire the wrecked scene before him.

Gregor turned and waved his hand. "Here, come and help me clean up *your* mess," he said.

Obediently, Adam wandered over to his adopted father and grabbed an empty rack.

"Are you mad?" he asked.

"I'm not too pleased, if that's what you're asking."

"We were just having fun."

"Fun? You somehow managed to wreck my shop! *You're* lucky nothing's broken!"

"Well," Adam said sheepishly. "You must not have seen the chain."

"*What?*"

Adam pointed to the pillar where two chain links hung limp against the stone wall. Gregor eyed the ruined contraption, and much to Adam's surprise, shrugged. "It needed to be replaced anyway."

"You're impossible," Adam remarked.

"Highly improbable, perhaps, but not impossible."

"What does that even mean?"

Gregor paused and thought it over for a moment, then he turned to Adam. "I have no idea."

A grin tugged at the corner of Adam's lips. "So how was business?"

"Same as usual. I sold a few swords, but that's about it."

"Did you meet anyone interesting?"

"You ask me that question every single day," Gregor said with a laugh. "Why? Are you expecting someone?"

"You know I'm not. It's just that everyone's so boring."

"That's not very nice."

"Well, it's true! Our whole kingdom is like this! It's almost as if everyone is sleepy all the time."

"I've never noticed," Gregor remarked.

"Well I have. I wish we could sail away to somewhere more exciting."

"Roddington is the only land that exists," Gregor said slowly.

"I know they all say that, but how do you really know?"

Gregor paused for a moment and a confused expression grew on his face. "I can't remember why."

"You're not that old yet," Adam teased.

"I'm getting there. So, did you win?"

"Did I win what?"

"Your duel with Tyrule."

Adam smiled. "No. But that's only because he didn't play by the rules."

"Well, get him next time. Pick up that last set, and then we'll wait for our visitor. I bet you it'll be a page. They usually deliver the messages."

Adam nodded and began gathering swords in his arms. When his hands became full, he deposited the weapons in an empty rack. Seconds later, several heavy knocks resounded through the empty air. He looked at Gregor in anticipation.

"Perfect timing," the mastersmith remarked and marched over to the front door.

Gregor disengaged the locks in a matter of seconds, and Adam noticed that it was a practice acquired only through years of experience. He threw the doors wide open, and Adam gawked at the figure in the doorway. A man dressed in armor from head to toe dominated the scene. Only his stern, muscled face was visible.

"Well, you're not a page," Gregor noted with amusement.

The massive knight turned to Gregor and spoke in a voice that matched his demeanor. "Now is not the time for jokes."

Gregor nodded quickly. "Right, my apologies. Would you care to step inside?"

"This won't take long. I need a sword," the knight grumbled.

"And I'm assuming it's for you."

"You assume incorrectly. It is for King Philip. Prince Nicolas is throwing a special celebration in honor of the king's fiftieth birthday, and he wants to give him a sword."

"I'd be glad to make it."

"That won't be necessary."

"And why is that?" Gregor asked with a raised eyebrow.

"He wants your boy to craft it."

Both the knight and Gregor turned to face Adam, who could not believe his ears. He stepped forward and glanced quickly at a confused Gregor, and then he settled his attention on the knight.

"You want me to do it?" Adam asked.

"Yes. It is a great honor."

"And it's for the king?"

"Yes."

Adam felt the color drain from his face, and his heart sank. "When do you need it?"

"You have four days."

"*Four days?*"

"That should be ample time."

"But what if I can't make it in time?"

The knight took a step closer to Adam. "Prince Nicolas thought that might be an issue. The way I see it, if you don't succeed, then everyone will remember your failure for many decades to come. The prince has another idea. If you do not make this sword, then you will be thrown into the dungeons for the rest of your life."

Adam swallowed fearfully.

"You can't do this! He's only a boy!" Gregor protested.

"I cannot, but the prince can do whatever he likes."

"Please let me help!" he pleaded.

"If you assist the boy in any way, then you'll spend the rest of your days in the dungeons as well."

"But why Adam?"

"I can only assume that the prince wants to use him as a symbol of youth, or perhaps he wishes to test the boy's abilities for something even greater. Now, I must return to the castle. Four days, boy. If you fail, the only thing you'll be making are scratches on your cell wall," the knight said sternly.

Adam nodded in reply, his eyes glued to the knight's feet.

"Adam?" Gregor prompted.

He did not reply.

"See to it that he finishes," the knight said.

He regarded Adam and Gregor once more before turning around and marching off. Gregor slammed the doors closed after the knight left and turned to his adopted son.

"Adam?" he repeated.

But Adam was not listening. He stared in fear at the spot where the knight stood only moments ago, trapped in the wake of inevitable doom.

CHAPTER TWO

A WORLD WITHOUT MAGIC

"We can't just sit here! I won't stand for this!" Gregor paced nervously back and forth around the shop as Adam weighed a metal rod in each hand.

"Like it or not, there's no choice," Adam said.

The mastersmith turned and faced Adam with an alarmed expression. "Do you really believe that?"

Adam looked up at his father. "Of course there's always a choice. I'm just taking the one that doesn't involve prison cells."

"If I could only provide a little assistance," Gregor said and headed towards Adam.

Adam pointed a metal rod towards him like a large finger, and his eyes were deadly serious. "No. You heard what the man said. It's got to be me. Besides, I'm not going to cheat at anything."

CHAPTER TWO

Glumly, Gregor turned away and began pacing even faster. The silence surprised Adam because his father always seemed to have a sentiment of advice ready for any occasion. *Why should this instance be any different?*

Shaking his head, Adam returned his attention to the task at hand. At the moment, he was deciding between two very different pieces of metal. One was made of traditional iron, and the other was a unique steel that Gregor had designed. His resources were severely limited, and the stakes were far too high to venture out and find more supplies.

"Which one should I use?" he asked, scratching his head.

"Which one of what?" Gregor replied, turning his head.

Adam held out the rods in reply.

"Well, seeing as the king is going to be fifty, I'd go with something more traditional."

"So the iron then?"

Gregor nodded firmly.

After carefully placing the iron rod into the refinery, Adam donned his dirty apron and bulky goggles, which made him appear somewhat owlish. He turned to a nearby shelf and snatched away a blackened mallet. As he watched for the metal to change color, he spun the handle along his skilled fingers over and over again. When the metal glowed a soft ruby hue, he tugged on his heavily-insulated gloves. At last, when the iron went from a burning orange to a blazing-hot white, Adam grabbed a nearby pair of tongs and tossed the metal on the worn anvil. The metal landed upon the hard surface with a boisterous clatter.

"Careful!" Gregor warned.

Adam made eye contact with him for a split second, which was enough to make the mastersmith turn away and return to his nervous activity. Tossing the tongs aside, Adam reached for the mallet and stared down at his project. Suddenly, he slammed the tool into the searing surface and turned his head to dodge the stray sparks that shot upward.

Bang! Bang! Clank!

Again and again, he delivered stroke after stroke with equal precision. The heat rising up from the forge seeped into the cracks of his eyewear and stung his weary eyes, making concentration difficult. He narrowed his eyes to slits as he swung again and again. Without warning, the searing hot piece of metal screeched loudly.

Adam stepped back for a moment to assess his work. The stress of the task at hand was beginning to encroach upon him. With casual orders, Adam performed just fine; the request was made, and he would deliver the expected results. This time, however, was proving to be quite a challenge. That unquenchable thirst to prove himself burned deeply within his mind, and he saw each failure as his own ineptitude. Not to mention that he certainly did not want to live in a cell for the rest of his life. Gregor's presence did not make things any easier, and his silence tortured Adam. He longed for a golden piece of advice that would ease his troubles, but the reality was sickening. Advice could not help him now.

Adam squinted again as the rod began turning orange. Gently, he tapped the rod back and forth across the anvil to restore the heat. When the iron had turned white once more, he resumed beating it into the anvil. At first, it seemed as if the strikes bounced off uselessly, so Adam furrowed his brow with concentration swung the mallet into the metal with full force. Finally, a section of the molten-hot metal gave way and took the shape of the blunt hammer's head.

Feeling a glimmer of hope rise within his chest, Adam watched vigilantly, because creating the correct impressions was vital to the craft. He swung again and again, watching as the metal's surface yielded to the pressure of the hammer and became flatter.

Yes! Adam thought to himself. *This is it!*

His heart raced at the thought that he was nearing the end. Watching closely for impurities, Adam timed his strikes with a trained eye. Indeed, it was beginning to look more and more like a sword with every resounding blow. His excitement reached a peak when the vertical line dividing the blade became visible.

Suddenly, Adam's grip loosened and created a blemish along the divider. The nearly perfect line now had an unsightly indentation smudged along its surface. He gasped sharply, and he paused for a split second. Nothing else happened, and he let out a small sigh.

Not a problem, Adam thought quickly. *I can fix this.*

At once, he began flattening the edges surrounding the flaw. For a moment, it seemed as if everything would be fine. With each strike, the edges began to even themselves out neatly, and the raised line became visible once more.

Suddenly, the metal shrieked loudly, and the rod snapped in two pieces.

Angrily, Adam smacked away both fragments onto the floor with the mallet, which he slammed down upon the anvil with equal fury. He aimed a swift kick at the wall behind him and stormed to and fro with a furrowed brow, his toe throbbing in pain.

"Why don't you let me prepare the rod. It's difficult, I know," Gregor offered.

"No! I've done it a hundred times before! This is embarrassing," Adam scowled.

"It was an honest mistake."

"No, it was a careless mistake!"

Gregor walked over to him. "Then be more careful with the next one."

"The next one? What happens if I break that one? We will have nothing left! You know what that means, don't you?"

"If that one breaks, then we can gather scrap metal and make a hybrid. They won't know the difference."

"They're the highest authorities in Roddington. They will notice!" Adam spat.

Gregor held out a hand. "Enough. I'm going to leave you alone for a while. Do yourself a favor and use the time to blow off some steam. You can't work properly if your emotions get in the way."

Adam nodded gruffly, and Gregor marched quickly through the double doors and out of the shop. Alone at last, Adam removed his goggles and wiped the soot from his face. The blazing coals in the refinery crackled hungrily, and he stood rooted to the spot, mesmerized by the glowing display.

His growing discomfort could only be matched by the ever-rising heat level in the room. The sooty clothes he wore clung to his slender body as if someone had plastered them there. His brown hair unfurled itself in an unsightly, dilapidated mess. All in all, Adam would hate to have someone wander into the shop and catch a glimpse at his miserable form.

As luck would have it, there came a sharp rapping from the door that Gregor left only moments ago. Adam swore under his breath and cursed his luck. "Come in," he shouted, doing his best to hide his rising temper.

One of the doors creaked open slowly, and a wave of light blinded Adam. Squinting, he discerned a crooked figure hobbling towards him. When the door suddenly slammed shut, Adam's vision wavered and adjusted slowly until the hunched man stood plaintively in the center of the shop. His aged, black eyes scanned the room methodically, and at last his gaze settled on Adam himself. A snakelike grin emerged across his features.

"So you're the mastersmith's boy?" he asked in a cracked voice.

"I am," Adam answered.

The stranger nodded with a bizarre sense of enthusiasm. "*Good.*"

Adam did not know what to make of the curious remark, so he shuffled about in discomfort.

"Well, you're awfully quiet," the man said.

"Just one of those days," he lied and shrugged.

The old man nodded slowly.

"So, do you need a sword? Anything?" Adam asked.

"I have no need for a sword. I require your services alone," the old man said.

"Look, I'm already busy with the prince's demands. You'll just have to take a number."

"I'm afraid it's just not that simple, Adam."

Adam stared at the man quizzically. "How do you know my name?"

Steepling his fingers, the stranger grinned incongruously at him. "Common knowledge, you could say."

"But it's not."

The stranger merely shrugged. "Call it what you wish. I'm not here to talk about myself, no matter how little I know. I'm here for you."

"Well, if you're really here for me, let's start with a name. Have you got one?" Adam asked.

"Mustafo," the man answered through crooked teeth.

"Well, if you don't want a sword, what do you want?"

A wholly serious demeanor fell over the old man. "Do not make the king's sword."

"I don't quite understand."

"It's simple. Don't make the sword. These people are not who you think they are."

"Who are you referring to?"

Mustafo shifted his weight uncomfortably. "This isn't easy for anyone, least of all, a teenage boy."

Adam scratched his head. "I have no idea what you're talking about."

"That's because no one else knows."

A strange kind of silence drifted between them for several moments, during which Mustafo would not let Adam escape his forlorn stare. His dark eyes were unnaturally youthful, but they also gleamed with a hint of secrecy.

"And you've discovered something," Adam finally said.

"Only what I have been allowed. Roddington has many secrets," he answered mysteriously.

"I highly doubt that. This place is as sleepy as it gets."

"Exactly!"

Adam stared at Mustafo with an eyebrow arched. "Well, what does that have to do with anything?"

"Everything! You are surrounded by lies. And I know how to uncover the truth," Mustafo said darkly.

"I don't think that's right. You've got the wrong guy."

"I don't like your attitude. Now, listen to me, because what I have to say is important. I know of things you wouldn't encounter in your wildest dreams," Mustafo snarled.

Nodding quickly, Adam said nothing in return.

"Now that's much better. There is a great evil at work here in the land of Roddington," Mustafo began.

"Evil?" Adam asked.

"A darkness. A darkness that everyone else cannot see through. I can't even see through it completely. My memories are damaged, and my past is lost. There is one person who can see the light, and I've found him."

"Who?"

"He's sitting before me."

"Me?" The sudden realization felt like a punch to the gut. Adam felt surprised, albeit wary, that Mustafo had placed him on such a high pedestal, even if it was for a string of unusual mind games.

Mustafo nodded. "I only remembered your name. That's how I found you, boy. Your name is the only piece of my past I have left. I know it's part of a great mission."

"I don't know. I'm just like anyone else around here," Adam said.

"Oh, but you're not. What do you know of your parentage?" Mustafo asked.

"Nothing. Gregor took me in."

"Interesting," the old man said and folded his long fingers together.

"I don't understand any of these questions," Adam said bluntly.

"I didn't expect you to. As I said earlier, an evil rests upon Roddington that no one can realize."

"Is the kingdom becoming more dangerous? Do they have secrets?" Adam asked.

"No. The kingdom is the least of our worries. It's the people who hide in the shadows that I fear."

"Then what is this evil, and when did it start?"

"No one knows when it began. Not even me. But I know now, after many years of meticulous searching, what endangers our world."

"What is it?"

"Magic."

Mustafo's dark, unblinking eyes hovered over Adam with an ominous intensity. Adam struggled under the weight of the old man's scrutiny. No one spoke for a while, and he looked to the floor.

"But magic doesn't exist," Adam finally said.

"Or so we've been led to believe."

"Even if it was real, how could someone make an entire land unaware? That's impossible."

"Indeed. Therefore, someone had to pay a hefty price," Mustafo answered.

"Something of that magnitude would have to be enormous," Adam noted.

"Correct. Someone paid a great price to ensure that no one in Roddington would ever speak, feel, hear, see, or know magic ever again. The only thing stronger than magic is—,"

"Magic," Adam breathed.

Mustafo nodded. "Perfect."

"So you're telling me that somebody stole all of the magic in Roddington. And not only that, but everyone who finds out about it gets quietly killed by a stranger. That seems a bit farfetched."

"You're not so clear on the details."

"Then explain."

"Very well," Mustafo said. "Many years ago, before you were born, there lived a terrible soul. I don't know who he was, but I have my suspicions. This man lived when magic was common to all, but he was consumed by power. Thus, when all of Roddington rested, he schemed tirelessly for a way to consolidate power into his own two fists. To take away the powers of everyone would not be enough. People would be angry, and the murder attempts would become a daily threat. With these powers, he needed to erase it from their minds. Magic, it seemed, would be lost to anyone but him.

"This task, however, required a great deal of sacrifice on his part. In order to hide the evidence, magic would have to be locked away entirely. Thus, our man is living among us as a seemingly normal human being."

"What did this man do exactly?" Adam inquired.

"I believe that all of Roddington is under a powerful curse. There are two people who know completely of its power. The one who created it, and the one who is destined to break it."

"Oh, me," Adam remarked.

"Absolutely. Which is why you musn't make the sword for your king."

Glancing over at the rod in the rack, Adam hesitated. "But the consequences are so much greater."

Mustafo shook his head. "No, they're not. As long as you are in prison, you're safe. It can buy us some time until you are ready to accept your role. I can think of something."

"Mustafo," Adam began. "You said that you had your suspicions as to who this man really is."

The old man merely nodded.

"I want to hear them."

"Well, it is only logical to realize that he traded his power for a lofty place in our society."

"It's not King Phillip, is it?" Adam asked fearfully.

"Definitely not. He is far too noble to lay a curse upon anyone."

"I say it's the prince, then. He seems like a dodgy one."

"I disagree. Being prince would be a disadvantage for him. No, I believe he is a figure of high influence."

"Like one of the Nobles?"

"I wholeheartedly think so. Only one comes to mind," Mustafo whispered.

"Well, I don't know of any nobles who would be twisted enough to dabble in sorcery," Adam said.

"I believe our man is none other than Alimzar Ramsgate."

Adam froze. "That is a very serious accusation."

"It's a serious curse," Mustafo countered.

"You do realize that his son happens to be my best friend," Adam said slowly.

Mustafo smiled in spite of himself. "It makes perfect sense now that I think about it. He uses his boy to get to you. Smart man."

Adam suddenly whirled around and shot the old man an icy glare. "If you think for a second that Tyrule is the son of some villain, think again. Now, I think you can show yourself out," he growled.

"The signs are all clear. You just need to put your preconceived notions aside," Mustafo remarked.

"I don't think you quite understood me. I said get out."

"If you need more proof, I live on a house on the outskirts of the town."

"*Get out.*"

Mustafo smirked at Adam and strode over to the back door. Taking one last look at the blacksmith shop, he placed a bony hand on the door handle. "I think I'll let myself out here. Wouldn't want to draw too much attention to myself," he muttered. When he heard the door creak and click shut, Adam turned around. The old man was nowhere in sight.

The encounter with the odd man made his blood boil, but Adam realized that he could not afford to dwell on any of Mustafo's preposterous claims. As he briskly walked over to the anvil, a soft knock made its presence known right as he reached for the mallet. Rolling his eyes, Adam begrudgingly marched within earshot of the front doors. "Come in," he spat irritably.

As soon as the words left his mouth, he wanted to recall them immediately, because the visitor did not wait for his permission before entering. This person was not here for business or tall tales. Adam's visitor was, in fact, a girl. She wore an emerald gown without sleeves that hung about her ankles. There was a daring gleam ignited in her sparkling hazel eyes when she regarded Adam, and her golden hair lay freely over her shoulders.

"You seem pretty upset about something," she remarked.

Adam looked up at his guest, his face tinted pink with embarrassment.

"Leira, I didn't see you there," he said.

"Of course you didn't. I was outside of the shop."

He could not help but smile in amusement. "Right. So what are you doing down here? And why are you so dressed up?"

"Oh, this thing?" Leira said and gestured to her gown. "I'll be wearing this to King Phillip's Banquet, or whatever it's called. My mother and I finally agreed on this one. I think it's pretty decent for a change."

"I agree."

"I was nearby, so I thought I'd drop by. Now, don't avoid my question," she said pointedly.

"Well, I've been trying to forge the king a sword."

"Don't you usually forge a bunch of swords? Why do you look so frustrated?"

"It's not that simple. There's a lot of pressure to get this done right."

"Well, just ask your father to help," she suggested.

"He can't."

"Why?"

"I was given very specific orders: work alone to make the sword or rot in the dungeons."

"Oh. Ouch."

"Yeah," he said. "Ouch."

The two of them exchanged amused grins. Adam scratched the back of his head.

"Well, you want to talk about it?" she offered.

He shook his head in reply. "There's not really much to say."

"So, what'd you have for breakfast?"

Adam shot her a funny look, and she shrugged in reply. "What kind of question is that?"

"I dunno. A stress-free one."

"Interesting. To answer your question, nothing. I had nothing."

"That's probably not the best idea."

"Well, I've had a lot on my mind."

"Haven't we all?" she remarked.

Leira made her way over to the fireplace and sat down in Adam's familiar spot. Noticing the shock on his face, she merely shrugged and examined her fingernails. Adam leaned up against a wall in resignation, and she laughed softly.

"Leira, can I ask you something?"

"Go ahead."

"Do you believe in curses?"

She paused for a moment. "As in ugly talk?"

"No, like magic stuff."

Her eyes regarded him blankly. "There's no such thing as magic. Anyone who says otherwise is lying."

"Okay," he said.

"If you're making the king a sword, I hope you got an invitation to the ceremony."

"Yes, I did actually."

Leira clapped her hands happily. "Brilliant! You can sit with Tyrule and me!"

A knowing smile came over Adam's features as he looked down at her. "You and Tyrule, eh? That ship hasn't sailed yet?"

She turned her scarlet face away from him. "That *ship* just happens to be a very real possibility."

"Oh really? Since when?"

"Since he asked me to be his guest at the celebration."

"And he asked you when?" he asked.

Leira turned a soft shade of pink. "Just the other day."

"So it's quite recent," he said as he walked over to the workbench.

"It's not that recent," she said indignantly.

Adam nodded his head and reached for the large chest that lay in the middle of the surface. He threw open the lid and jammed his hand inside of the box, searching blindly for a new mallet because his eyes were fixated on Leira's mirthless features.

"Recent is a subjective word," he trifled.

"Say what you want. It's progress," she scoffed.

"At least one of us is moving along."

"We both know you'll get there."

"But you *are* important," Leira said reassuringly.

Adam smiled and said, "Aw, thanks. What brought that up?"

"Why else would they pick you?"

Another answer, a response she could not have anticipated, formed in Adam's mind. He thought of Mustafo and his curse theories, but a firm shake of the head wiped away all doubt. Leira laughed softly. "What's with the head shake?"

Adam blinked twice. "Oh, nothing. I was just lost in some weird thought. But to really answer your question, I suppose Roddington has run out of useful smiths. I'm probably the last resort."

She raised an eyebrow. "You know that's not true."

He shrugged in reply. Leira clapped him on the back with a bit of extra force. Adam coughed loudly and noted the satisfaction that shone through her hazel eyes.

"What was that for?" he asked.

"Don't question my methods, Adam Crescent," she said lightly.

"I question your madness, which has nothing to do with your methods."

"And there's always a method to the madness."

"Whatever," Adam breathed in resignation.

"I always win," she said gleefully.

Rolling his eyes, he closed the lid and made his way over to the refinery, where he gently placed the silver mallet on the anvil's head. Leira looked at the instrument with obvious interest.

"This one," Adam said, noting her attention, "is a special mallet that Father himself designed. He created a sort of hybrid-metal, I guess you could call it, that won't take much of an impression from the average set of tools. The only piece of material I have left happens to be one of these, so I've brought out the special mallet."

Nodding slowly, she said, "Will it turn out to be silver like the others?"

"Actually, no. If anything, it will be gold."

"A gold sword? That sounds really neat," she said.

"Well, we wanted the traditional silver, but I broke all of the silver rods."

Leira smiled brightly. "Maybe that just means you're meant to make it gold!"

"You think so?"

"I don't see why not?"

"So you believe in luck, but not curses," Adam noted.

"Luck is fun. Curses are rubbish."

"You're probably right," he admitted.

Neither of them said anything for a while. Leira turned her head and surveyed the shop, and Adam nervously tapped the mallet's head against his palm.

"So you will come?" she suddenly asked.

"Come where?"

"To Tyrule's house, of course!"

"Oh, oh yeah. I probably will," he answered.

"That's only if you get this done. It must be pretty difficult. You know, having to provide perfection to the highest authority in all of the land." She looked at him with a mischievous expression.

"Yes, and your saying that didn't really help."

"Sorry," she replied with a shrug.

"Anyway, I'm doing a miserable job of it. I am not the mastersmith. I'm just some kid. They should just brace themselves for a failure. I don't really fancy the idea of the dungeons."

Leira patted him gently on the shoulder. "You're overworking yourself. Listen, I've seen some of the things you've made. They're really good. Don't let anyone overwhelm you. Just keep trying, and I'm sure everything will be fine."

"That's nice of you, but what if this sword doesn't work out?" Adam asked.

"It will work. In the extremely unlikely case that it doesn't, well, that would be really unfortunate. Perhaps we could get Tyrule's father to help."

"Leira, I've only got about a day left to finish the sword. I can't afford to make any more mistakes. No one can pick up the slack for me. You know that."

"Adam, will you stop worrying already? You will make it correctly. I have faith in you, so why don't you? You'll get it, *I promise*! Anyway, I should really get going. Mother's going to murder me when she finds out that I skipped the trip to the market!" Leira rushed out of the workshop, her long blonde hair in a crazy swirl behind her.

Adam waved to her as she left, and she waved back right before the door slammed shut. He looked back at the mallet in his hand and thought about their conversation. For some reason, the anvil did not seem as daunting as before. Her words lingered in his mind, and he realized that she was telling the truth. Without hesitation, Adam picked up one more rod and placed it in the heat. He clasped the hammer firmly in his fist and looked down upon the forge with a renewed sense of mastery. He raised the hammer up to eye level once the rod turned white-hot. As he brought it down with a mighty swing, Adam felt a surge of confidence rise up from within him.

CHAPTER THREE

ROOFTOP RUN

The following day was exactly the breath of fresh air that Adam so desperately craved. With the dilemma of the sword out of the way, he could finally relax. Even doing the chores he normally despised came as a great relief. Gregor, who closed the shop to give his son some freedom, appeared genuinely pleased at the finished product. Unlike most swords, the blade was golden in hue, and it looked like a weapon only nobility would carry.

For the most part, all Adam really wanted to do was get some sleep and rest for the big day. Of course, his hopes proved to be unrealistic, because Gregor continually hounded him about proper attire. In the end, though, both agreed on one of Gregor's old traveling suits, a garment he wore as a young man.

When the day of the ceremony finally arrived, Adam rose earlier than usual and carefully put on the suit, which consisted of a snow-white shirt, black pants, and a cobalt jacket with golden fringes and buttons. Upon seeing his reflection, he did a double take and stared at the charming boy in the glass. Adam was so caught up in his appearance that he failed to notice the footsteps trailing into his bedroom.

"Well, don't you look dapper?"

Adam whirled around and spotted Gregor leaning against the doorframe, his face aglow with amusement.

"Thanks," Adam breathed.

"Represent us well today."

He smiled and answered, "Don't I always?"

Gregor shrugged. "Don't you?"

"I try, at the very least."

"Good. So, I had the strangest dream last night," Gregor said.

"Which was?"

He shifted his weight to his feet. "It was a memory actually. I wouldn't have been able to recall it any other way."

"I'm not going to know unless you tell me."

"No, I can't imagine that you would. It was actually how you came to me in the first place."

Adam froze for a moment. Could Gregor possibly remember something about his parents? Adam learned early on that his father, the man who adopted him, had little information on his origin.

"About my parents?" he asked.

"Possibly. There was only one person though. A man. Anyways, he knocked on my door one night, and asked that I take you, which was really odd. He must have known somehow that I've always wanted to raise a child. My wife, died about two years before you came along, as you know. I took you in this house without a second thought. Now, this man didn't say much, no unnecessary questions, but he did tell me something. Before

30

he left, he just said, 'it's urgent,' and left. I didn't ask anything of him, nor did I follow him. I had what I wanted, and I was happy. I don't know how I could have forgotten that. Must be old age," Gregor said and rapped a fist lightly against his head.

The account was one Adam had heard many times before with one exception. He never knew that a sense of urgency hovered above the scenario. For a moment, the prospect excited him. He realized that his parents were in a hurry, and a child would only be a detriment to their safety.

"Do you know who my parents are, then?" he asked.

Gregor scratched his head. "I have no idea. If I did, I would have tried to find them. I know what it's like to grow up without parents."

Adam nodded and stared at the ground. There was another possibility, but it was just too farfetched.

"I should probably get back in the shop. You need to finish getting ready. Things are starting to get busy outside. I'm so proud of you," Gregor said and stepped towards Adam.

Father and son embraced one another warmly, and Gregor finally stepped away and disappeared through the doorway. As Adam watched him leave, an unsettling feeling rose in the pit of his stomach. It was as if a sense of dread, a mundane finality, followed Gregor into the room. He shook his head forcefully and began searching for his black dress-shoes.

He found the old pair of shoes under his bed and slipped them on quickly. Once more, he stopped in front of the mirror just to smile at his pristine reflection. Satisfied, he raced into the kitchen and grabbed a red apple. Adam stood in a corner as he ate the fruit as quick as he could. When he was finished, he tossed the core into the rubbish bin and hurried to the shop, which took up half of the house.

A wave of relief washed over him when he spotted the open case lying on the workbench. He walked over to the bench and looked down at his handiwork. After many attempts, Adam finally made a near-perfect sword. For a weapon, it possessed an aura of artistry. After he was done admiring his creation, he reached across the bench for the case's lid. Adam stole one more glance at the sword in the violet fabric before closing the box tightly. Grabbing the case, he walked briskly towards the large double-doors. A withered satchel hung from a hook on the wall. Adam snatched it away and jammed the case inside before slinging the pack over his shoulders. Exhaling sharply, he marched out of the doors with conviction.

The second he stepped foot on the road outside, Adam had to hop backwards to avoid being trampled by horses. The traffic to the castle congested the street as far as the eye could see. To make matters worse, Adam needed to move against the flow in order to reach Tyrule's house.

Even though the crowd was moving away from where he wanted to go, Adam had another plan up his neat sleeves. While the others jostled past one another, Adam slipped back into the alley behind his house. The building next door had a crudely constructed wall, and several of the bricks protruded from the surface. Many times before, he scaled the bricks and made it up to the rooftops, a world of its own. In this case, he realized, the rooftops would be his only surefire way to make it to Tyrule's on time.

Adam slung the case over his shoulder, rolled up his sleeves, and clasped the nearest stone his hands could find. Not once did he glance down, but he gazed upward and moved with the grace and proficiency of an expert. Besides his work in the forge, Adam felt his toned physique could only be attributed to his frequent climbing excursions. The wall towered over the small, crowded street, and people would normally spot a boy trying to make his way to the roof; however, everyone frantically hustled towards the castle, leaving Adam free to do as he wished.

At last, he exhaled sharply as he heaved his body onto the roof. His feet scraped against the red tiles when he stood at full height. Dusting the dirt off of his trousers, Adam peered into the distance and observed the titanic castle behind him. Even from where he stood, he could easily spot the serpentine line of people and horse-drawn carriages spiraling into the castle gates.

The azure skyline behind the grand castle extended beyond the vast horizon and over the expansive sea. Adam turned his head and looked back at the sprawling mass of architecture before him. The entire land of Roddington was one enormous city, which made navigation confusing at times. A bell tower chimed from the distance, and Adam checked the satchel to secure his precious cargo. After slinging the pack over his shoulder, he inhaled slowly and closed his eyes for several moments. Suddenly, his vivid blue eyes flew open and he leapt forward.

The warm air cradled him for a moment, then his feet landed on the next rooftop with a dull crunch. He broke into a brisk jog, his focus directed forward, the familiar russet tiles clicking under each step. The buildings in the marketplace were spaced far apart, so Adam had to be creative. Many of the roofs were joined by fabric canopies, and most of the buildings were at different heights. Adam hopped on one such canopy and slid down onto the next rooftop. One-by-one, he bounced, slid, or ran up the taut fabric and covered substantial distance. Most of the people below were too preoccupied with the trip to pay him any attention.

As the marketplace scene melted into a residential area, the buildings gradually grew taller. After years of practice, finding obscure footholds and foundations was second nature to him. The climbing was rigorous, but his frequent excursions kept him in excellent shape. The houses were closer together than the market shops, and Adam found himself hopping along in short intervals.

Far ahead, he spotted a gap among the rooftops where a wide road cut through the neighborhood. Usually, Adam would climb down and simply cross the street. On that particular day, though, the street teemed with several horse-drawn carriages, all of them looking like miniature replicas from Adam's lofty height. Looking down, Adam spotted a rope near his feet that connected to another house across the street. With no other plausible options, he bent down and tugged at the cord. When it was clear that it was secured tightly, he grabbed the rope with both hands and slid off of the roof.

Most passerby were not accustomed to watching a boy dangle precariously overhead, but the few that were merely scowled and continued on their way. He shimmied quickly, but deliberately, along the rope. The height did little to bother him, but the occasional glance at the astonished passengers made him anxious.

"Oi! You there!" a deep voice shouted from behind him.

Adam swiveled his head and caught a glimpse of a red-faced, balding man stomping angrily on the rooftop behind him. In a beefy hand, he brandished an enormous pair of shears, and the sunlight reflected brightly off of the freshly sharpened blades.

"You can't be serious!" Adam called back.

The man glared at him, and Adam knew he meant trouble. He barely managed to travel halfway across the rope before he heard a loud *twang*! Suddenly, the tension in the rope vanished, and he hurtled forward at an alarming speed. The ground below did not look particularly inviting. Adam stifled a scream as he readjusted his body and moved his legs out in front of him.

When he struck the side of the wall, most of the force traveled into his kneecaps, and the remainder jolted painfully through his legs. Looking down, Adam noticed that he hung uncomfortably close to the ground. The pain subsided in a matter of seconds, and he began the ascent.

"That'll teach you!" Adam heard the disgruntled man shout from the other side of the street.

ROOFTOP RUN

The climb up the rope was arduous, but he made it to the rooftop remarkably fast. Adam turned his head and saw that the man responsible for his near-death-experience was nowhere in sight.

"That'll teach me to avoid crazies like you. Go on back to your skulking," he muttered crossly.

The other side of the street featured ornate houses decorated with balconies, verandas, and emerald-green roof tiles. Tyrule's house was not far. Without missing a beat, Adam vaulted onto the next rooftop. For Adam, these parts of Roddington were the most fun to navigate through. The rooftops required farther jumps and faster reflexes, which excited Adam every time. These houses towered over most of the other buildings, and one misplaced step could be fatal.

He approached a dome-shaped clock tower that would be too slippery to climb; however, a balcony loomed below the clock's archaic face. It was a far jump, but Adam took a running start and propelled himself through the air. Transferring his motion downward, he caught the edge of the balcony and grunted under the impact to his chest. He heaved himself onto the walkway and continued jogging, his feet matching the tempo of the loud gears. Adam placed a foot on the other end of the railing and launched himself forward.

The next roof, a flat one, was at least two floors shorter than the clock tower. Suddenly, he felt his pack slip off of his shoulders. The moment his feet touched the stone tiles, he leaned forward and rolled, landing with one hand on the tiles. A fearful glance backwards revealed his satchel dangling from the corner of the building. Breathing a sigh of relief, Adam popped up and treaded carefully to retrieve the special gift. In one deft movement, he stooped down and snatched the pack free. Adam clutched the fraying satchel to his chest as if he was assuring himself that it was still real. At last, he reset the straps and took off running.

CHAPTER THREE

For about a mile or so, Adam continued leaping along the tops of the houses. Far off, he spotted a large wall surrounding an impressive estate. When he was close enough, Adam forsake the thrill of the rooftops for a perch on the edge of the wall. Adam looked to the entrance of the manor and noted with a frown that the gates were closed. He crouched slightly and hurried along the top of the wall, taking care not to fall. The enormous house within the enclosure belonged to none other than Alimzar Ramsgate. The dominating estate stood at three floors, and an impressive courtyard accented the beige walls.

In the rear of the garden, Adam spotted a gazebo. Seizing the opportunity, he climbed carefully past the gates and hurried towards the garden side. Taking a quick glance around to make sure no one was watching, Adam leapt onto the top of the gazebo and dropped to the ground. The impact stung his ankles, but he ignored the discomfort as he ran out of the garden.

When he stood before the large front door, Adam took a moment to unroll his sleeves and push his hair back into place. After wiping a stray bead of sweat away from his brow, he reached for the enormous brass knocker, which read *Ramsgate*. The metal felt cold in his hand as he knocked twice. His answer came in a matter of seconds. The door slowly opened inward, and out stepped one of the most orderly men Adam had ever met. Alimzar Ramsgate's straw-blonde hair was tied back neatly in a ponytail, and his close-trimmed beard sat perfectly on his strong chin. If his facial features were not enough to suggest the man's prestige, then his ostentatious clothes would. He wore a scarlet jacket with frilly white sleeves and gloves, all of which radiated importance.

"Good day, Adam," he said in a smooth voice.

"Same to you, Mister Ramsgate," Adam replied.

Alimzar smiled at him through tight lips. "Tyrule tells me you made the king a sword. I must confess my interest."

Adam paused for a moment, knowing that he never breathed a word of his project to Tyrule. "Er—yes I did," he finally answered.

"Well, he and his friend, Leira Dawes, are upstairs. I believe you are acquainted with Miss Dawes, am I correct?"

"Yes, that's right," Adam said and took a step forward, but Alimzar held out a hand.

"A moment, please, if you will. May I see it?"

Reluctantly, he answered, "Of course you may."

Alimzar smiled graciously as Adam removed his satchel and withdrew the elongated case. Handing it cautiously to Alimzar, he watched carefully for any unusual reactions. Tyrule's father slowly removed the lid and looked upon the golden blade stoically.

"Such beautiful craftsmanship. The king will be most pleased in your work. May I?" he asked and gestured to the handle.

Seeing no harm in it, Adam nodded. Alimzar carefully removed the sword from its velvet bonds. For a moment, he held the sword up and stared plaintively at the flawless blade. He made no attempt to hide his amazement.

"Yes indeed, a fine sword," he said airily.

"Thank you," Adam said.

Suddenly, Alimzar placed it back in its case and handed the package back to Adam, who received it with startled hands.

"Must be off," he remarked tersely.

Before Adam could get another word in, Alimzar abruptly brushed past him and hurried to a lone carriage that waited for him outside of the gates, which were now fully open. He watched as Tyrule's father climbed inside of the craft, and four beautiful, white horses whisked him out of sight.

For a moment, Adam did not move. Tyrule's father was behaving quite strange, but not strange enough to justify an evil spell. Shrugging, Adam put the case back in his pack and walked quietly inside the house.

The first sight that greeted Adam was the black and white tiles that formed a neat checkered pattern. Several portraits and busts adorned the halls, and many of them featured Tyrule's mother, who sadly passed away during Tyrule's infancy. Closing the door behind him, Adam stepped out into the entrance hall. "Tyrule?" he said loudly.

"Adam, is that you?" Tyrule's voice called from nearby.

"Yeah! Where are you?" he replied.

"The dining hall, so come quickly!"

Adam followed the voice up a gleaming marble staircase and around a narrow corridor. At the very end, he spotted Tyrule and Leira at a long, mahogany table, both of them sitting at opposite ends. When Tyrule spotted Adam, he gestured for him to join them. Walking briskly, Adam entered the dining hall and pulled out a chair from the middle of the table. Looking up, he stared at a dazzling chandelier in awe. Tyrule coughed quietly, and Adam quickly removed his pack, placed it on the table, and sat down.

"We're so glad you're here! We were worried you wouldn't make it on time," Leira blurted excitedly.

Tyrule nodded in agreement.

"Well, my time management skills are not the best. I can't always be fashionably early like Tyrule," Adam quipped.

Tyrule replied, "You might want to try it sometime. Now you're here, and that's what matters."

Raising an eyebrow, Adam asked, "Have I kept you waiting or something?"

"No, no. Tyrule is just giving you a hard time. We can't go anywhere until our ride gets here. Speaking of which, how did you get here? You look like you just finished a long run," Leira said.

"You could say that," Adam answered, making eye contact with Tyrule.

Tyrule smiled softly. "He finished running along the rooftops."

Leira looked at him with a serious expression. "Come on, Adam. You couldn't take the road like a normal person? You could get into serious trouble if you keep this up."

"I've been a magnet for trouble lately. You can ask Tyrule. And, no, I couldn't have taken the road like a normal person. The streets are terribly crowded today. Think about it. People from all over are coming to see the king," Adam remarked.

"Still, I'm sure you could have found a better way," she insisted.

"Probably not."

Tyrule glanced at Adam's pack. "Is that the sword?"

Adam nodded in reply. "Let's not open it in here. I'll show you on the ride over."

"Why?" Leira and Tyrule asked in unison.

The curious expressions on both of their faces made Adam uncomfortable. "Does it matter? It's not a big deal, really. It would only slow us down at this point."

Before either of them could reply, a faint knock echoed from downstairs.

"And there's Roger. We'd better get going," Tyrule said and rose from his chair.

Adam breathed a sigh of relief and followed them out of the dining room, through the cramped corridor, and down the large staircase. A middle-aged man stood complacently in the middle of the entrance hall. His gray hair was interrupted only by a receding hairline, and he wore a small monocle on his left eye. The man, whom Adam could only assume was Roger, smiled warmly at the three of them.

"Good morning, young master Ramsgate. Would you be so kind as to introduce your friends?" he asked in a soft voice.

Tyrule stepped forward. "Of course. Roger, this is Adam and Leira. Adam and Leira, Roger."

"Pleasure," Adam and Leira said together.

Roger's kind smile widened. "The carriage is outside, sir. Let us make our departure now."

Tyrule nodded, and Roger went over to the door, holding it open with a gloved hand. Adam, Tyrule, and Leira slipped through and entered the courtyard. Halfway to the gate, Leira stopped abruptly.

"Oh, I left something inside. Would you mind if I went and got it?" she asked Tyrule.

"Not at all. Allow me to come with you," he answered.

Before they disappeared back inside of the house, Tyrule stole a bold glance back at Adam. Adam ignored the look and followed the driver to the carriage. The black carriage, unlike Alimzar's own, appeared to be drawn by four black horses. Roger climbed up into the driver's seat with unusual speed for a man of his age.

"Roger, Mister Ramsgate's carriage had white horses. Does the color mean anything?" Adam asked.

"White represents nobility, like Master Ramsgate. Black is generally for family members or guests," he answered.

"Oh," Adam said and climbed up the small steps into the carriage.

Sitting alone in the cabin, Adam leaned back in the seat and took a close look at the cozy interior. It reflected Tyrule's picture-perfect world, a world he would not mind living in for a few days. He looked at himself in the brightly polished metal of the carriage and saw his reflection staring back at him, especially his serene blue eyes. Suddenly, they grew unnaturally dark. Adam gasped in shock and directed his gaze elsewhere.

Something is going on here!

Adam stared awkwardly at his feet while he waited for Tyrule and Leira to return, being extra cautious not to look at his reflection. Those dark eyes were definitely not the ones he was accustomed to looking at in the mirror.

At this thought, something else occurred to Adam. *What if Mustafo wasn't completely wrong about me?* The idea seemed ridiculous at first, but nothing else could adequately explain the change in eye color.

His train of thought was halted when he heard Leira and Tyrule's voices engaged in lively conversation. In an effort to help Tyrule, Adam sprawled himself over the entire bench. As the voices drew nearer, he did his best to appear lazy and lifeless.

Finally, the door swung open, and Adam turned his head slowly toward his friends. Leira climbed up the small set of steps and saw Adam. She smiled at him kindly and took a seat on the bench opposite to him. When Tyrule entered the cabin, Adam managed to catch his attention with a heavy stare. His eyes flickered quickly in Leira's direction, then back to Tyrule, who understood the unspoken message and mouthed *thank you* to Adam. Adam responded silently *you owe me one*.

Once they were all seated properly, Adam cast aside the charade and sat up like any self-respecting person would. Tyrule shut the door behind Leira quietly and smiled to himself as if he had just won an award.

"Are you ready, young master?" Roger called out.

"Yes, Roger. Everyone's here and ready."

"Very well, then. I shall try to deliver you and your friends to the castle as swiftly as possible!" the driver shouted.

Adam peered out of the window and watched as the mass of people hurried by. Suddenly, the entire carriage jolted unexpectedly as Roger signaled the horses. Caught by surprise, Adam smacked his forehead against the window frame and winced in pain, tears coming to his eyes. No one said anything, but another jolt rocked the carriage once more, and Leira's head hit the wall behind her.

"Ouch!" she cried, rubbing the back of her head.

Tyrule looked at her, his eyes filled with concern. Adam watched through squinted eyes.

"Are you all right?" Tyrule asked.

Adam opened his mouth to answer, but Leira spoke before him.

"Yes, of course. It's only a bump on the head." She laughed lightly.

"Just making sure," Tyrule said.

Even in his pain, Adam stifled a laugh when he saw Tyrule's reaction. Unfortunately for Adam, the expression on his face betrayed him.

"What?" Tyrule asked, slightly red-faced.

"Oh, nothing." Adam repressed the smile that tugged at the corners of his lips.

"Well, I'm excited to be here with you both today," Leira piped up.

"And we're glad you've graced us with your presence," Tyrule said.

Leira blushed and let out a small giggle. Adam rolled his eyes when he saw the smile on Tyrule's face widen. "Is 'graced' the right word?" Adam commented.

Leira laughed and replied, "Well, I can only hope so."

All three of them laughed at the remark. Leira laughed quietly, her nose wrinkled. Tyrule laughed, of course, to compliment her. *Oh, the things you'd do, Tyrule,* Adam mused. For a moment, he felt a sudden twinge of jealousy. Seeing Tyrule and Leira flirting with one another only reminded him that he was alone. For a split second, he wished that he was escorting someone to the king's party.

"So, Leira," Adam said to distract his thoughts, "what have you been up to?"

"Me? Oh, not much, really. I've been at home with Mother getting ready for the ceremony. Adam, can we see the sword?" she asked.

"Can you?" Adam replied, holding up the case.

Rolling her eyes, she nodded, and Adam handed it over. When she lifted the lid off carefully, her eyes widened in amazement. She touched the handle lightly and examined her fair features reflected in the golden blade. "Wow, Adam. This is incredible. I knew you could do it! I told you so!"

Adam laughed softly. "Yeah, maybe."

Leira carefully put the lid back on the case and handed it back to Adam, who graciously received it. She offered him a friendly smile, and their eyes met. Her smile faded into a rather curious expression. She studied his face for a moment, and he remained perfectly still under the scrutiny.

"Adam, is it just me, or are your eyes darker?" she asked innocently.

Adam swiveled his head away. "I don't think so," he answered quickly.

Leira shrugged and leaned over Tyrule to catch a glimpse of the parade outside the other window. She turned back quickly, her eyes aglow with youthful excitement. "We're almost there! I can see the castle gates!"

Adam casually turned his head in that direction and spotted the wrought-iron gates. From this distance, it looked as if someone had taken a black string and curled it around in an intricate web. But as they drew closer to the gate, Adam saw that it no longer resembled string, as the twisting bars were as thick as a child's forearm. They all waited eagerly as the carriage finally slowed down to a crawl before the gates. From the window, Adam saw the knight who had visited him previously with the demand for the sword. Adam fidgeted uncomfortably as he watched the knight march towards Roger.

"Name?" the knight inquired.

"The three children? Tyrule, Laura, and Adam," Roger answered.

Adam did not take kindly to being called a child. He looked to Leira and noted the scowl on her face.

"Affiliation?" the knight grumbled.

"Tyrule? He is the son of Alimzar Ramsgate."

"Oh, of course he is expected! It must have slipped my mind. Wait one moment. Did I hear you say Adam?" the knight asked with interest.

"Yes."

"Adam Crescent?"

"I don't know any other Adam."

The knight walked out of sight. Suddenly, the door flew open, and he stood in the doorway. "Adam Crescent?" he nearly shouted.

Startled, Adam sat bolt upright.

"Do you have the sword?" the knight asked.

"Yes. Right here," Adam held out the case.

"May I see it?"

Adam shrugged and handed it over. The knight opened the case and removed the sword. He placed the empty case on the bench next to Tyrule. In the light, the sword looked truly wondrous to behold. The golden color of the blade gleamed boldly in the sunlight, and the hilt sparkled like a gemstone. Adam felt a bead of sweat on his brow as the knight took his sweet time inspecting the sword. The knight, satisfied with the results, placed the sword back in the case. "I need to take this and prepare it for the presentation," he said.

"Go ahead. I've seen enough of it," Adam remarked.

Without another word, the knight nodded gruffly, scooped up the case, and marched past the gates. Before he was out of sight, though, Adam, Tyrule, and Leira saw him wave an armor-clad hand to admit them. At last, the great burden had been lifted from his shoulders. Adam let out a sigh of relief because he knew the sword could no longer cause him any more trouble.

The gates screeched with age as they slowly opened to receive the group. The carriage jerked slightly and inched past the iron gates and into the estate. Adam and Leira watched with awe as they moved further onto the property. The gardens were as green as the juiciest pear, and the hedges were all groomed to resemble animals: tigers, eagles, and many other magnificent creatures. The road beneath the rickety wheels of the carriage was constructed of scarlet stones spiraling in an elaborate pattern.

Several people and other carriages were also moving in the same direction, and Adam could tell that other guests were just as awestruck as he was.

The colorful landscape seemed to stretch out indefinitely. Adam thought all of the different sights, sounds, and smells he absorbed were simply fantastic. The scent of the freshly manicured estate floated about them. The clatter of the crowd's footsteps resembled the sound of a discordant drum. Only one more surprise awaited Adam as he and his friends neared the castle where bountiful festivities awaited them.

CHAPTER FOUR

BIRTHDAY SURPRISES

The castle, by far, was the most impressive spectacle Adam had ever encountered. The dominating structure appeared to swallow the red bricks of the road like a mighty giant. The steely gray bricks all meshed together in an intricate pattern much like that of the road. The emerald tips of the towers coming off of the colossus were so high that they seemed to scratch holes in the cloudy sky, allowing the sun to cast a golden cascade of light off of the many flags that adorned the towers.

The carriage inched towards the enormous estate. Adam tore his attention away from the massive castle to catch a glimpse of his friends' reactions. Leira seemed to be just as impressed as he was, as her eyes were wide and her jaw dropped. Tyrule did not appear all that impressed. Adam supposed that this lack of excitement could be explained by the frequent visits Tyrule and his father made to the lovely castle.

"I've never seen anything like it! It looks like something from a story-book!" Leira exclaimed.

"Yeah, it's really amazing," Adam said breathlessly.

"Just wait until you see the inside," Tyrule said. Adam had not even thought about the interior yet.

"You mean to say that the inside is even more impressive?" Leira asked.

Tyrule nodded with a friendly smile. Leira noticed and smiled back, though her cheeks were slightly tinged with pink. Adam rolled his eyes at the silent flirtation. He was well aware that he was becoming the awkward third wheel in this scenario, but he really could not have cared less; he was just happy to be at the castle on such a beautiful day.

At last, when the carriage drew up parallel to the castle doors, Leira cast away all restraint and fidgeted in her seat with nervous excitement. "Ooh! This is just wonderful!"

Adam smirked at her. He also felt the same overwhelming sense of excitement, but no one in the carriage paid him any attention.

The carriage took a moment to stop, as if it were allowing its occupants to steal one last glimpse of the awe-inspiring castle's exterior. The vivid aroma of flowers hung in the air like a gentle curtain.

"Alright, young master! We have arrived!" Roger announced jubilantly.

"Thank you, Roger! Just wait for us nearby. I wouldn't want Leira to get sore feet from walking," Tyrule called back.

Coughing, Adam made a poor attempt at concealing his laughter, which seemed to work, for no one paid him the slightest bit of attention. Instead, Tyrule got out of the carriage swiftly to help Leira down the tiny set of steps. He extended a well-manicured hand, which she proceeded to grab with much excitement. She giggled and allowed him to guide her out of the carriage slowly. Adam wasted no time in getting out; the carriage was cramped, and he honestly wanted nothing more than to step into a wider space, and he wanted to do anything but watch Leira and Tyrule flirt like little schoolchildren.

When Roger bade them goodbye and left, they turned around to face the large castle doors. The doors, which were made of what appeared to be sleek mahogany, extended to a lofty height; their surface was etched with elaborate patterns. Adam stared intently at the massive marvels. It seemed that royalty had no blemish.

Adam's stare was broken by a group of tiny women trying to get by. He politely stepped aside and allowed them to enter, and only one member of the large party stopped to thank him. After the group had entered, Tyrule took a large step forward and caught the door before it swung shut. Chivalrously, he held the door open wide so that Leira might be the first to enter, beaming at her the entire time.

"Thank you. That's very sweet of you, Tyrule," she said bashfully and entered.

"It's only the right thing to do," he said while trying to maintain a noble expression.

He waited for Tyrule to follow her, but instead he remained holding the door ajar. "Aren't you coming?" Tyrule asked with a hint of impatience.

"Oh, you're waiting for me? Well, I feel honored. *That's very sweet of you, Tyrule*," Adam said.

Tyrule forced a laugh, and Adam stepped through the doorway. Once he had gone through, Tyrule released the door and followed suit. Adam's and Leira's reactions to the interior were similar to those they experienced when they first arrived, except that Adam nearly tripped over the threshold upon entering.

The castle interior was truly magnificent. At least Adam thought the places he could see were incredible, among which were several impressively tiled hallways lined with expensive pottery and austere portraits.

CHAPTERFOUR

The uniformity of the chandeliers that graced the ceilings added a pleasant touch to the flawless architecture. The main atrium was crowded with all sorts of people, and most of them appeared to be obscenely wealthy given the lavish clothes and golden bracelets he spotted. He hardly had any time to make any further observations, for at that moment, a plump woman burst through the large mahogany doors. Her face covered in horrifying waxy makeup, she rushed toward the crowd. Poor Adam, Tyrule, and Leira were shoved forward by the obnoxious rotund woman. Adam moved away like a small creature, wrinkling his face in discomfort.

"Faster, faster! Come on, children! With your youth, you should be even faster than me!" she yelled in a grating voice.

Despite the obvious desire to get away from the woman, Adam and his friends could not get very far. There was a slow-moving group ahead of them, and rushing through them would be very rude. Adam could barely make out the small man at the front of the crowd who looked remarkably similar to a turtle. For the next several minutes, the three of them were sandwiched uncomfortably between the people in the crowd.

Finally, when the undulating mass of people arrived at what appeared to be the ballroom, the throng dispersed. Suddenly their view became unobstructed, and Adam was able to get a good look around. The ballroom was filled with a vast number of chairs lined up in orderly rows. Row after row filled up with impressive speed, and Adam realized that he and his friends needed to fill their spots soon. The sea of chairs was divided along the center of the room by a spacious aisle. He took the initiative and pointed out the seats on the edge of the divide to Tyrule and Leira. Attending such ceremonies was uncommon for Adam, and he wanted to get as close to the action as possible.

After they sidled along a row until they reached the edge, Adam immediately took his seat along the aisle. Leira sat next to him with a wide grin. Tyrule, however, remained standing as he peered around the room.

"Tyrule, what are you looking at?" Leira asked.

"Oh, I'm just seeing who's here." He took the seat next to her.

Adam was primed and ready for the ceremony to begin. His hands trembled in excitement. Before he knew it, a colorful fantasy materialized in his active imagination.

The king stood at the front of the room, smiling kindly at those who stared back at him with equal excitement. A knight rushed forward to the king with the case. The king waited patiently as the knight opened it and handed him the sword. His eyes widened in amazement, and he rushed at once to grab his present. In awe, he held up the sword in the light, and then a wide smile formed on his face.

"This type of handicraft is unparalleled! Would the creator of this fine spectacle please—"

"Adam, are you okay?"

Adam snapped back to reality. Leira stared at him with a concerned expression. He looked back at the front of the room. No one was there. "Yeah, I'm fine."

With a turn of the head, Adam looked over at Tyrule, who sat next to Leira and was tapping his foot impatiently as he waited for the ceremony to begin. Leira must have noticed his impatience too because she quickly turned to face him. "Oh, Tyrule! Won't this be absolutely incredible? I'm nervous myself, yet I'm not even part of this!" she exclaimed.

"I am excited, too. Say, have you any engagements following the ceremony?" he asked with a charming smile.

"Tyrule, the ceremony hasn't even begun, and you're already worrying about what we're doing afterwards!"

Adam smiled subtly to himself. Tyrule and Leira launched into a colorful conversation, and he did not really feel like listening, nor did he care to fantasize about the king and his gift. Instead, he remained still and let his mind wander.

At first, nothing interesting came to mind. But after a while, Adam began to entertain himself by counting all sorts of different things, such as people with hats, people wearing white, and even people with too much makeup. He spotted the angry woman with an unnaturally rigid expression sitting on the other side of the room. When her narrowed eyes flickered toward him, he quickly turned his head and looked to the front of the room.

Tired of listening to them, Adam closed his eyes for a few moments. He certainly was not sleepy by any standards; he just wanted to relax. Not long after, a fresh image—Mustafo's face—flashed in his mind. His eyes flew open at once.

Why is this bothering me so much?

Before he could even begin to answer his own question, a loud brass fanfare blasted out to every corner of the room. Everyone stood up immediately, except for Adam and Leira, who had obviously never attended such an event.

"*Get up!*" Tyrule hissed.

They both jumped to their feet, feeling slightly embarrassed. They joined Tyrule and the rest of the crowd in facing the back of the vast room.

"On this wonderful day, we have all gathered to commemorate the birth of our noble King Phillip! Join us now in the festivities as the king and his court enter in procession! Long live the king!" a booming voice announced.

"Long live the king!" the people shouted back.

Adam and Leira mumbled unsuccessfully with the crowd, and they were quite thankful that no one noticed them.

At once, two long lines of armor-clad knights marched gallantly down the center of the aisle. All of them, even Tyrule, watched with rapt attention. The knights continued their march all the way down until they reached the very front row. The lines parted in perfect synchrony and the knights in each line stood along the edges of the aisle. One knight was so close to Adam that he had to take a step toward Leira, who took no notice at all.

Following the knights was a large party of noblemen, one of which was the notable Alimzar Ramsgate, Tyrule's father. Neither father nor son waved to the other, as it would have appeared highly inappropriate to do so. The group of noblemen walked with an air of extreme importance. Tyrule himself was already beginning to acquire such an aura. The noblemen passed the knights at the front row and followed a small set of marble stairs leading to an elevated platform. Like the knights, they parted, except that they traveled in opposite directions, filling the seats located on either side of two enormous thrones.

Finally, every last member of the throng, including the knights and the noblemen, bowed their heads as the king and another man walked side by side. The king walked at a humbled pace, waving to several people in the audience. He had a delighted smile on his face, which was not obstructed by his neatly trimmed, light-brown beard. Under the ornate gold crown on his head, a pair of cool blue eyes twinkled at the people. The good King Phillip was a man of virtue and justice; he was hailed by many and hated by few.

When the king and the other man had passed them, Adam glanced over at Tyrule. "Who's the other man?" Adam whispered.

"The king's brother, Prince Nicolas." He spoke quickly.

Adam nodded and continued watching; however, even knowing that the two men were brothers, he found it quite odd that the prince was nearly as old as the king. He had always thought of princes as being younger than kings; this he blamed on the old fairy tales he used to read as a youngster.

When King Phillip and Prince Nicolas reached the large chairs at the middle of the elevated platform, they made an about-face to the crowd. Everyone in the crowd offered an even deeper bow out of sincere respect.

"Rise, friends!" the king waved his hands and called out cheerfully.

Everyone rose at once. *"Long live the king!"*

The king smiled at this and raised a hand to quiet the crowd. "I am quite honored that you think so highly of me. Believe me, it means a lot to me that you all care so much that I have managed to rule yet another year. Even if I were to die today, I have the satisfaction of knowing that I have ruled such loyal people."

The crowd became excited, and many people whispered hurriedly amongst themselves. Finally, the prince stepped forward, and the people fell silent. For brothers, the two of them appeared to be quite different. Prince Nicolas's hair was jet-black, and he had no beard. His eyes were a steely gray color, and he stood considerably taller than King Phillip. His very demeanor radiated a sense of self-importance. For reasons he could not explain, Adam felt slightly uneasy as he watched the prince's still figure.

"Alas, let us hope that my dear brother does not fall prey to death anytime soon! Let us hope he lives a good, full lifetime. And now, let us begin! Squires! Bring forth the gifts!" the prince announced in a commanding voice.

Both King Phillip and Prince Nicolas took their seats, and a single, slow-moving line of squires moved forward from the rear of the room along the aisle in the center, each of them carrying different gifts. When the first of the squires stood before the king, he bowed humbly and presented the king with an unusually large bottle of wine.

"Excellent! I look forward to having a good birthday drink!" The king laughed.

The squire bowed once more and traveled along the outside of the chairs to the last row of seats.

One by one, each squire followed suit. Adam watched the king graciously receive each gift, and sometimes he would make a clever remark that would cause the whole throng to erupt in laughter. He fidgeted in his seat as he watched carefully for the sword.

The king received a plethora of gifts. Apart from the bottle of wine, he received a fine stallion, a new robe, a small dagger, a new bow with a neatly designed quiver of arrows, a new banner, and a new crown-polishing kit. At last, Adam caught sight of the familiar case in the hands of a squire walking forward. He squirmed with excitement as the small man drew nearer to the king.

The squire bowed just as the others had and handed the case to the king, who accepted the gift with a smile. He hurried away and joined the others in the last row. King Phillip carefully removed the lid and his mouth fell open in surprise. He removed the shining sword from its case and held it up for all to see. "Wow! This is a beautiful sword! Surely it must be the work of the mastersmith! Am I correct?" he asked, enchanted.

"No, my brother. This is the work of his apprentice—the boy, Adam Crescent," Prince Nicolas replied coolly.

"Well, let him be commended for this fine piece of art!" the king roared.

Adam felt his ears turn red, and he bashfully directed his eyes to the knight standing stoically next to him. He recognized him as the knight who had met him and his friends at the gates. The man's sword and scabbard was hanging only a couple of inches from his reach.

When the king placed the sword back in the case, Adam looked back up. Another squire was already on his way up to the front of the room. Suddenly, King Phillip coughed violently and looked to his brother. "I don't feel well. I—I think I need something. I need water," he said in between coughs.

"It will pass, my brother," the prince replied calmly.

"No, no! It won't!" the king cried, and he leapt out of his chair.

He stumbled down the set of stairs, and everyone in the room gasped in terror. Prince Nicolas raced down to his brother, who ran down the aisle in fright. He fell over, but crawled manically to escape. King Phillip coughed and writhed in pain. Leira tore her gaze away, apparently unable to bear watching another human endure such pain. Adam watched fearfully as the king clawed at the marble floor.

Suddenly, King Phillip fell deathly still, and his eyes stared vacantly at the frigid floor. Prince Nicolas dashed over to his brother, knelt by his side, and placed two fingers on the king's neck. Feeling no pulse, he quickly stood up.

"How has this happened? Who could do such a thing? My brother! He is dead!" he cried out in horror.

Some of the knights broke formation and stepped toward the fallen king. The atmosphere in the room quickly had turned from joyousness to icy shock.

"Knights, stay where you are!" the prince shouted.

The knights tensed up, but they returned to their positions. Prince Nicholas ran back up to the gathering of noblemen. Adam could not believe his eyes, for surely they betrayed him. The whole crowd was suspended in absolute silence and nervous apprehension as they watched the prince.

"Someone check that sword!" the prince shouted angrily.

One of the noblemen hurried over to the case, which lay closed on the floor where the king had dropped it. The nobleman reached into his pocket and withdrew a white handkerchief. Carefully, he removed the top of the case, using the handkerchief as protection. He wiped the handle of the sword and stood up to his full height.

As the others waited for something to happen, Adam was in shock. *How can they think* I *did this?*

When the nobleman withdrew the piece of fabric, an unmistakable violet stain stared the audience in the face. Horrified, Adam felt the hairs on the back of his neck stand up.

"It's poisoned!" the nobleman shouted.

The prince turned to the crowd. "Adam Crescent! You unspeakable menace! How dare you murder our king, my brother! Stand up and show yourself!"

Adam stood up quickly. "Sir, I didn't kill him! I swear!"

The prince eyed him skeptically. "All right, then, who did?" he asked with a sneer.

"I—I—I don't know, sir!" Adam stammered.

"Lies! Adam Crescent, you have murdered a good king and an even better man! You shall pay dearly for this monstrous crime! *You shall pay with your life! Guards, seize him!*" Prince Nicolas roared.

Adam struggled to say something, but he could not find the words. Out of some bizarre instinct, he turned to the knight next to him, snatched the sword from his scabbard, and faced the prince with a daring gleam in his eyes. Leira and Tyrule looked at him, both equally horrified. The members of the audience gaped at Adam in terror.

"I told you! I didn't kill him!" Adam cried, holding out the sword.

"You dare point that blade at me? The evidence is overwhelming! You shall be punished! *Guards!*" the prince screamed.

Adam looked to Leira in desperation. "Come on, you know I would never—," he began, but he instantly forgot what he meant to say when he saw the angry knights rushing at him.

Reflexively, Adam kicked the knight closest to him in the chest, and he flew backwards into a group of approaching attackers. Shocked by his display of strength, Adam leapt into the aisle and darted toward the exit. Several of the knights ran toward him, swords pointed angrily at him.

An energy like no other surged through his veins, and Adam yelled and swung his sword in the cold air. One of the knights raised his sword to block the blow, but Adam's sword cleaved the other blade neatly in two. He threw a punch at the bewildered knight, hurling him into a wall. As more and more knights surrounded him, he dueled with unparalleled speed. He shattered several more blades and sent many other knights soaring in different directions.

He was amazed at his unnatural strength, yet somehow he could feel himself getting even stronger. Adam let out a fierce cry and swung his blade in a wide arc. All of the knights flew back against the rear wall and fell to the floor unconscious. For a split second, he stared in horror at the unconscious knights littered all over the room. Suddenly, he remembered that he was a moving target.

With inhuman speed, Adam sprinted out of the ballroom, aware that several more knights would be in hot pursuit. Frantically calling to mind the memories of the jostling crowd, he nimbly navigated through the large number of vacant rooms until he reached the atrium. Just as he expected, a group of knights had already blocked the door. When they saw him, they too surrounded him. He became locked in a wild frenzy of slashing swords. Much to his own amazement, he fought quickly enough to dodge and deflect every last one of their blows. Suddenly, Adam felt a force from inside him intensify. Unable to contain it any longer, he screamed, and what appeared to be an azure hybrid between lightning and fire leapt from his fingertips and blasted the knights backwards and into unconsciousness.

Recoiling in shock, Adam stopped abruptly and stared at his hands in terror. A fresh wave of knights encircled him and held their blades out dangerously. One member of the scarlet rank leapt forward for the kill, but a loud voice stopped him dead in his tracks.

"Do not kill the boy!"

Everyone, including Adam, turned and watched the tall figure of Prince Nicolas enter the ring, a crooked smile on his smooth features.

"What do you want with me?" Adam spat.

Prince Nicolas laughed quietly to himself. "I just wanted you behind bars, but now that I've seen what you really are, I think we have something to discuss."

"No, we don't. I was framed! Framed by you!" he shouted.

The knights that encircled the two of them broke into discordant laughter. Prince Nicolas held out a calm hand to silence them.

"An amusing claim," he mused.

Adam glared at him. "It'll be about as amusing as your downfall."

The prince shot him an icy glare and removed a sword from his side. "On your knees!"

"And if I don't?"

"Don't test me."

Neither of them moved, and Adam returned the glare with one of unbridled determination. Snarling in rage, the prince kicked Adam's feet out from under him. Adam fell to the ground with a crash. Slowly, he rose to his knees, his face glowing with courage. "You may be able to hurt me, but you can't touch the truth."

"You fail to recognize that I can do whatever I wish, boy! Now then," Prince Nicolas said and brought his face closer to Adam's. "I'll give you one more chance. Will you obey?"

No one spoke for several moments. The prince smirked darkly, much to Adam's irritation. Suddenly, Adam look directly into the prince's eyes and spat in his face. "There's your answer."

Prince Nicolas snarled and pointed his sword at Adam's throat. "And to think I would have let you live!"

"Do your worst," Adam growled.

"My worst?" the prince said in amusement. "You underestimate what I'm capable of, Razorwolf."

Suddenly, Adam saw a glint of gold, and he felt a titanic force collide with the side of his head before the world around him became consumed by darkness.

CHAPTER FIVE

CLOAK AND DAGGER

Always, always, the waters flow.
Onward my child, onward go.
Seek the soul in eternal blue,
Enter a world with visitors few.

Come ye, and leave precious land behind
And journey deeper, deeper you'll find
Secrets and mysteries slumber away
Your kingdom, lad, awaits you today.

The water's edge whispers a secret.
Listen, child, and you shall keep it.
Be wary, the waters steal breath.
Tarry not, lest you wish silent death.

CHAPTER FIVE

The seas are not silent, but alive.
Through calm and rage the waters survive.
To tame them, man has not yet learned
Victory cannot be found, but is earned.

Always, always, the waters flow.
Onward my child, onward go.
Seek the soul in eternal blue.
Enter a world with visitors few.

The power of the words withdrew Adam from the vault of slumber. His head throbbed dully from the prince's heavy blow, and the cold air only exacerbated his aching joints as he sat upright. The small bed creaked in protest, for it had spent a great number of years supporting a vast variety of prisoners. As for the jail cell, Adam found it no more welcoming than a tiger with its fangs bared. Rust slithered down the metal enclosure, and the dank, gray bricks eerily reflected the soft yellow candlelight. He stole a glance at one of his cell's corners and spotted an appalling apparition. A skull glared at him with terrible, empty eye sockets, and its wicked jaw was drawn up in a horrific grin. Adam gasped and shrank against the wall.

"Who goes there?" a voice whispered from nearby.

Adam quickly jumped from his bed and pressed his body against the bars. "Only me."

"You can't be older than sixteen!" the stranger noted.

"I'm only fourteen."

There came a ragged noise from the shadows of the dungeons, the sound of long-forgotten laughter.

"How has your luck brought you here?" the man asked.

"Open defiance," Adam answered truthfully.

"That doesn't sound like Phillip's doing," the stranger said hesitantly.

"He's dead."

A shroud of silence drifted between them momentarily, and both reflected over the tragedy of the fallen king.

"How did he die?"

Adam inhaled slowly. "Murder."

"Who would dare?" the man asked in shock.

"They think it was me. I was framed. Someone poisoned his sword, the sword that I made."

"Now what would they gain by framing a boy?"

"I don't know," he breathed.

There was an explanation, but he did not want to acknowledge that Mustafo had been right the whole time.

"Maybe you have something they want."

"Maybe," Adam paused. "Do you believe in magic?"

The stranger chuckled in reply. "Why do you say that?"

"One of my friends told me a story," he lied.

"And what was this story?"

"Supposedly, the king of the land put a curse over everyone so that no one could touch magic. Not only that, but they forgot that there were other realms. The caster is said to hold total control over those who have been cursed. Anyways, some man knew about this curse, but he didn't want to believe it."

"That's an interesting story. I wouldn't be surprised if magic was real," the stranger remarked.

Adam was surprised by the prisoner's reaction. Unlike his friends and his own father, this man expressed amusement, possibly even remarkable sentiment.

"That song you were singing earlier," Adam began. "Where did you learn it?"

No reply came for what felt like several minutes, but it was easy to exaggerate time within the confines of a prison cell.

"I dreamed about it, actually. Me grandmother sang it to me once. It's been long forgotten."

"Long forgotten," Adam echoed.

"I don't like the prince," the stranger said.

"Prince Nicolas? Me neither," he said darkly.

"That's him. He took my boy. Said it was punishment for my crimes."

"Have you heard anything of your son?"

"Nothing. I sometimes wonder if he still lives," the man trailed off.

"Well, what's his name?" Adam asked.

"Balian. He was a good boy, and I miss him terribly. There's so much I wish I could have told him. You remind me of him. What is your name?"

"Adam."

The man savored the name. "It's a good name. I don't usually get names in here. Lots of horrible people. I'm Halbern."

"Nice to meet you, Halbern."

"The pleasure is mine. You have given me great comfort. This has been a great day, or is it night? Either way, I must rest," Halbern said.

"Rest well," Adam replied.

Not another word passed between the two of them. Halbern's gentle snoring was the only sound in the dark prison besides the sound of dripping water. It was to this unusual symphony that Adam spent many hours listening to as he yearned to be free.

As the days melted into weeks, and weeks into months, Adam gradually lost sense of time. Despite the bleakness of the situation, Adam's sharp tongue never faltered. During meal times, when the knights would deliver food to the prisoners and jeer at them, he always found the most irritating insults to their intelligence. Soon, they began calling him Snark.

Of the prisoners themselves, hardly anyone ever spoke except to quiet Adam and Halbern. Even though Halbern was much older than he was, Adam found him to be a suitable companion in the dreary prison. Everything the man had to say interested Adam, even the small accounts of trips to the market. Since he could not see Halbern, Adam imagined him to be a round man with thing hair and thick spectacles. As far as he could tell, Halbern was not a threatening person.

One day, Adam asked him, "Halbern, why did they capture you?"

Adam heard movement from the cell next door. "I merely explored. I didn't steal, certainly didn't kill."

"Where did you explore?"

"The seas."

His answer surprised Adam. No one in Roddington, by royal decree, was allowed to venture into open water.

"Halbern, that's forbidden."

"So are many other things in this kingdom, but the prince was absolutely furious that I went anywhere. See, Balian and me, we wanted to see how far we could go. Suddenly, a wild thunderstorm came over our boat, and we were forced to turn back. I can imagine that you know who waited for us back at the port," Halbern said gruffly.

"Prince Nicolas."

"Yes, and before chaining us up and separating us, he made sure to tell us that only certain knights were able to sail. The crime of venturing out is punishable by death, a fate that I await."

"Death?" he asked.

"Oh yes. I am sentenced to die."

"What happened to Balian?"

CHAPTER FIVE

A stagnant pause found its way into Adam's cell. Suddenly, the sound of choked sobs filled the dank air. "I don't know what's become of my boy. I don't want to believe that he's really—really—," Halbern struggled.

"I'm sorry. I didn't mean to bring it up like that," Adam apologized.

"The fault is not yours. I do not weep only for my boy, my Balian. I weep for you, Adam. I have heard others in here who have done unspeakable things, things that would make you cringe in the hours of the night. But you are different. I know that you're innocent. I know who you really are, and I don't want the world to lose someone like you," Halbern said.

The sentiment caused a memory to surface in Adam's mind.

"Halbern, what is Razorwolf?" he asked.

"I've never heard it. Where did you hear it?"

"Before the prince knocked me out, he said something about Razorwolf. I don't know if that was directed at me, you know like an insult, or if he was talking to the knights who captured me," Adam answered.

"Well, I have no idea," Halbern admitted.

The conversation returned to the familiar, but in his mind's eye, Adam could not help but wonder what Prince Nicolas's unusual words actually meant. After a while, Halbern suspended speech and went back to sleep. By the time the knights returned for supper, Adam could hear him snoring quietly. One knight came to Adam's cell with a bowl of cold soup.

"Snark," the knight acknowledged him.

"And what's your nickname?" Adam asked.

"I beg your pardon?"

Adam smiled in spite of himself. "You geniuses call me Snark. Surely they have a name for you."

"No."

"Then allow me. Let's see, you're so skinny it's creepy, which also leads me to wonder how you ever achieved the rank of knight in the first place.

Your voice reminds me of a twelve-year-old girl, and you walk like a confused bird. Twiggy sounds good," he said.

The knight grabbed the cell bars in rage. "You dare make a mockery of me?"

All the while, Adam watched in amusement. "Not necessary. You've done an outstanding job of that yourself."

"I can't wait until they off you."

"You and the rest of the knights. Anything else?"

The knight glared at him once more before turning away and storming off. When the sound of the metal boots disappeared into the darkness, Adam could hear Halbern chuckling.

Meals in the prison often resulted in lively, and sometimes strange, conversation. For the past four meals, Adam explained to Halbern how he navigated Roddington by the rooftops, and Halbern found the whole idea fascinating. Since he met the old man, Adam could sense that Halbern's energy waned with each passing day. That evening, Halbern suspended their trivial conversations for something more sentimental. At first, they ate their cold soup in silence. Deep in remote parts of the prison, Adam listened to the arrhythmic sound of dripping water. At last, Halbern spoke first and dissolved the silence.

"You are the only friend I've had in years, you know," he whispered.

Adam stopped eating. "Surely there have been others."

"No. The only two people who have ever been near me were horrid. Heathens."

"I'm sorry," he said.

"No, don't be. I wish I could see your face though. That's the thing about these cells. The design is absolutely horrible. You can barely see the empty walls through the bars, yet you can't see who the guy next to you really is," Halbern said.

Pausing for a moment, Adam asked, "And who do you think I am?"

Halbern answered slowly. "I think that you are a boy who doesn't deserve this life. I know that you're not. That's what I've learned to hate about Roddington. The innocent don't have a voice against those who are more powerful."

"You mean to say that King Philip has done bad things?"

"No, and that's why I'm sad that he's gone. He was a champion for the weak, the last good thing. Well, that is until you came."

These words came as a shock to Adam. "You mean it?"

"Every word," the ragged voice answered.

"I wish I could see you, too, Halbern. You've been kind to me, and I know you don't deserve to be in here either."

"I chose to leave. You are but a boy. I believe you Adam, and I hope that the monster who framed you will find justice. I used to dream about my freedom, you know. Now, I find myself more concerned with yours. It is my wish that you will somehow escape and clear your good name."

"I don't think I have it in me," Adam said.

Halbern chuckled softly. "I think you'll soon find out that you're better than you think you are. I can see it in you."

* * *

Several days later, as Adam and Halbern were discussing their favorite spots in the market and how those places changed over the years, the sound of jingling keys echoed across the prison. Their conversation suddenly came to an abrupt end, for they knew what the noise meant. Someone was about to die. Adam wished he could see Halbern just to gauge his reaction. A tremor of fear rippled down his spine. The sound of footsteps came closer to them, and he watched apprehensively. When the skinny knight walked by his cell, he breathed a sigh of relief.

"Oh, Twiggy. It's only you," he said.

But Adam spoke too soon. Three other knights walked past his cell, and at the end followed the sinister figure of Prince Nicolas. Immediately, Adam shrank back.

"What's the matter, Snark? Cat got your tongue?" Twiggy sneered.

"We are not here to play with the brat," Prince Nicolas commanded.

Releasing an imperceptible sigh of relief, Adam felt the color return to his face; however, something was still amiss. The footsteps stopped after passing his cell, and he could not see what the prince and his cronies were doing. In the far corner of his cell, the ugly skull stared blankly at him. Hesitating for a split second, Adam kicked the skull aside and pressed himself into the corner. From this location, he spotted none other than Prince Nicolas and three of his knights standing at the neighboring cell. The prince's malicious features snarled against the yellow glow of his lantern, and his lips were drawn up in a hideous sneer.

"Halbern, I have a choice for you."

No reply came.

The prince laughed softly. "Surely you want to live?"

Adam heard movement from the cell. "What do you want?" Halbern croaked.

"It's simple, really. I can free you."

"At what cost?"

"The life of another prisoner or your own," Prince Nicolas whispered.

"What is your offer?"

"I thought you'd never ask. Would you, Halbern, be willing to forgo your own execution if another took your place? Here are the terms: you go free, and Adam Crescent takes your place."

Biting his lip in terror, Adam tasted blood. He waited with bated breath for Halbern's decision. After their friendship, such a decision would be extremely difficult to make. Adam expected Halbern to pause for a moment, but the man's sudden reply startled him.

"No."

Relief drifted over Adam momentarily, but the realization slowly dawned on him.

"How noble of you, Halbern. There is something else that you might want to consider. Don't you have a son of your own? Perhaps I could free him as well, and father and son would be reunited once more," the prince said coldly.

The knights watched Halbern's cell carefully as he paused to make a decision. One knight, the one called Twiggy, glanced quickly at Adam's cell.

"Is he still alive?" Halbern asked.

"That is not our agreement. You have a choice to make. Leave here untouched and let Adam Crescent take your place. Or you can die," Prince Nicolas said.

"Then I will die."

Horrified, Adam leapt forward and clutched the bars tightly. "No Halbern!"

"Silence, boy. I am speaking to Halbern and Halbern only," the prince growled. "Now, Halbern, this is a serious choice. Why won't you save yourself?"

"My boy wouldn't want me to do it. And something tells me that you fear this one," Halbern said firmly.

"I have no fear of any boy, you fool. You have clearly sealed your fate."

"And so I have."

"So be it. Halbern, your time has come. What will your last request be?" he whispered.

Halbern, Adam could tell, was thinking deeply about his last wish before the tragic death. His choice would be difficult to predict. Then Adam's mind wandered into darker corners, and he wondered what he would eventually be forced to choose.

"The boy must be my witness. He comes."

Halbern's answer shocked Adam to the core. Surely he heard incorrectly.

"What?" the prince hissed.

"The boy comes to watch. That way, he will be the last thing I see," Halbern insisted.

"Very well. Guards, escort this man. I want to have a word with the witness."

Prince Nicolas remained motionless as the guards entered the cell and withdrew the bent form of Halbern. When the clattering of prison chains disappeared beyond earshot, the prince stepped over to Adam's cell and regarded him with a truly venomous expression.

"I don't approve of your meddling," he growled.

"You think I arranged this?" Adam protested.

"I don't know what your intentions are. Let me be clear to you, Adam Crescent. I don't like you. Do you know what happens to people I don't like? I ruin them, so don't test me."

"I have no intention doing so."

The prince smiled at him. "It doesn't matter now. You'll be the next one to visit that room, and I'll be watching from the front row. What a pity."

"And why is that?"

"You could have confessed, and I might have pardoned you. Instead, you decided to put on a show."

"You and I both know that wouldn't change anything," Adam remarked.

"It is possible. Either way, you've made many of my knights angry."

"Because of my magic?" Adam asked.

Prince Nicolas paused for a moment. He narrowed his black eyes and glared at Adam with the utmost disgust. "I don't know what you mean by that."

Adam smiled cleverly. "Your features betray your words, Your Highness."

"You know magic doesn't exist, boy."

"Or so you've led everyone to believe. I know what you are," Adam growled from behind his enclosure.

"Do you now?" Enlighten me," the prince sneered.

"You're the one who cursed Roddington." The curse, real or not, was the only possible leverage Adam had against the prince, and he was not about to let such a cruel man gain control.

Prince Nicolas laughed gleefully and folded his hands. "You're a bright one. How tragic, though, because you won't be with us much longer."

"And why not?"

The prince took a spider-like index finger and slid it across his throat. "Execution. Believe me, I've got something special planned for you."

"It doesn't matter."

"Oh, but it does."

"No. Look around you. This curse you've created, well, it's starting to come undone. It's only a matter of time now."

"You'll be dead in a matter of hours. There's nothing more you can do."

"Wrong. I will find a way. You can bet your entire kingdom that I won't stop until your spell is broken. You will lose," Adam spat.

The prince smiled scathingly. "How can I lose when I have nothing?"

"You have everything." "Or so it would appear. And that is where you're wrong. I have nothing to lose and everything to gain. Tell me, how do you plan on beating that?"

"First, I'm going to destroy this curse. Then, I'm going to come back, and I will defeat you once and for all," Adam said boldly.

"It's all admirable, really," the prince began with a twisted smirk. "But how can you prove anything? Who will believe you, a murderer? As far as everyone else is concerned, you're insane because magic does not exist.

You'll walk the path of the doomed. And every moment you throw away, I will spend in laughter as I watch you fail."

"There are others who know the truth. I happen to know a few."

The prince's grin disappeared briefly, but the wicked snarl that replaced it took Adam aback. "Your fate is already sealed."

"No. It is only beginning. If I used magic once, I could do it again. I will escape," Adam said, hoping to scare him.

Suddenly, Prince Nicolas brought his face nose-to-nose with Adam, and the only thing that separated them was the rusty bars. "If you try anything, I will destroy you. Make no mistake about it. It might just be the last thing you do."

"Then let's get on with it. Lead the way," Adam replied.

"My pleasure." Prince Nicolas begrudgingly unlocked the cell, and Adam slipped out into a long hallway illuminated by very few torches. He gripped Adam's arm tightly as they marched down the corridor. "You're in luck. The execution chamber is just down this hall, and it's not a long walk. Look at the bright side. You won't have to walk back."

Adam said nothing in reply. Prince Nicolas clutched tightly onto Adam's chain, pulling him around like a dog. Every once in a while, he would yank sharply, and Adam nearly toppled over. With each and every blind step, he hated the prince more and more. If he ever got out of the castle alive, a possibility that seemed highly unlikely, he would seek Mustafo for guidance against the prince's tight grip.

Prince Nicolas forcefully dragged him along a steep set of stairs. Adam tried finding time to find the steps in the dark, but the prince would not allow it. Many times, he pulled the chain harshly, and Adam fell against the cold brick, the last time on his face. When they reached level ground, his breath became harsh and ragged. The sound of jingling keys sliced through the still air as Prince Nicolas unlocked the door. Suddenly, the door swung open, and a bright light flooded the space and blinded Adam.

"This light is the last you will see, boy," Nicolas said smoothly before leading him down a long corridor.

Unlike the rest of the castle, from what Adam could see, the walls were not covered in archaic portraits, and cracked tiles lined the floor. He realized that he walked along the path of the doomed, a path from which no man returned. There were so many things Adam had left undone. His friends thought he was a murderer, and he did not even get a chance to say goodbye to Gregor. Tears streamed down his face as the prince led him further into the heart of despair.

At last, they arrived at a wide door, and for the first time, Prince Nicolas let Adam enter first. When he stepped over the threshold, Adam stared blankly at the enormous amphitheater before him. Several benches surrounded a round stage in the middle of the room. A few people held seats in the rows, most of them masked to preserve their identities. A single aisle divided the seats and led directly to the stage, where Halbern waited solemnly for the journey into the netherworld. On either side of him stood a knight. In the center, a large tank stood, the waters within untroubled. As Nicolas led him to the front row, an uneasy feeling rose in the pit of Adam's stomach. Before taking a seat, the prince whispered in his ear, "If you try anything to escape, I'll have you begging for death."

Adam glared into his cold eyes and said nothing as he sat down. The prince walked forward to the knights. They both regarded him with a loyal salute, and he nodded at them.

"Where is Calder?" Nicolas asked.

"Preparing, my liege," the knight to the right of Halbern said.

"Very well. Tell him that there will be two executions today, and the second one will follow right after the first. If he asks what method, reply that he is free to use his imagination. As for me, I must return to the people. Being king isn't an easy business."

Both knights bowed to their king, and Nicolas turned to leave. Before exiting, he made a point to walk by Adam slowly and smile wickedly at him. The sound of a slamming door told Adam that the prince had left. Only seconds later, the door swung open again and admitted a portly man with scarlet hair and a beard to match, his black robes dragging along the floor. When he reached the stage, he turned and faced the grim audience through thick spectacles.

"I must apologize for my tardiness. I am Calder, Master of Ceremonies. Today we are gathered to witness the demise of the unspeakable cad, Halbern Thorn. Please rise and recite the oath with me," the man said in a callous voice.

Everyone, except for Adam and Halbern, stood bolt upright and placed a hand over their heart.

"For the truth, justice, and prosperity of Roddington we are gathered here. I solemnly swear to make the right choice, the choice our good King Nicolas himself would choose. Furthermore, I swear myself against all practices of evil, even in the face of my own demise. To the king, I swear my utmost loyalty now and forever," the people spoke unanimously.

Calder nodded. "Very good. Please be seated." He paused for a moment as the audience sat down once more. "Now, today we are here because one of our own, Halbern Thorn, has committed an atrocious offense, and I presume you are all aware of the injustice. You see, our man violated one of Roddington's most crucial laws. Would anyone care to recite the decree?"

A masked figure stood at once and spoke in a deep voice. "Unless authorized by the king or the prince, no one may use a sea vessel for travels beyond the port. Infractions of this decree will indubitably result in death by execution."

"Precisely. For Halbern Thorn, one life was not enough. He took his own son with him on that day as they tried to sail away into forbidden territory. Their quest was, of course, proved useless when a storm drove them back into our ports where we seized them. Needless to say, the boy is no longer with us," Calder reported.

Halbern dropped to his knees and sobbed bitterly. "No! My son! You killed my son! Murderers! All of you are murderers!"

One of the knights delivered a forceful kick to Halbern's side, and he crumpled feebly.

"Enough of your babble, you criminal. Halbern Thorn has been in our cells for sixteen years, and his son for six of those years before his death. Now he must pay for his crimes. Does anyone object?" Calder asked.

No one spoke, which bothered Adam. Looking braver than he actually felt, Adam stood up and faced Calder daringly.

"I do," he said firmly.

"Your opinion does not matter, boy. Look around you. The decision is unanimous. Halbern Thorn, you are guilty of heinous offenses, as stated earlier. What have you to say for yourself?" the Master of Ceremonies asked.

"Naught. I accept it all for my son. Do with me what you wish," he replied through tears.

"Very well. Because King Nicolas has ordered punishment to be proportional to the deed, you are to die within the waters. Do you object?"

Halbern shook his head no. The whole situation repulsed Adam. Death by forced drowning. What a horrible way to die, he thought. As the Master of Ceremonies continued, Adam looked around at the small crowd gathered to witness such a terrible injustice. As the new king, he acquired a great list of duties, and watching executions did not fit very well on the agenda.

"Now, Halbern Thorn, you are to die. Please, knights, escort the prisoner to the tank and prepare him for submersion," Calder ordered.

Immediately, both knights seized Halbern's weak figure and secured his arms, legs, and mouth. Once it was clear that he could not escape his bonds, the knights lifted him up, one for his arms and the other for his legs. They marched over to the enormous tank, and Halbern remained unflinching. Calder nodded in approval.

"Very well. You shall die in the waters just as you have used the waters to commit your crime. May you find mercy in the netherworlds, fiend. Immerse him now."

The knights raised him high into the air and pushed him over the tank's edge. With a large splash, Halbern's body sunk to the bottom. Adam watched in horror as the man squirmed and writhed to be free. As precious seconds trickled by, Halbern's movements gradually slowed, and his efforts visibly dwindled away. Suddenly, the glass shattered into millions of tiny pieces, and a wild rush of water flooded the stage. Halbern tumbled free and lay motionless on the floor.

Calder and the audience looked around in anger, for they had seen the silver glint crash through the glass. No one stood in the rear of the amphitheater, which puzzled everyone, including Adam. Furiously, one of the masked viewers stood up and shouted. "Who threw it?"

No reply came, and Calder's face turned a furious shade of scarlet. "Show yourself now! I know it was one of you!"

Again, no one spoke up, and Calder marched angrily down the aisle. Meanwhile, Adam watched in horror as the members of the audience began to argue bitterly amongst one another. In the blink of an eye, the quarrels went from verbal to physical. As the cacophony began to spin out of control, Adam struggled against his restraints. Suddenly, a forceful hand grasped his shoulder and spun him around. A man clad in armor looked at him with stern, gray eyes and held a finger to his lips. From one of his many shoulder bags, the man withdrew a key and deftly disarmed every chain that trapped Adam. He wiped a wave of long, black hair from his face before addressing Adam.

"Follow me," he whispered.

But Adam did not follow. Instead, he ran to Halbern's side and tore the fabric away from his mouth. Terrified, he pressed two fingers against the old man's neck and felt the weak remains of a pulse.

"Halbern! Halbern! We've got to go! We've got to get out of here!" he cried.

Halbern looked at him through droopy eyes. "I can't," he croaked.

Adam refused to accept this. "I can help you! I can, I will!"

"It's over, Adam."

Blinking back tears, he asked, "What do you mean?"

Halbern smiled weakly. "You must escape, my boy. I know you can stop the evil that poisons Roddington. Promise me something."

"Anything!" he choked.

"Promise me that you will become the hero the world needs. You have the makings of greatness. Please," Halbern rasped.

Adam sobbed bitterly. "Halbern, I'm no hero! I can't save anyone!"

"You already have. Promise me, Adam. Give me your word so that I may pass peacefully. I beg you."

"I-I-I promise, Halbern," he said.

"Swear it. Swear by me."

Adam opened his mouth to speak, but a scarlet flash caught his eye. An object hurtled towards him at an alarming speed, and he moved aside out of pure reflex. As he fell to the ground, Adam realized his grave error. There was a sharp gasp beside him. Adam turned and saw the arrow lodged below Halbern's neck. His eyes were lifeless, and Adam knew that his friend was gone. Before he could break into profuse tears, something pulled him off of the stage.

"Noooooo!" he screamed.

Suddenly, a hand clamped over his mouth. Despite his efforts to free himself, the stranger maintained a tight grip.

"Do you wish to leave these halls alive?" a whisper rasped in his ear. "If so, you'll do exactly as I say. Understand?"

Adam nodded quickly and followed his dark rescuer past several rows of benches as they headed upward bound. It was not long before the onlookers spotted them and shrieked. Adam's heart raced furiously as he rushed to keep up with his savior.

"Don't worry. By the time we escape, the royal guard will be far too late," his deep voice called back.

Cries of "stop them!" shook throughout the amphitheater, but the mysterious rogue had time on his side. Without warning he turned and snatched Adam by the hand with a sharp jerk, and the rogue pulled him through a small doorway. When the door slammed closed from behind them, the only sound that remained was their hurried footsteps. As far as he could tell, Adam and the rogue were running alone in the marble corridor.

"Who are you?" Adam asked.

"I am Talan, and you need to get out of here," he answered quickly.

"Why are you doing this?" Adam cried.

"You have a vendetta to settle with the prince. So do I. We're on the same side. I'd love to chat, but I'm busy escaping," Talan answered.

The shock of the rescue forced the pain away, and Adam fell silent and continued following Talan down the corridor. Quietly, they ran down the dark hall until they reached a single door at the end. Talan pressed an ear against the door and closed his eyes while Adam fidgeted nervously.

"There's a lot of commotion outside. We don't have long," he remarked, reaching into a bag. When Talan withdrew a set of lethally-sharp, steel spikes, Adam eyed them with fear.

"What are those?" he asked.

"Throwing knives," Talan answered.

"You're going to kill them?"

"Have you a better plan?"

Adam fell silent. With great deliberation, Talan mouthed three, two, one, and he turned sharply. His foot met wood, and the door was knocked off of its hinges. Talan wasted no time admiring his theatric performance and grabbed Adam again. Together, they ran headfirst into the light and onto the main castle staircase; however, they were not alone. Several men dressed in light armor sprinted after them at once. Talan peered backwards for a split second, but it was long enough for Adam to spot the scowl on his face.

"Archers. One tried to kill you earlier," he grunted through clenched teeth. "Stay close."

Suddenly, Talan flicked a hand backwards, and Adam looked back just in time to see the silver streaks strike the soldiers' chests. Many of the mobile archers tripped and fell over their fallen comrades. Talan smiled in amusement.

"Jam the doors!" a furious archer screamed.

"Talan, what do we do? They're blocking the exits!" Adam cried.

"You thought it'd be that easy?" Talan retorted with a smirk.

With that, Talan reached out and snatched Adam close to him. Adam yelped in protest as they both raced to the floor. Half-a-second later, he heard the sound of arrows as they whipped by overhead. He tried to get up, but Talan kicked him back down before hurtling a deadly knife at their assailant, who cried out in pain and toppled backwards over the balcony.

"We're on the fifth floor," he panted. "And we need a change of plan. See the second floor landing?"

Adam looked down past the balcony and spotted the intended floor. "I see it!" he shouted.

"Good. Duck!"

Without a moment's hesitation, Adam snapped his torso forward just in time for Talan to release another wave of knives. The rogue's brow was furrowed in concentration, and his teeth were clenched in rage. "There's a stained-glass window down there. That's our exit," he ordered.

"Are you mad?" Adam protested.

"If you want to live, you'll jump. Now down the stairs!" Talan roared.

A quick glance upward revealed a vibrant wave of warriors, their arrows nocked and trained on the escapees. There was no way that could take all of them out. Throwing caution to the wind, Adam dived at Talan, and the two of them hurtled down the staircase. They collided against the floor with a loud slam, and Adam had to blink stars from his eyes.

"Thanks," Talan huffed and leapt to his feet.

Dozens of agile warriors jumped down from their perches in hot pursuit, but Talan's knives met all of them in midair. He snatched Adam up once more and sprinted down the next staircase. Only one more flight remained, but a band of knights now stood in their way.

"Time for some close combat," Talan remarked and ran towards his foes with a mighty yell.

Talan leapt and kicked the nearest warrior directly in the face, causing to drop his shield. In a swift movement, Talan swept the knight off of his feet and slammed him into the remaining enemies. During this time, Adam hurried down frantically and grabbed the shield. It was large enough to cover most of his body, but the area below his knees was exposed. Boldly, he raised the shield and charged at a lone knight. The impact caused Adam to bounce off the seasoned warrior harmlessly; however, it distracted the knight long enough for Talan to kick him over the edge. Adam glanced down at the ground floor and watched in horror as the another fresh battalion of knights headed their way.

"Talan! There are more!" he shouted as several arrows broke against the shield.

"Then toss me the shield!" Adam flung the piece of armor to Talan, who caught it with expert skill. The rogue swung the shield with all of his might and slugged the knights to the floor. Though they groaned and tried to get up, both Adam and Talan leapt over their crouched figures and sprinted down the next flight of stairs. At last, they stood back-to-back before the stained-glass window.

"Now what?" Adam shouted.

Talan lifted the shield in front of them to deflect another wave of arrows. "When you jump, run as fast as you can out of here!"

"Mustafo's house," Adam replied instantly.

"Where?"

"It's the only house on the outskirts!"

"Then I'll—," Talan was interrupted by an onslaught of angry knights.

In fear, Adam watched as his rescuer fought at least seven men at once.

"Go!" Talan roared and hurled the shield against the window.

Glass of every color rained down upon them, and Adam had to shield his face from the wreckage. Quickly, he looked past the window and down at the castle's extensive lawn. Escape was so close, but it was a dangerous fall. He inhaled deeply and bent his knees to prepare for the inevitable.

"Adam! Look out!" he heard Talan shout.

He looked to Talan, but a searing pain suddenly erupted along his shoulder. Adam howled in anguish and looked over his shoulder to find the tail of an arrow lodged in his skin. The pain spread like fire, and he allowed the fire to consume him. A knight broke free of Talan's attacks and ran full force towards Adam. Without hesitating, he snarled and delivered a powerful punch to the man's gut. The armor clanked in protest as the knight crashed through the stone balcony. The pain flared up even worse, and Adam reached over his shoulder and ripped the shaft free from his skin. He growled in pain, but he tightened his fist and snapped the arrow in two. Talan regarded him with incredulity, but Adam took one last glance of the castle's interior before vaulting out of the window.

The blue skyline and the green world meshed together in an unsightly blend. The fall only lasted an instant; the impact was nothing to him. Adam landed on his hands and feet and leapt forward. He broke into a blazing sprint and ran straight for the iron gates, his feet moving faster with each passing second. The gates were slowly closing, and that was his only hope for escape. The knights guarding the gates hurried towards him, but Adam batted them aside with apparent ease. As the gates were about to make contact, Adam dashed forward and threw himself against them. The impact threw the iron gates into the distance like a child would throw a stick.

At last the castle lay behind him, so he waited for the adrenaline to simmer down. Suddenly, his energy began to drop at a dangerous speed, and he could sense that the end was near. There was a loud noise from behind him, and he turned his head quickly to steal a glance backwards, but the castle was already far behind him. Adam turned his head and saw green for a split second, then nothing. He took one more step, and the world around him disappeared in a violet haze.

CHAPTER SIX

FACES WITHOUT NAMES

The chilling air stung with a vicious bite. The wind swept about in a rage, and the trees bowed under the pressure. Lightning flashed violently, and thunder rumbled ominously overhead. Although the trees shielded most of the earth from the rain, drops of water still invaded the forest floor.

Adam realized he lay facedown on the ground. Slowly, his eyes fluttered open, and everything was a blur. His whole body ached dully even though he lay still as a stone. The rain trickled down from his already soaked hair down to his face, but he did not care at all.

With all the effort he could muster, Adam groaned and rolled over, his face turned to the overcast sky. The water ran down his cheek as if nature itself sought to ease his pain. He breathed softly, and then he closed his eyes and drifted back into heavy slumber.

CHAPTER SIX

There was nothing except for the grass that extended in every direction. Men clad in colors of blue and silver were hurtling toward him at an alarming speed. They were wearing armor, but they were not knights. They followed him like hungry wolves inside the castle walls. But he was powerful; with relative ease, he defeated the men, but more were still coming. They were coming, and he had to flee.

His footsteps thundered powerfully, and they rocked the earth. A fierce growl escaped from the overcast heavens. The noise frightened the men, and they arrested pursuit. He peered into the clouds and waited for the sound to subside. As the growl grew louder, he realized that it came not from the sky, but from within.

"Leave me!"

But it did not leave. It hungered even more. The beast howled from within him and sent a shock wave through every fiber of his being. He shook again, but he did not fall. He desperately needed an escape, and he would not last much longer on his own.

Then it dawned on him: it saved me.

The beast saw this as a moment of weakness. It clawed violently to be free. Still, he fought it. The fight was wearing him out, and the beast was only getting stronger.

Then it whispered to him, and he listened. "You cannot run from me, Adam. You and I are one."

He protested against the beast. "No! No! We are not!"

It continued whispering from the shadows. "I have slept a long time. You must trust me! Only I can help you!"

He hesitated. "How can you help me?"

The beast whispered again to him. "I have immense power. Let me help you! With my help, none of those men will find you! No mortal could ever hope to overpower me!"

He thought for a moment. "Help me!"

The beast curled its thin lips, exposing its fangs in a smile, and it howled louder than anything he had ever heard before. It slowly freed itself from the tightly fastened bonds that held it. He and the beast existed as equals. Still, he clutched tightly to his identity, fearing it to be lost.

"You must let go! I can only help you if you trust me! You shall return once we are safe!"

He hesitated once more.

"Why don't you trust me?"

He paused. "I don't know you!"

The beast rasped. "Yes, yes you do! Mustafo! He knew! He knows what you are! I am still you, Adam!"

He remained quiet. "This cannot be!"

The beast smiled. "It is! And you must let me help you, or they will catch you! More will come, and they are dangerous men. Trust me!"

He hesitated for a moment. At last, he released his very essence.

As he surrendered all control, the beast roared once more and took the fore-front. Then his vision became gnarled and twisted. Suddenly, the world around him became unbelievably sharper; the beast could see everything with impossible clarity. No longer was he running with human speed; the beast blasted forward with incredible speed. His human shape dissolved and in its place was something far more powerful: the wolf.

There had to be a nearby place, a piece of the world hidden from enemies. The wolf looked all about and watched as a copse materialized along the horizon. A roar of thunder echoed from the heavens above. The forest, it appeared, would be his shelter for the night. The wolf hurried toward the dense foliage to avoid the impending threat of rain.

Quickly, he got closer and closer to the forest, and the sky grew increasingly darker. Everything seemed to become silent as he burst past the first grove of trees. Further and further, he delved into the heart of the forest. A blast of mighty thunder shook the ground, and finally the wolf skidded to a halt under a thick canopy of trees.

CHAPTER SIX

Sensing it was safe, he lay down on the cold ground. All was quiet. All was safe.

"Your trust has been well placed. You are safe now."

He resurfaced and replied to the beast. "What do I do now?"

It answered him. "For now, sleep . . ."

Adam gasped and sat upright. Looking around, he could spot only the trees that surrounded him. Any hint of pain he had felt earlier had vanished without a trace. In fact, Adam felt fully rested, which was odd, because he had spent the stormy night on the forest floor.

How did I get here? he wondered.

Nothing came to mind. Adam looked down at his shirt, and was surprised to find it torn in several places. The once white fabric was now covered in unsightly grass and dirt stains. Luckily, his black pants had not suffered the same fate, but his shoes were nowhere in sight. He was truly perplexed and could not remember much about the past few days at all.

Adam grew increasingly frustrated. He needed answers, and he needed them now. He remembered the boring day in the blacksmith's workshop. Tyrule had come to visit, but then what?

The knight!

Adam remembered the order he had received for the sword, and his difficulty in forging it. The old man came, but what was his name? For a moment, he squinted as he struggled to recall it.

Mustafo.

Mustafo told him something, something that did not make sense. After he left, Leira came and offered him encouragement, which helped him finish the sword. Then everything blurred once more.

The ceremony.

He rode in a cramped carriage to the beautiful castle with Tyrule and Leira, who flirted like children. They were uncomfortably sandwiched within the vast crowd. Then the procession rolled in, followed by the king, who received many gifts, and then Adam's sword. Adam was extremely excited. King Phillip was about to get another gift, but something happened.

The king was murdered!

Adam was safe now, but something unpleasant dawned on him. He leapt to his feet and looked up through the leaves of the dense canopy. Adam's heart pounded like a savage drum as he raced beyond more of the trees. He desperately hoped that he would not find a sign. But he resolved that he could not escape the inevitable; only one thing could satisfy him now, and it was the discovery of evidence.

Adam's bare feet slammed against the damp earth as if the ground beneath him were the source of all his troubles. He had no idea where he was going, nor did he care. Several stray twigs and rocks on the forest floor scratched and cut his feet, but Adam felt no pain. Fear clung to him with a violently tenacious hold.

Without warning, Adam yelped as he scraped his foot against something rough. It was a large gnarled root sticking out obtrusively from the soil. He abruptly fell down, and a fresh wave of pain shot through his foot.

Adam lay facedown in the gritty mud for several moments, as the impact of the fall had knocked the breath out of him. After what seemed an eternity, he lifted his head up from the earth and spat out mud. His eyes met a thick tree that blocked most of his peripheral vision. The roots that issued forth from the trunk were enormous, and they cradled him uncomfortably.

He moved his arms out from under his body to get up, but then something in the mud caught his attention. Between two of the large roots was a heavy impression. From his distance, he thought that it resembled that of a rock or a leaf. He crawled closer to it and saw that the mark did not bear any similarity to either. The shape was clearly discernible, and Adam stared at it for a moment in astonishment. There, pressed into the cold, damp soil, was the unmistakable impression of a boot.

He fell on his knees and stared at the large impression. Adam placed a trembling hand on the mark and felt the cold soil on his fingers. He gazed up at the heavens, devastated. His worst fears had been realized. Halbern was dead.

So it's true.

Adam lowered his head and, for the first time in years, his eyes stung with gathering tears. He wanted nothing more than to remain on the forest floor, for surely no one would accept him now. Adam sniffed and continued staring at the ground. Even in this pitiful condition, he could not ignore the looming thought.

All of the king's men—no, everyone in the kingdom*—is out to get me. I'm some freak of nature. To make matters worse, I'm lost in the middle of a giant forest.*

He looked at the dense canopy of leaves that lay overhead. Feeling trapped, he bowed his head and sobbed bitterly. He crawled over to the massive trunk and sat against it as he wept. A few stray raindrops fell from the leaves and mingled with his tears. Crying, he noticed, felt unbelievably good under the circumstances. Suddenly, an image of Leira flitted across his mind, and he felt ashamed of himself for what he had become. Wiping away tears, he gazed back at the ground.

Remembering Halbern's last words, Adam's face became stern and he glared towards the sky. "I swear by you, Halbern, that I will become the hero Roddington needs. I will stop at nothing until Prince Nicolas is no more, and you will be avenged."

As his words drifted into the air, Adam knew he could not remain on the forest floor forever. The king's men would be waiting for him, so he could not step foot in the town. He peered through the dense cover of leaves above him; a small ray of light seeped through a tiny opening.

Adam squinted at it for a moment, and then the answer came to him as if by magic.

"Kid?" a voice called out.

Adam whirled around and spotted a figure emerge from behind a wide tree. In the dim light, his features were hardly discernable, but the damaged armor he wore was a giveaway.

"Talan?" Adam asked.

The man nodded and walked towards him. "I thought I heard your voice. Are you feeling any better? You were out cold for a few days."

"I guess."

"That was a pretty bad wound to the shoulder," Talan said.

"I almost forgot about it," Adam remarked.

"Well, let's see it then."

As Adam removed his shirt, Talan moved closer to him. Upon first glance, he blinked and rubbed his eyes in shock. "That's impossible."

"What's impossible?" Adam asked.

Talan pointed at Adam's shoulder. "There's no wound."

"*What?*" He looked down at his shoulder. Sure enough, it appeared unscathed. Adam looked at Talan, who eyed him suspiciously.

"Who are you?" he asked.

"I don't know how to explain this. I'm just Adam, really. But I do know that I could ask you the same question. Who are you?"

Talan blinked. "Someone you can trust."

"That's all you're going to give me? Seriously?"

"I have my secrets just like you have yours. We'll leave it at that," Talan answered.

"Why are you out to get the prince?" Adam pressed.

"Revenge. He stole something of mine, and he has to pay. The only problem is that—"

"He's untouchable. Trust me, I know."

Eyeing him conspicuously, Talan asked, "How do you know so much? You look like you are no older than twelve."

"*Fourteen*," Adam snapped indignantly. "And I've had a run in with him. Luckily for both of us, I know someone who can help us figure out his weakness."

Talan scoffed. "And just who might that be? One of your little friends?"

"No. His name is Mustafo, and he lives on the outskirts."

"This is the one you told me about before we got away?"

Adam nodded.

"And you're sure he can help? I don't want to drag everyone into this."

"Positive," Adam said firmly.

"Very well. Let's go find this Mustafo," Talan said firmly.

Finding their way out of the forest proved to be the hardest task Adam had ever endured. The forest sprawled out in an enormous expanse, and trying to navigate through it was like trying to move through a labyrinth blindfolded, but he haphazardly stumbled upon a way out. By the time they actually walked out from the forest, the sun had nearly finished its daily race across the horizon.

Adam was thankful for the impending darkness, as it would help conceal him. Luckily, he recalled that Mustafo's dwelling place was located on the outskirts of town, and the old man had insisted that security, oddly enough, was virtually nonexistent. If Mustafo was correct, slipping unseen into the house would be all too easy.

The grass beneath Adam's feet felt incredibly soft, especially after his expedition through the forest. Far off in the distance, he spotted a lone speck of light. He realized that the tiny source came from a house. With the precaution of a stray cat, Adam and Talan moved stealthily into the elongated shadow that followed the setting sun. In the dark, he found an odd sort of comfort, as he felt nearly invisible. Still, there was no time to waste, so they hurried toward the dimly lit house.

As they drew closer, the silhouette of the house formed a rather unusual shape against the velvet backdrop of the sky. A skinny, bent chimney hung awkwardly over the house at a peculiar angle. The windows were positioned in weird places, and most of them were strangely misshapen. The whole house itself seemed to lean precariously to one side. If Adam had entertained any doubts earlier about whose house it was, they were erased, for such a house could only belong to the mysterious Mustafo.

At last, Adam stood before the unusual house. At first, he remained deathly still while pondering his options. Was this a foolish decision, or could Mustafo really help him? Adam bit his lip in uncertainty. He did not want another encounter with the knights. Then it occurred to him that his newfound powers could cause much more harm, even to innocent people, if he did not find out what was going on.

"Are you sure about this?" Talan whispered.

Nodding, Adam swallowed his fears and summoned all of his courage as he marched up to the short door before him. Without the slightest hesitation, he knocked twice on the door, which felt light under his touch. Standing and waiting, he stared straight ahead, bracing himself, for surely Mustafo would appear shocked that an alleged murderer and an armor-clad rogue stood at his doorstep.

When the door finally creaked open slowly, Adam looked directly at the ground, fearing the old man's reaction.

"Ah, Adam! There you are! I was beginning to worry that you had lost your way! Come in!" Mustafo's voice rang out.

"Hang on a minute. You don't think I killed the king?" Adam asked in disbelief.

"Hardly. I see you brought a friend. Good reasons, I can only think," the old man replied and gestured to Talan.

Adam merely shrugged and stepped forward. The old man slipped back inside the house in a hurry. Adam ducked under the small doorway and closed the door behind him. The inside of the house was very unkempt. Several books and all sorts of items, such as pointless trinkets and coins, were strewn all over the place. Adam stepped carefully around a jar filled with wooden beads.

"Come on, m'boy! Hurry up! We must speak!" Mustafo called from another room.

Adam did his best to move faster toward the voice. Once he had made it across the sea of Mustafo's belongings, he saw Mustafo sitting at a table. Surprisingly, the table was cleared off and appeared to be impeccably clean; it did not seem to fit in with everything else in the house.

Adam walked over to a small chair at the end of the table, opposite to where Mustafo was sitting, and sat down cautiously, as if he expected a surprise of some kind. He looked up at Mustafo, who appeared to be very interested. Talan slowly entered behind them, but he stood quietly in a corner, watching carefully.

"Er—thank you, sir," Adam said.

"The pleasure is mine, boy," Mustafo replied with a twisted grin.

Adam nodded politely.

"I've forgotten you've been out on the run! Would you care for anything? You must be starving." Mustafo hopped up from his seat.

"If it's not any trouble."

Mustafo disappeared to another room for a moment. After a couple of minutes, he came back to the table carrying a cup of water and what looked like mystery meat of some sort. At this point, Adam did not care what he was served as long as it was edible.

Mustafo took his seat and waited patiently for Adam to finish the food and drink. When Adam was finished, he looked to the old man. "Do you really believe it wasn't me who killed him?"

"I know it wasn't you."

Adam's eyes widened a bit. "You mean you know—."

Mustafo cut him off. "No, I don't know who the real culprit behind it is, but I know for a fact that it wasn't you."

"Er—sir?"

"Oh please, call me by my name. *Mustafo*."

"*Mustafo*," Adam said. "You came to me a few days ago and claimed I was special."

"That I did."

"Well, you didn't mean I was talented at my job, did you?"

Mustafo smiled cryptically and answered, "I didn't mean that at all."

Adam peered out of a window and saw the faint outline of the town in the nighttime. "You spoke to me as if you thought I might be different. Abnormal."

"Ah, some of us are different from the rest. That much has always been certain."

"Well, I think there are people out there who are *very* different," Adam said.

Mustafo smirked again.

"What do you know about magic?" Adam asked.

"Magic? I thought you'd never ask. Well, it is said that there have been those in history who have possessed certain abilities that transcend the normal traits that all are born with, those who are endowed with special gifts. Why do you ask?" Mustafo inquired.

"That day at the ceremony. I don't think I would have been able to escape on my own."

"You believe it is magic that saved you?" Mustafo asked with obvious interest.

"Well, yeah. There's no other way I can think to describe it. But do you think that's foolish of me?"

"Not at all. Tell me more about this magic."

"Well, this magic, could it cause you to change?" Adam said, looking at the old man intently.

"By change, you mean what?" Mustafo asked.

"Just change in general. Is it possible?" he pressed.

"Yes, I think. Have you experienced any unusual dreams as of late?"

Adam paused for a moment, but not once did he remove his gaze from Mustafo's eyes. "Yes, actually. When Talan and I were in the forest, I had a dream that a wolf was talking to me."

Mustafo's eyes widened and a large grin appeared on his face. "A wolf, you say?"

"Well, yes. Does that matter, though?"

"There is one legend..."

"There's a legend?" Adam asked with no attempt to subdue his excitement.

"Yes, and it is about a man who changed his form."

"Into a wolf?" he asked quickly.

"Not like any wolf you're thinking about."

Adam pressed him for more information. "Could you tell me anything about it?"

"Well, it was a long, long time ago, but legend says that there was once a man who possessed incredible power. This power enabled him to change into a mighty wolf. This wolf was unlike any other. He walked on two legs, for one, so a name was needed to distinguish it from the others," Mustafo said slowly.

"And the name?" Adam said persistently.

"He was called Razorwolf."

The very name sent a tingle down Adam's spine; it seemed to resonate with a sense of might and power. Adam was struck by an odd feeling that he, too, had such power.

"*Razorwolf*," he said breathlessly.

"Yes, Razorwolf. Here's the curious thing, though. There has been only one Razorwolf, ever. I mean, it's legend, after all," Mustafo said.

Adam pressed on. "Do you believe it? The Razorwolf?"

"What are you hinting at, boy?"

"I'm not too sure, but could there ever be another?"

"Oh yes. And it makes perfect sense, because the Razorwolf is the only being strong enough to destroy such a powerful curse. It's all coming together now. You've probably noticed by now, if you haven't already, that your senses are beginning to sharpen."

Adam glanced at Talan, who remained motionless. Looking back to Mustafo, he asked, "The Razorwolf, did he have any enemies?"

"Well, of course, Adam! Every hero has enemies!" Mustafo exclaimed.

"Who are they?"

"There are some people who use their abilities for good, and others for evil. The evil ones we know as the Shadowlords. They have great power," Mustafo replied darkly.

"Shadowlords? I've never heard of them," Adam said breathlessly.

"I wouldn't have expected you to. Not in these parts. Few in this town have."

"Well, what exactly are they?"

"Like you, they have extraordinary magical abilities. To understand, you must know of the Age of Resplendency."

"The Age of Resplendency," Adam repeated. The words felt light on his tongue.

"Yes. In the early days of this land, there were only the Pentacular Reximen," Mustafo said.

"The Pentacular Reximen? Who are they?"

"All in good time. I'm getting there. The Reximen were the first wielders of magic. They governed the land under one man called Talimand. This man had two powerful students named Zailuron and Phenon.

"Zailuron and Phenon were the best of friends. Some claim that they were practically joined at the hip. Together, they were a fearsome force that few would dare to challenge. For many years, Talimand watched as they brought justice to even the farthest corners of Fallador. The wise man realized that they needed to grow as individuals, so he separated them and sent them on different missions. To the East went Phenon, for he was to bring down a powerful and cruel lord. To the far North went Zailuron to look for reinforcements for the Reximen."

"Like a battalion?" Adam asked.

"In some regards, yes," Mustafo continued. "What Zailuron found was not more men, though. After wandering in a cave, he stumbled upon an old spell book. Curious, he flipped through the ancient pages and discovered spells unlike any others he had seen before. Powerful spells were exactly what he believed could turn the tide in any battle. He discovered a secret of sorts. When he returned, he told only Phenon of his findings. Phenon claimed that such powerful magic ought to remain a secret because no man could ever hope to control it.

"Zailuron agreed with his friend, but he did not rid himself of the book. Instead, he earnestly studied its pages every night. Soon, visions of power began to float in his mind. Not even his closest confidants had any idea of the truth.

"One day, Zailuron had a quarrel with one of the Reximen. In his anger, he unleashed one of the hidden spells and directed it at the other man. The magic smote his enemy on the chest, and he fell to the ground. Zailuron had killed the man, and he greatly feared that his error would soon be discovered. The few who witnessed the attack agreed to help him conceal the body on the condition that Zailuron teach them the ways of this new magic. He agreed, and they practiced during the darkest hours of the night.

"The power, potent as it was, soon began to exert a hold over their minds. On another lone mission, Zailuron used the power to kill all of his enemies with a single wave of his hand. The Shadowmagic was much too powerful to control, as Phenon had predicted, and of course the deaths he caused were irreversible.

"Soon, Zailuron and his followers were immersed in the Shadowmagic. Phenon sensed that something was amiss in his closest friend, so one day he cornered him alone. Zailuron excitedly told him of the mighty power he had acquired and his proficiency in using it. He spoke of the deaths he alone had brought about. Disgusted, Phenon hurried to Talimand and told him of the Shadowmagic. Zailuron learned of this and knew he would certainly be expelled from the Pentacular Reximen. Thus, he gathered his followers and planned to surprise Talimand.

"The following morning, Talimand sought Zailuron, intending to remove the traces of evil from his honorable halls. Zailuron was ready, though. He engaged Talimand in a deadly battle of spells. When Phenon arrived, he was stunned to find his friend attacking their teacher. In one swift movement, Zailuron unleashed a powerful spell, a strike to the chest, and Talimand was no more.

"The murder of Talimand was the final blow to Phenon. Zailuron had turned, and Phenon, sad as he was, stood his ground. He led the Reximen against Zailuron's army of Shadowlords. The battle was long and arduous, but it was Phenon who dealt his old friend a mortal blow when their magic clashed. In anger, the Shadowlords retreated, swearing vengeance against the Pentacular Reximen.

"And so Phenon taught the Reximen to defend themselves against that very force until the day that he died. Some say that even after Zailuron died, his uncanny leadership survived for generations. The Shadowlords were truly powerful," Mustafo said with a dark grin.

Adam remained silent for several minutes as he pondered the story the old man related to him. It certainly struck a chord within him. Had it been he and Tyrule who were at such deadly odds, Adam knew that he would not have had the strength to defeat him. But the legend was a chilling subject, and he wanted to move away from it for the time being.

"Mustafo, as you know already, I can't stay here. I'm a wanted criminal, and I don't think they'd welcome me as this Razorwolf monster," Adam said gravely.

"Well, there is another place."

"How do you know so much about these magic tales? I mean, I've never heard of them before, and I've never met anyone else who does."

"Never mind that! Safety is what you seek, is it not?" Mustafo said urgently.

"Sorry, just wondering."

"That is fine. Now, according to an old legend, there is a place far away from here where you can go. It won't be easy; in fact, it'll be very dangerous. They've been known to do terrible things to those they perceive as a threat. Some of the victims I used to know. After running into a Shadowlord, if they weren't already dead, they went mad. I suppose there really are things worse than death after all."

"I don't have any other options."

"Well, you could stay here. If you're interested, the legend says that you must go to the Reximen Heights."

"The what?"

"The fortress built into the side of the mountains!" Mustafo insisted.

"Where is this place?"

"Well, I know there is a cluster of mountains," Mustafo began. "This is the part you won't like. First you must go to an island way beyond this town. In order to get to it, you must sail across the sea."

"Well, I'm done for," Adam said flatly.

"No, no, you're not. You have your friends."

"My friends? They think I'm a murderer. And besides, how can I get anywhere near them with the knights on patrol?" Adam asked, feeling increasingly hopeless.

Mustafo was quick to reply. "They know you. And as to the communication problem, no one will expect an old man to cause any harm. Let me send the message to them."

"Do you really think they will come?"

"If they are your true friends, I think they will come."

"I trust you, Mustafo."

"And I am honored, especially to be trusted by a Razorwolf."

"Thank you, but where am I to stay?"

"Well, I thought that part was obvious," Mustafo said.

"You mean here?"

"Where else?"

Adam fell quiet for a minute. Everything was happening incredibly fast. Then, something occurred to him. "Mustafo, I'm the Razorwolf. If I'm the new one, what if the Shadowlords return?"

"Mortal peril. After all, they possess some of the most incredible powers this world has ever known. Come now, it's getting late! You'd best be off to bed!" Mustafo said quickly. Rising with unusual haste from the table, the old man walked over to where Adam sat and picked up the plate and the cup. Adam, too, rose.

"I just have one more question for you," he said.

Mustafo turned and eyed him suspiciously. "What would that be?"

"How do you know so much?"

The old man froze for a split second, then he answered, "Everyone has secrets, Adam."

When Mustafo disappeared from the kitchen, Talan stepped away from his post and walked towards Adam, an unsettling expression forming on his face.

"I don't trust him," he said.

"You said the same thing about yourself. Everyone must have secrets," Adam said.

"There's a difference. I don't like talking about my past. From what I've heard the two of you speaking of, this is bigger than any one of us. He spoke of another land, not to mention a specific landmark. I'm warning you now, Adam, that this one's a shady character."

"Well, we should wait a little bit longer before jumping to conclusions. But I suppose you're right. Both of us should be on the lookout for anything suspicious," Adam said.

Talan nodded. "So magic does exist. It will be a useful weapon against the prince."

"About that. The prince has magic of his own."

"Then you'll have to take it from him," Talan said.

"I'm told I'm the only one who can."

"And I will be with you every step of the way. Our two quests are now one, and I will never waver. Betrayal is not a weapon in my arsenal."

"Good. You know what I want in my arsenal? Sleep," Adam remarked.

"There's an empty room just behind this room. There's the door right there." He pointed at a doorway directly behind Adam.

"Thank you." Adam turned to leave.

He ducked under another low doorway and saw the white sheets of the bed in the dim light. Without further delay, Adam threw himself onto the bed and lay still. As he lay there, he could not help but recall Mustafo's odd sense of reverence for the Shadowlords. He spent no more time on the thought, for his heavy eyelids drooped, and he did not resist. Sleep found him quicker than ever before.

CHAPTER SEVEN

SKELETONS IN THE CLOSET

For the first time in several days, Adam felt the comforting presence of silence soothe his ears. After the rushed events that had transpired in the last few days, the quiet felt unusual. He could also sense a soft light against his closed eyes.

Fully rested at last, his eyelids slowly flickered open. What appeared to be an off-kilter ceiling slowly came into focus. Adam turned his head to one side, and he saw the dazzling sunlight pouring through a rather peculiar-looking window. He could barely make out buildings of the town in the background.

Adam suddenly remembered where he was. The memories of the past few days flashed through his mind in a blur. King Phillip's birthday ceremony seemed like years ago. He felt a twinge of sorrow when he thought about the smiling king's fate. A good man had been murdered, and the awful truth was that someone was out there getting away with such an atrocity. Even worse, Prince Nicolas had pinned the impossible deed on him.

What troubled Adam even more was the truth about his own identity. Several days earlier, he was the son of the blacksmith, a boy of humble beginnings. Now, as the Razorwolf, he supposedly possessed incredible powers he neither understood nor felt he could harness. The very name Razorwolf seemed to resonate within him every time it echoed in his mind. Only the day before had he learned everything: the Razorwolf and the dark magic of the Shadowlords. The name of the villainous band of warriors left a repugnant taste on his tongue.

He slowly sat upright and his eyes met the small doorway, which was constructed of several different types of wood, so it was an odd collection of various earth tones. Adam lifted his legs over to the edge of the bed. When his feet found the floor, he stood up and stretched his arms wide in a gaping yawn.

Adam walked lazily toward the doorway. He ducked under the low frame and found himself standing in the room where he and Mustafo had sat only hours ago. For some reason, he expected to find the old man sitting down at the same table, wearing that crooked smile as he waited for his guest to sit down and chat.

But Mustafo was nowhere in sight. He felt awkward standing in the house alone. "Mustafo?" His voice cracked from disuse.

The wizened voice did not answer.

"Mustafo?" Adam repeated even louder.

Again, there was no reply. Suddenly, a muffled thump came from another room. Adam felt jolted by the startling noise, and his head jerked to the right as if it were controlled by some phantom impulse. Was Mustafo actually at home? Perhaps he can't hear that well, Adam assumed.

There had been an obvious improvement in his hearing since the episode in the woods. Adam knew it had to be the Razorwolf part of him that was responsible for this because fourteen years' worth of enduring the sounds of the blacksmith's craft could hardly have been healthy for his ears. He chortled to himself at this thought and realized that it was the closest he had come to a laugh since the carriage ride with Tyrule and Leira.

Adam brushed past the table without giving it the slightest bit of attention. He moved toward the source of the noise, which was straight ahead through another small doorway. The business of ducking under the small frames was already becoming commonplace to Adam, even though he had only spent one night in the odd house.

A small room was ahead of him, yet there was another doorway to his immediate right. Adam's acute hearing suggested that the source of the noise came from the right, so he ignored the room in front of him and turned to slip through the other doorway.

Unlike all the other doorways in Mustafo's house, this one had an actual door preventing Adam from simply passing through. It had a normal-sized frame, and the door's wooden surface had a strange lump of rock crudely plastered on it. Raising an eyebrow, he supposed that he stood before Mustafo's sleeping quarters, and he felt a little uneasy at the prospect of entering.

"Mustafo?" he called.

There was no answer. Instead, Adam heard the thumping noise again. He became concerned that Mustafo was in some sort of trouble, so he thought it best to forget about the niceties and just open the door. He placed his hand on the doorknob, inhaled sharply, twisted it quickly, and pushed the door wide open.

Adam saw a small bed placed in the center of the room. This was easily the largest room in the house. He looked about in a rush, but Mustafo was nowhere in sight. The thumping noise sounded again, and Adam's hearing caused him to snap his head in its direction.

CHAPTER SEVEN

One of the casement windows had fluttered open, and the wind had caused the window frame to hit the wall. Adam felt incredibly foolish for rushing inside his generous host's room only to find that the window frame was banging against the wall. He shook his head in embarrassment and was very thankful that no one was around to witness his little mistake. As he stepped away, a voice caught his attention.

"Where are you going?"

He whirled around and spotted Talan examining the map of Roddington that hung on Mustafo's wall.

"What are you doing in here? This is his private space!" Adam hissed.

"Looking for evidence. I told you before, Adam, I don't trust him," Talan answered.

"He could still be here!"

"Not so. He's out in the market looking for your friends. I'm an early riser, you see."

Rolling his eyes, Adam remarked, "You're one of those 'by-the-book' people, aren't you?"

Talan looked to him, unamused. "By-the-book might have just saved your life the other day. Now, come help me look."

Even without Talan's command, Adam could not help but take a quick peek at the room. Curiosity got the better of him. Opposite the wall was another open window, and in front of it was an old desk with several papers scattered all over it. In another corner of the room was an archaic chest of drawers. The room itself was impressively tidy compared to the other rooms of the house.

An unusual thought occurred to him. Mustafo could not have accumulated such a vast store of knowledge about magic through mere hearsay. No, Adam realized, he had to have some written record of the stories. He wanted to know more of the fanciful things, of Mustafo's compelling stories, that danced within his dreams.

"Have you tried these papers already?" he asked.

Talan shook his head. "Can't read."

"You serious?" he gawked.

Talan shot him a stern look, and Adam quickly looked away. After a quick glance at the door, Adam placed his hands on one of the knobs. Quietly, he pulled the drawer toward himself, revealing a large collection of stray papers.

He quickly glanced one by one at a few of the pages. For the most part, they appeared to be letters to people with names he had no hope of pronouncing. With a sense of disappointment, he placed the messy pile on the desk and peered through the open window. He sighed, picked up the stack of papers, returned the letters to the drawer, and closed the compartment.

As he turned to tell Talan about his unremarkable search, Adam spotted a small movement out of the corner of his eye. A strong gust of wind blew in from one window and caused the window frame to smack against the wall. As the wind swept through the room, it traveled through the other window, picking up a single piece of paper he must have accidentally left on Mustafo's desk and tossing it outside.

Adam looked at Talan in horror.

"What are you waiting for? Go get it!" Talan barked.

In the blink of an eye, Adam ran out of the room. He nearly dove through the small doorway that led to the dining room as he raced to get the paper. Running through the sea of Mustafo's belongings, he nearly tripped on several occasions, but he managed to reach the front door safely.

If Adam had been hiding out within the town, it would have been too risky to retrieve the paper. However, he was on the outskirts of town, and he knew that the knights would not be looking anywhere near Mustafo's house. With this in mind, he threw open the front door and immediately spotted the piece of paper lying at the base of a large tree.

Adam darted over to the tree and stooped down to snatch up the paper. Once it was in his grasp, he quickly turned around and dashed back into the house.

Once he was behind the door, he slowed his pace. He neatly sidestepped all of Mustafo's things that lay scattered on the floor. After stopping to catch his breath in the living room, he took the familiar route back into Mustafo's bedroom.

"Be more careful next time," Talan admonished.

"Okay," he answered.

Before reaching for the drawer handle, Adam hesitated for a moment. Once more, curiosity got the better of him. He looked down at the piece of paper in his hand and could make out the ink bleeding faintly through the page. Turning it over, he saw that it was a letter. The writing was exceedingly neat and ornate. Before he could stop himself, Adam began reading.

Dear Mustafo,

I hope this letter finds you in good spirits. It has been a long time since we last met. If I remember correctly, you still owe me a visit. At this point, I'd say it's long overdue, old friend.

It seems like only yesterday that we were at the very peak of our abilities, does it not? A lot has changed since then. I know you live far, far away, and a visit would be quite difficult; however, I realize you are in a strategic location if our predictions are correct. This boy you speak of seems to possess the very attributes that we once expressed when we were younger.

If your predictions are indeed correct, then we must be careful. There will be those who will find him and try to convince him that their side is dedicated to what is right. We must try and make sure this never happens. If you can already sense his attributes, it is obvious that he must have considerable power. We cannot afford to lose him.

There will come a time, if I am correct, when his abilities will become apparent, so I think it best to prepare for when that time comes. Send him to me so that I can educate him properly in ours ways. I know there is that tower where others like him gather, but as I mentioned earlier, I'd like to work with him individually to help him manifest his power.

At this point, I believe it is safe, but you never know for sure what's out there. At any event, I am beginning to get suspicious about the king. You must get to him first! There is a will, and there is a way. I believe you'll know what to do when the time is right. The threat must be stopped, and you and I both know that you are the best choice for the job.

With that, I bid you farewell, old friend. I hope to cross paths again in the near future.

Rhys

"Talan, I think you need to see this."

Talan strode over to him and said, " Read it out loud."

Reading over each word carefully, Adam relayed to Talan the strange letter. When Adam was done, Talan grabbed the letter and examined it in the light. He gingerly pressed his tongue to the parchment and examined the handwriting.

"What are you doing?" Adam asked with an eyebrow raised.

"I may not be able to read," Talan replied. "But I can recognize characteristics. This is not a recent letter, Adam. This paper is several years old, which means that he's filed it away for quite some time."

"Secrets," Adam whispered.

"Yes, and this is a dangerous one. This is our evidence, Adam!" Talan exclaimed.

"Hold on now. We can't just take this out of context."

"And ask him about it? How foolish," Talan remarked.

"Will you let me finish?" Adam snapped.

Talan folded his arms.

"As I was saying, we should keep watching him," Adam said.

"No. That letter was about you. Don't you get it? He plans to use you. Maybe he is against the prince, but that doesn't mean he has his own plans for you. And, think about it, he has an ungodly reverence for those Shadowlords. Adam, listen to me, we have to get out of here," Talan warned him.

"You're right. If that is an old letter, he knew about my powers way before I did. I just want to know where he gets his secret knowledge from."

"I don't think it would be wise. Things like that can really twist a man's mind."

"I never thought about that. Can we at least wait for Tyrule and Leira before making any serious plans?" he inquired.

"Perhaps. In the meantime, though, I will be spending every waking hour in preparation for our departure," Talan said.

"That sounds reasonable."

Talan abruptly left Adam's side and hurried out of the room. All alone, Adam gingerly opened the drawer and placed the letter back on the stack where it belonged. After closing the drawer, he left the room slowly, carefully closing the door behind him. As he stepped back into the dining room, he could not help but recall something about the conversation he and Mustafo shared the previous night.

Mustafo suggested the possibility of Reximen Heights, but he was frustratingly vague about how to get there. In fact, it seemed that, by being so vague, the old man was trying to dissuade him from finding it. At the first mention of "the boy" in the letter, he knew that Talan was right in saying that Mustafo and his mysterious friend were referring to him. They seemed genuinely interested in Adam, which chilled his blood. He wondered whether Mustafo was planning to send him to this Rhys character or if he would allow him to make the journey to the mountains of the other land.

Adam pulled a chair out from the table. As he sat down, a very exciting thought occurred to him: There are others like me!

For once, Adam felt proud of his power. The prospect of others with magical abilities was so thrilling. Many questions began to swirl around in his mind. Who were they? What were they like? Did they also turn into something? What powers did they have? Would they like him?

Even with thoughts like these, however, he recalled his shortcomings. He had yet to freely access this power, nor had he ever been fully conscious during an episode. There was no telling what other people would think of him. After all, if he was the only Razorwolf, surely he would be excluded. Perhaps he would go pay Mustafo's friend a visit.

Still, one thing lingered in Adam's head, and it was an uncomfortable thought. Somehow, Mustafo and his friend had known about King Phillip ahead of time, and somehow they knew something about Adam. If they knew that something the king was in mortal danger, then he should still live.

Mustafo's correspondent had mentioned something about powers. Everything seemed to be falling into place like an elaborate puzzle. Mustafo knew a lot about this other side of reality, so could he actually have magical powers himself?

You must get to him first.

A shiver rippled down Adam's spine as the truth became clear. If Mustafo had such powers, he could have easily tampered with the sword at the ceremony. Adam wrinkled his nose as he thought deeper and deeper. Why would Mustafo defile the sword? What could he possibly gain from it?

If Mustafo really had murdered the king, why did he let Adam, who was supposed to be special, take the fall? Mustafo's words echoed in Adam's head like an old song.

CHAPTER SEVEN

The evil ones we know as the Shadowlords. They had great power.

If Mustafo knew there were people who would try to persuade Adam to their side, what were the lengths he was willing to go to keep Adam on his side? After the death of the king, there was no one for him to turn to, and Mustafo had greeted him with open arms. And the old man seemed to have a twisted obsession with the Shadowlords; he practically revered the dark warriors.

I know it wasn't you.

Mustafo had arranged the whole thing so that Adam would trust him completely. The old man was already surrounded by an impenetrable shroud of secrecy.

Adam knew that the letter was meant to be kept secret. Had he not seen it, he would have blindly followed Mustafo. He felt a small twinge of fear, yet he also felt the keen sting of betrayal. He resented that Mustafo had manipulated him so. In his time of need Adam had not found help. Instead, he had found someone who was only interested in using the remarkable powers he exhibited.

Suddenly, Adam's thoughts disappeared when he heard the front door swing open. Mustafo was back. Adam sat up in his chair as he heard the footsteps grow nearer.

"How do you walk around in here?" the familiar voice of Tyrule Ramsgate remarked.

Adam was a bit perplexed. If Mustafo had such selfish intentions, why in the world would he bring Adam's closest friends into his home? Mustafo came into the dining room first, followed by Tyrule and then Leira.

"There he is," Mustafo said simply.

Tyrule and Leira both eyed Adam suspiciously as if they were ascertaining his guilt. Their scrutiny weighed upon Adam, causing him tremendous discomfort. He looked away from them and stared blankly at the table.

"Adam." Tyrule's voice was monotonous.

"Tyrule," Adam said blandly.

"Adam, where have you been?" Leira cried.

Adam stared back at her with an eyebrow raised, as he was not expecting such a reaction. "I—I—wait, aren't you going to ask me if I did it?" he asked incredulously.

It was Tyrule who spoke next. "Did you?" he asked, with a hint of venom in his voice.

Adam was taken aback. "How can you even think that?" he asked defensively.

"Well, what I saw at the castle was pretty convincing."

"Look, it wasn't me!" Adam spat.

Tyrule squinted at him in contemplation.

Leira, on the other hand, seemed to believe him. "Well, you must have some idea who it is," she said softly.

"Yes, actually, I—," Adam began.

"Have you now?" Mustafo interjected suddenly.

Adam had nearly forgotten about the sudden revelation of Mustafo's true nature through the letter. In fact, he felt increasingly uncomfortable in the old man's presence. For a moment, he was at a loss for words. He struggled desperately for something to say.

"Yes, Adam. Who was it?" Leira asked again.

"Er—I have no idea. What I meant to say was that I actually wish that I knew." He forced the words out.

"Don't worry, Adam. These things have a way of presenting themselves," Mustafo said quietly.

"I—I suppose you're right," Adam stammered.

"Adam, you seem nervous," Tyrule noticed.

Adam looked up at him. "I'm not," he said, trying to convince himself as well as the others.

"Looks like it to me."

Briefly, for a couple of seconds, no one spoke. The silence was uncomfortable, and Adam wished that someone would say something.

"Well, perhaps the lot of you should discuss the next step," Mustafo finally said, and he disappeared to his room.

Once he was gone, Adam felt as though someone had lifted an incredibly heavy boulder off his shoulders. He was glad Mustafo was gone, for now he could share the new information with his friends.

"Listen," Adam whispered.

Leira bent closer to him at once, but Adam noticed Tyrule's slight hesitancy. Leira shot him an angry look, and he bent down in submission.

"What is it?" she whispered back.

Adam looked around to make sure that no one except for his friends could hear him. Once he was sure of their complete privacy, Adam let out an uneasy breath. He looked into Leira's warm hazel eyes and then into Tyrule's cool ones. The truth had to come out sooner or later. With a growing sense of trepidation, Adam glanced nervously at Leira.

When all was absolutely still, he spoke in a low whisper. "I know who killed the king."

"Who is it?" Leira asked quickly.

"Mustafo."

Tyrule and Leira exchanged skeptical glances and looked back at Adam.

"I don't think he would be capable," Tyrule remarked.

"I beg to differ," Talan's voice spoke quietly as he entered the room behind Leira.

Tyrule and Leira whirled around in surprise.

"And just who are you?" Tyrule asked.

"A friend," Adam answered quickly.

"You two know each other?" Leira inquired.

Talan nodded before speaking. "If not for me, Adam would not be with us today. Hear me out. Mustafo has dark plans up his sleeves. He's not who you think he is. Ask Adam. He seems to be a harmless old man, but he knows a lot about things we can't even begin to imagine."

Tyrule and Leira looked at Adam fearfully. "Like what?" they asked in unison.

"Evil things. I won't speak of them here. We're already being risky just by talking about him," Adam answered.

"So what are we going to do?" Leira whispered.

"I'm still working on that part," Adam said.

"Don't worry, Adam. I have a plan, and your friends can help us," Talan said.

"We can?" Tyrule asked.

"Let's stop with the pointless questions," Talan said flatly. "Now, you're the son of Alimzar Ramsgate, which could work quite nicely for us. Here's what you need to do. You're going to tell your father that Adam Crescent is hiding in a house on the outskirts of Roddington."

Adam looked to Talan in panic. "What?"

Talan nodded. "You heard me correctly. I know there's probably a huge sum on his head, so most, if not every, member in the royal guard will come down here. Of course, by that time, I'll be at the harbor. Ramsgate, once you alert them, come straight down to the harbor. Lara—"

"Leira," she corrected.

"Right. You'll be helping our friend get down to us safely. You'll have to hide him convincingly just in case some of the guards are on duty. If we play our cards right, and with a little bit of luck, we'll be on our way without a fight."

"You've been working on this for a long time, haven't you? And by a long time, I mean all night," Adam remarked.

"You really have a mouth, don't you?" Talan said bluntly.

"You have no idea," Leira replied.

"Oh, that reminds me. Adam, I'm guessing that crossing from Roddington to the other side is no easy business, especially when the prince rules. See if you can convince Mustafo to tell you how to get past it. You're his golden child, the one who can make all of his dreams come true. It shouldn't be too hard," Talan said.

Adam smiled daringly. "I'm good at talking."

"I've noticed. Now, we're finished here," said Talan as he rose and disappeared into his room.

When he was out of earshot, Tyrule whispered, "Who is he?"

"He saved my life. I don't know much about his past, but we will definitely need him, especially where we're going," Adam answered.

For the next several minutes, Tyrule and Leira set aside their preconceived doubts and openly conveyed to Adam the detail of the newly christened King Nicolas's dealings. From what he heard, Adam sensed that a shadow was beginning to fall over Roddington.

"He's not King Philip in any sense," Leira informed him. "He is much more rigid, maybe even darker."

"Well, we should probably return home, Leira. My father will be wondering where we are. Knowing your mother, she won't be too pleased," Tyrule said.

"Both of my parents are in other parts right now. They'll have no idea. But you're probably right," she said and both of them rose from their seats and headed for the door.

Leira left first, but Tyrule stopped before passing through the front door.

"Adam?" he asked.

"Yeah?"

"Does tomorrow morning sound good for our next meeting?"

"Sounds great."

"And one more thing," Tyrule continued.

"Go on," Adam said.

"It's good to see you."

With that, he disappeared behind the door just as a smile reappeared on Adam's face, the first in a long time. His happy moment faded quickly, because he had a mission to complete, one that could mean life or death.

CHAPTER EIGHT

MOONLIGHT ESCAPE

Mustafo spent an unusually long time locked away in his bedroom, much to Adam's growing apprehension. The plan was simple, of course, on paper. It would not be easy to execute by any standard, but it could be done.

But Adam could not ignore the sad fact that, since he was wanted for murder, there would be no return to Roddington. Several times, he mentioned this to his friends, and each time they firmly agreed to carry on with him. Adam insisted that they write farewell notes to their families explaining the circumstances.

What worried Adam was his silent escape from the old man's house. If Mustafo had killed the king and got away with it, then preventing a teenage boy from leaving a small house would be a simpleton's chore. Escaping the house seemed to worry Adam more than the possibility of running into the knights. It was not easy to keep a stiff upper lip because his insides churned terribly.

Luck, it appeared, was in Adam's favor this time. Talan's expertise was a valuable weapon in their endeavors. Not to mention, Leira possessed unmatched charm. If she so much as batted her eyelashes, anyone would be agreeable to her request. This part of the plan was crucial, as Adam needed Leira to effectively hide him from anyone that they might encounter during their escape. Plus, Adam felt no inclination to charm the old man.

When the sky outside became dark, Adam suspended his watch and went to sleep. The next morning, he rose exceptionally early and waited for Mustafo to stir. Before seeking the old man, Adam wandered into Talan's room and found that the rogue had already left. Being alone with Mustafo unnerved Adam, but he hid his feelings effectively. For several hours, he sat alone at the empty table and waited impatiently for Mustafo to make his presence known.

Suddenly, there came a loud knock from the front door, and Adam tiptoed to the peephole. Expecting Talan, he was caught off guard when he spotted Leira staring through the glass. Quickly, he opened the door and let her in.

"What are you doing here so early?" he whispered.

Leira shrugged as she entered the house. "There's not much to do at home. Plus, I can't stop thinking about the adventure. It'll be so great!"

"Let's hope so," Adam said complacently and followed her to the table.

Leira took a seat immediately, and Adam picked up a glass bowl from the center and studied the swirling patterns etched into its glossy surface.

"Adam, where have you been since the celebration?" she asked.

"Look, it's a long story," he replied quickly.

"I'm sure I can keep up."

"I'm sure you can, too, but I'll tell you once we're on our way."

Leira paused for a moment. "Is there a reason you don't want to tell me?" she asked.

"No, no. I'm going to tell you everything during our voyage."

"A voyage? Where are you planning on going, m'boy?"

Adam nearly jumped out of his skin when he heard Mustafo's voice crackle. Before he could stop himself, he released the glass bowl, and it fell to the floor with a crash. Both Adam and Leira looked at the old man with equally horrified expressions.

"Didn't mean to spook you two," Mustafo said.

"That's okay," Adam said.

Mustafo wandered over toward them and took his familiar seat at the other end of the table. He smiled kindly at Leira, and then he looked to Adam with a serious expression. Adam quickly bent down and gingerly picked up the broken shards.

"Adam, I've been thinking. Perhaps the Heights are not the best place for you right now," he said with a wheeze.

I knew it! He's going to send me to that other person! Adam thought. He was grateful that his face was hidden from Mustafo's view, for it would have betrayed his fear.

"It's not?" Adam asked blankly.

"No, there's another place. It's off in that general direction."

"Er—I wanted to ask you something," Adam stammered and glanced quickly at Leira.

Getting the hint, she nodded firmly and disappeared off into another room.

"Where is she going?" Mustafo asked.

"No idea. She can be odd sometimes, but it's always harmless."

"I see. Well, what did you want to talk about?"

"Perhaps we should sit down," Adam said.

Mustafo nodded, and Adam took his seat at the opposite end of the table.

"What's on your mind?"

"Well," Adam began uneasily. "I know that crossing between lands might be difficult, especially if Prince Nicolas didn't want anyone crossing."

"An obstacle, you mean," Mustafo said.

Adam nodded.

"I think I might have an answer for you. Many years ago, when you were probably just learning how to speak, someone tried to sail away from Roddington. I know he was punished somehow, but talk of a powerful storm rose amongst the people."

"Was his name Thorn?" Adam blurted.

"I believe so. How do you know?" Mustafo asked suspiciously.

"Oh, my father told me about him. Used him as an example," he lied.

"Makes sense. You and I both know, by now, that powerful storms don't just materialize out of nowhere. I strongly believe that this storm is a keyhole."

"What do you mean by keyhole?" Adam asked.

"Prince Nicolas's spell divided both lands Roddington and Fallador. The only thing that exists between them is the sea. I'd be willing to bet that his curse is weakest in that storm."

"But that doesn't make any sense," Adam remarked.

"Oh but it does. The reason the storm is so powerful is because it has not been unlocked by the key. Every curse has a key," Mustafo said.

"Don't tell me that I have to find some key. I'm not going back in that castle."

"You've already got it."

"I do?"

"You are the key, Adam. That's why the prince is so strict about forbidding passage across the waters. He fears the person who can pass through the storm because the curse will begin to come undone."

"So I just have to sail across?" Adam asked in disbelief.

"That's right."

"Well, that's convenient if I'm heading for Reximen Heights."

Mustafo raised an eyebrow suspiciously. "Actually, there is another legend that speaks of a teacher."

"Well, perhaps I might go there instead. I'm still a bit tired, so can we make these travel arrangements tomorrow?" Adam asked quickly.

"If you're sure. In the meantime, I am going to sort out some of my papers. They are not as well organized as I previously thought," Mustafo replied quietly.

Adam gulped nervously and looked at the floor.

"Mustafo?" Leira piped up all of the sudden.

Mustafo and Adam spotted Leira standing in the doorway.

"Yes?" Mustafo asked.

"I was wondering if I could possibly stay here. My parents are out of the city, and I could help you and Adam. I'm good at housework."

Adam knew for a fact that Leira was just awful when it came to housework. Luckily for them both, Mustafo was not aware of her inadequacies. Adam clamped his teeth down upon his tongue to prevent himself from smirking.

The old man hesitated for a moment, and then he smiled lightly. "Well, I suppose there's no trouble in that."

"Thank you, sir," Leira said with a phony smile.

Mustafo nodded kindly to her. "Well, Adam, I suppose we shall discuss the arrangement tomorrow, then. If that's it, then I think I shall be off to the market again. I think those papers can wait." He rose from his seat.

Adam and Leira remained frozen until they heard the door slam, and they listened as the waddling footsteps gradually faded away. Once they were sure the old man was gone, they simultaneously drew in an immense breath of air. Leira looked at Adam with nervous apprehension.

"I can't believe it. He seemed so sincere when he explained that you were here," she said.

"Yes, neither can I. He murdered King Phillip, though. No one would ever suspect that an old man did it. He's playing a charade, Leira. We can't fall for it," Adam said darkly.

The light of protest was in her eyes, but Adam returned the look with a bold glance of his own.

"Adam, I still don't understand why you won't tell me anything. It's not fair. I tell you everything, even my deepest secrets."

"I told you already. You'll find out soon enough. Now's not the place. Besides, he might not want me to tell others. It could put you in danger."

"He knows what happened to you?"

"Well, yes. Remember when I told you about the time he visited?" Adam asked.

"Yes, but what happened?"

"Well, he knew something was going on."

Leira arched an eyebrow to prompt Adam to reveal more. "And?"

"And you will find out later," he said flatly.

Leira narrowed her eyes. He merely shrugged in reply.

"Fine. But this had better be good!"

"Trust me. You've never heard anything like it," he assured her.

"Now why would you tell me that?" she whined and stomped her foot.

"I don't know. It just seemed the best way to put it. I've done my part of the plan. Now, we can stay here chatting all day, or we can play our roles so that Mustafo doesn't get suspicious," Adam said brusquely.

Leira said nothing and rose from her seat. She walked over to a nearby cupboard and removed a broom. Without another word, she took to sweeping the dirty floor with furious swipes. Adam also realized it was time to do something, so he went to clean up his room.

For several hours, both of them cleaned, dusted, and did all sorts of dirty work. Leira had the misfortune of finding several dead rats in unsightly corners. Adam's eyes quickly became red and watery from all of the dust that flew into the air when he started cleaning off the furniture. Between Leira's screams of surprise and Adam's loud coughs, the day seemed to pass rather slowly. Just when they thought that they had finally completed their tasks, they discovered to their dismay that there were other compartments and things to clean or organize.

At midday, Adam and Leira dropped their mops, brooms, and dustbins without the slightest hesitation and rushed into the kitchen. He reminded her that she needed to give Mustafo a decent meal in order to seal the deal. Leira whined, protesting that she could not cook even the easiest things without creating a disaster.

Adam suggested cooking eggs, but she quickly turned that down, reminding him of the time that she had set fire to a table. He continued to offer ideas, but she always found a previous incident that ruled his possibilities out.

In a last-ditch effort, Adam suggested salad. Leira thought about it for a moment, and she realized that she had never attempted to make salad before.

"But salad's incredibly easy—it's an idiot's dish," he claimed.

"Oh, so you think I'm an idiot, then. Is that what you're saying?" she asked indignantly and whacked him in the back of the head.

The tutorial Adam gave her took a while for her to absorb. But after many failed attempts, she actually managed to make edible decent arrangement of carrots, lettuce, and other various vegetables.

"Remember, Leira, everything I told you. We don't want him to have any reason to be suspicious."

"And speaking of suspicious, where's Talan?" she asked.

"He left early this morning," he replied and returned to cleaning.

After the kitchen was nearly spotless, Adam and Leira went back to working. She went to all of the rooms except for Mustafo's bedroom and another cluttered room. She felt rather proud of herself for deciding to wait until twilight to clean up that messy room. One quick glance told her that it would take hours to clean it up, and she knew she needed to allow plenty of time for nightfall.

Adam floated about from room to room looking for something that Leira had missed in her wake. As time crawled by, there were fewer and fewer spots to clean up, and Adam was beginning to get bored. The inactivity did not wear him down. All he could think about were the events that were to transpire in several hours. He longed to be free of Mustafo and his wickedness so that he might finally discern how to use his new powers.

Finally, the door flew open, and in came Mustafo with his prizes from the market. He waddled into the dining room where he proceeded to place an unusual assortment of items on the table. Apart from the regular edibles, Mustafo brought in several little gold rods, a couple of stones, and another jar of carved beads.

When he had finished sorting his collections into several different piles, he took a glance around his house. Noticing its newly attained cleanliness, he nodded in approval. "Well, well, well. I don't think this place has ever looked this good."

Leira rushed into the dining room at once to meet him. "Well, I did promise, didn't I?"

"Well, you deliver quite nicely on your promises. I just have one question," Mustafo said.

"Anything you ask."

"Can you fix that mess in the other room?"

"Oh," Leira answered with a light, phony laugh. "I'm saving that one for last."

Mustafo nodded and returned to shuffling through his things.

Adam was watching Leira at one end of the room and Mustafo at the other. Mustafo seemed to be looking at him out of the corner of his eye.

"Adam, are you feeling more… robust yet?" Mustafo asked.

"What—er—yes, I'm getting there. Had a nice nap just a moment ago," Adam answered quickly.

"Ah, that's always nice to hear." Mustafo didn't seem to notice how rushed Adam's words were.

Leira must have sensed the awkwardness rising, so she interjected herself into the conversation. "Mister Mustafo, sir?"

"Yes, Leira, isn't it?" Mustafo turned around.

"Yes, that's it. It's almost time for dinner, wouldn't you think?"

"Well, isn't this a treat. I'm not used to this kind service. What d'you have in mind?" he asked gleefully.

"Oh, I make a good salad. Is that all right? I mean, I would hate to serve something displeasing," Leira cooed.

"I'm sure that'll be fine."

Adam was relieved when Mustafo accepted salad without another remark or question. So far, everything was going according to plan.

"Well then, Adam, why don't you come and have a seat?" Mustafo gestured to a chair.

Adam smiled lightly and acquiesced. He sat with his hands in his lap at the end of the table opposite to Mustafo. The old man smiled at him, and Adam forced himself to smile in return.

Leira ran about collecting the various vegetables needed for the salad while Adam and Mustafo talked to one another.

"So, Adam, you have quite a friend in Leira there," the old man remarked.

"Yes, I agree. She's good."

"Are you two together?" Mustafo asked as if it were the simplest of questions.

Adam noticed that Leira nearly dropped one of the vegetables she was busy mincing.

"Er—no, we're just friends."

"Oh, my mistake. Just wondering."

"That's all right."

An awkward silence followed Adam's last remark. Mustafo played with his odd toys, and Adam twiddled his thumbs uncomfortably under the table. He was relieved when Leira finally rushed over to the table carrying three identical bowls.

She handed what appeared to be the neatest salad to Mustafo. Adam did not care what his food looked like. In fact, he was not even all that hungry. How could he be at such a crucial moment?

When the three of them sat at the table eating the colorful salad, Adam forced himself to swallow bite after bite. He fulfilled his role in the plan as best as he possibly could. He did not want to give Mustafo any reason to suspect that something was afoot.

Mustafo ate his salad quickly, and Leira had barely even touched hers. When he was finished, Mustafo looked to her. "Dancing deltyres! That was good!" he exclaimed.

Leira nodded shyly and ate more of her own salad. Adam followed suit. Mustafo looked to them both and raised a curious eyebrow. "Why are you two so quiet?"

Adam froze for a moment. He searched for a reply, but nothing would come. Had Mustafo caught on? He and Leira quickly exchanged nervous glances. Finally, all traces of nervousness disappeared from Leira's face. She looked Mustafo squarely in the eyes and opened her mouth to speak. For a split second, Adam worried that she was about to say something that would give them away.

"We're just tired after cleaning, that's all," she said simply.

Adam exhaled slowly.

"Oh, I should have known. Well, perhaps after this, we'll all be off to bed," Mustafo said.

"I'd really like to, but I just wouldn't feel right leaving that room in that condition. I simply must finish it before I go to bed," Leira said.

"Are you sure? I've never heard of such dedication."

"Oh yes. In fact, some of the things in it would look absolutely wonderful outside. If I see anything that really catches my attention, I might just have to put it out right away!"

"Oh, well, of course. You've done so well in this house and on this food. I trust your judgment," Mustafo said.

When he looked down to continue messing with his things, Leira gave Adam a nearly imperceptible wink. Adam smiled to himself because he knew exactly what she was doing. He had to hand it to her for her quick wit. For the plan to work, cleaning the room was the final thread that needed to be woven, and Leira had done so with brilliance. Now, if Mustafo heard the door open during the night, he would dismiss it as the innocent Leira retrieving items to add to the décor outside of the house.

Finally, when all three of them were done eating, Leira scooped up the dishes and washed them thoroughly. Mustafo bid them goodnight and went to his bedroom. Adam did the same, except that he had no intention of sleeping. He smirked wryly, finding amusement in the old man's ignorance of what was to come.

Adam lay awake in his bed, waiting. He heard Leira working in the other room. Several times, he heard her nearly slip and fall. Had the circumstances not been so grim, Adam realized this would have been rather funny.

Still, he listened carefully. His acute hearing was incredibly useful, as he could hear Leira muttering when she knocked over something. Adam listened to the sounds outside the house, such as the twittering birds, the occasional rustle of leaves, and the low whistle of the wind. Listening kept him from getting mired in boredom, for he was impatient and ready to execute the plan. Everything hinged on Mustafo remaining asleep.

Finally, he heard Leira leave the room. She might have been tiptoeing, but with his keen hearing, it sounded as if she were stomping angrily along the floor. He peered out of his doorway as she drew closer. When she became visible, he quickly got out of bed.

Leira came in quickly and saw him. "All right, we're ready," she whispered.

"Are you sure?" he whispered back.

She nodded. "He's snoring. It's quite loud. It's a bit annoying, really," she said breathlessly.

Adam nodded back. He had heard the snoring a long time ago, but he wanted to wait. Of course, had Leira known the full truth about Adam's little secret, they might have already been out the door and on their way to freedom, for his hearing would have been an immensely useful tool.

But this was no time to dwell on what could have been. Adam followed carefully behind Leira until they reached the dining room. She paused for a moment to listen for the snores, but he was ready to leave.

"Keep moving. He's still asleep," he whispered tersely and went into the room Leira had cleaned up.

She paused for a moment in confusion, apparently wondering how Adam could have possibly heard the snores already. She shook her head and followed him into the next room.

The formerly messy room was actually spotless, much to Adam's great surprise. If he had not spent countless hours earlier helping Leira, it would have been just as dirty as before. He stared out and saw the front door. Escape was so close that he could practically taste it.

Adam spotted a large, navy-blue blanket resting by the door. Of all the things required to make the escape successful, the blanket, Adam thought, was the most unlikely. He did not particularly fancy the idea of galumphing about in a veil. But when he considered the alternative of remaining at the leaning cottage, he suddenly realized that traveling under a shroud did not seem half as bad.

Leira noted his hesitancy and snatched up the fabric boldly.

"Leira! Do we really have to do this?" he hissed.

"Shhh! Yes! It's the only way! You're the one the knights are looking for!" she whispered back.

Adam sighed in resignation and stood over by the front door. Leira crept carefully over to him and threw the blanket over his face. Suddenly, everything turned dark. He waited patiently as Leira made several adjustments so that the blanket resembled a veil. With a smirk, Adam realized that he probably looked quite outlandish. If they could make it to safety unseen, it would be a miracle.

When Leira arranged the fabric around his face, some of it tickled his nose, and without expecting it, Adam sneezed. They both remained deathly still, as he could no longer feel Leira's deft fingers. All they could hear was the old man's snoring, calm and uninterrupted. Sensing it was safe, Leira wasted no more time on his appearance. She grabbed his hand and led him into the cool air.

Through the thin fabric, Adam could see that the landscape outside was shielded from the eerie glow of the full moon by several trees. He and Leira slipped outside and closed the door silently behind them. They quickly tiptoed away from the front door towards the back of the house and found themselves standing next to the tall tree that towered nearby. It seemed to have expanded to twice its normal size in the darkness that enveloped them.

CHAPTER EIGHT

Adam and Leira went around to the other side of the tree, and they used the large trunk to shield themselves, so that they could not be seen from the house. He waited patiently for some further instruction, but he received none.

There were only a few irregularities in the fabric that Adam could see through, but he was still able to make out the sky. They waited behind the tree for what felt like several hours. Neither one of them moved a muscle, keeping perfectly still for fear that Mustafo might catch them.

Adam waited for Leira to signal him to move. He really could not understand what the delay was. The irritation of boredom was beginning to sink in the corners of his mind. For a moment, he considered moving first and making Leira follow. Of course, this idea was instantly reduced to vapor when he realized how much he depended on Leira's vision to guide him. It slowly dawned on him that she was waiting for the clouds to cover the sky so that they would not be moving under the light of the moon.

Finally, when a curtain of shadowy clouds obscured the moon, Adam heard the sound of marching nearby. He heard Leira's heartbeat begin to race. From their hiding place, they could clearly see the torches that contrasted with the night sky. As the line of knights curled around to the front door, Leira gave him a nudge, and with one hand on his arm, guided Adam along their journey. He found it extremely awkward with his vision partly obscured. He took small, sharp baby steps as she led him onward.

Had Adam seen a girl travelling alongside a veiled figure, he would have probably suspected that something fishy was going on. Still, Adam mused that a veiled face still appeared much friendlier than that of an alleged murderer. The thought of being found guilty made him shudder. Naturally, the last thing he wanted to be known for was killing. This thought bore down upon him like an anvil, and even his steps became more labored.

Leira must have noticed Adam's slow pace, so she walked a bit slower, apparently to make things look a little less strange. He could only see parts of Leira's face as well as the sky. He felt a bit odd staring at her face in such a way, so he focused his attention at the sky. The moon's pale face glowed softly behind the shadows of the clouds, and Adam remained staring upward at the dark dome of the sky. The stars twinkled softly in the dark fabric that made up the heavens.

As they continued, Adam heard the faint knock on the door, followed by the command, "We demand to search your house by order of the king."

"*Go, go, go!*" Leira hissed.

The order sent a shiver down Adam's spine, and he hastened his pace. Their journey seemed to take quite a while, as they spent most of their time taking a circular route around Roddington to avoid even the slightest suspicious glance. Unfortunately the town's port was not obscured by any buildings. There were fewer trees in that area, which meant less cover, but they were protected by the night. The moon, it seemed, faced them like a watchful guardian behind a veil. The night itself was eerily silent, and Adam knew that no one would be out and about at this time. He had been awfully lucky lately, and he hoped that this chain of good fortune would see him through the voyage.

Adam began to hobble a little faster when he heard the nearby sound of gentle waves undulating endlessly. They were so close! His heart began to flutter as the sound of the water grew closer and closer.

Suddenly, Leira stopped dead in her tracks and stopped him by clutching his arm.

"What is it?" he whispered.

"Don't say a word. I'll handle this," she hissed.

At last, he heard a set of footsteps draw nearer. From what he could tell, a heavy man was approaching, for the footsteps were more like stomps upon the earth. The man's putrid scent grew stronger, and Adam had to hold his breath.

"Oi, you! Girl! What are you doing out so late?" a scratchy voice called out.

"I am taking my friend here to his ship."

"Oh really? Why's his face covered, then?"

"He has a disease."

"And what's this disease called?"

"Oh, cripes," Leira said under her breath.

Adam felt his heart sink. The only ailments he was acquainted with were headaches, stomachaches, and the occasional cold.

"Cripes, did you say?" the man asked.

"Yes, have you heard of it?" Leira said quickly.

"Never before."

"Well," Leira said dramatically, "my poor friend has only ten hours left until he dies from a horrid infection. If we don't get him out of here soon, the whole town could become infected. I'm sure you wouldn't want that, now would you? Quarantining sounds like a tiresome business if you ask me."

"Never! Get him out of here!"

"A wise choice. Who, may I ask, are you?"

"Tamberland. I'm on patrol of the ports tonight. Trying to catch that murderer on the loose."

Adam twitched involuntarily.

"Well then, Tamberland, your noble kindness shall never be forgotten. Thank you for ensuring the safety of Roddington," Leira said quickly.

After that, no more was said. As he and Leira walked away, Adam heaved a great sigh of relief. That was a close call, and Leira had handled the situation with surprising resourcefulness.

Once the sound of waves lapping against the hulls of sea vessels became discernible, Adam knew the fulfillment of their carefully laid plans was only minutes, if not seconds, away. Suddenly, Leira stopped and held an arm out to prevent him from moving any further. At first, Adam thought they were encountering another official, but he realized that she would have given him some order if that was the case. She looked at him, and Adam watched.

"Wait here."

He nodded and remained standing. He waited, absolutely still as he listened to Leira's footsteps trail off toward the boats. Another set of footsteps met hers. Adam listened to the motion of feet, wrinkling his brow with concentration.

"Have you got him?" It was Tyrule's voice.

"Yes. I've got him. He's right over there," Adam heard Leira whisper.

"All right, then. I'm glad you're safe."

Adam was listening closely to their conversation. Had he heard that last bit correctly? It sounded as if Tyrule was softening considerably for Leira. He did not mind this at all, but he was greatly surprised at the closeness that Leira and Tyrule had managed to reach in the past few days. He supposed that he'd had a small role (if it could be called small) in this interesting development.

"Oh, Tyrule. I'm glad you're okay, too," Leira said. Adam could sense a hint of bashfulness in her voice.

Adam chuckled softly so they would not hear him. Despite the present circumstances, he welcomed the entertainment.

"Well, I'd love to chat some more, but we've got a bit of a journey ahead of us. I'll go get him. I reckon it'll look less suspicious if I actually helped him up," Tyrule said. Adam heard his footsteps grow nearer.

He let out a tiny groan as Tyrule got closer. He remained perfectly still as his friend's tight grip clamped around his arm. Adam followed blindly, making a barely audible grunt. He felt awkward and uncomfortable as Tyrule guided him from platform to platform.

Finally, after what felt like a century, Tyrule released him. Adam knew that he was on the boat at last, but he remained just as still as before. He held his breath, for he could not afford to throw their carefully planned efforts away at the last minute.

He listened to the sound of Tyrule and Leira's footsteps scuttling all over the boat.

"Hurry, Leira! Get the ropes on that side!" Tyrule whispered.

Adam heard Leira shuffle the ropes with much difficulty. Tyrule, it seemed, was adroit at this business from years of practice. After all, he had owned the boat since he was eleven years old.

The sail rose in the night with a gentle flapping sound. Adam could sense that a windy voyage awaited them. A slight wobble came from the floor beneath him, and he knew they were off. A glimmer of excitement wavered in his heart, for adventure was on the horizon.

He waited ever so patiently for his friends to announce when it was safe for him to remove the veil. After what seemed like several minutes, during which he could hear only the sound of the hull gliding along the water, he finally heard footsteps.

"All right, Adam. You can come out now," a familiar voice whispered.

Adam did not need to be told twice. Eagerly, he tore the veil from his face, and it fell to the floor without a sound. He was glad to be rid of that awful thing. The cool night air gently caressed his face, and he smiled in the stark moonlight. He looked to his side and spotted Talan staring mysteriously at the moon.

'Well, I take it that you're excited to be free," Tyrule said and walked towards them.

"You have no idea." Adam said breathlessly.

"Don't lose focus. We still have to get out of here. Let's get on with it," Talan said briskly.

MOONLIGHT ESCAPE

After that, not another word was said. Adam and Tyrule watched from the handsome sailboat as Adam's hometown, Roddington, disappeared behind them. Slowly, it became smaller and smaller until it hurt their eyes to squint at it. Finally, they looked ahead to the great unknown. Onward they went, to a new world where untold magic awaited them.

CHAPTER NINE

ON STORMY SEAS

The small cabin rocked gently from side to side. Adam woke up slowly and sat on the edge of the small bed with his head propped in his hands. At first, the small quaking movements the boat made upon crossing the crests of the waves were a bit unsettling, but after several hours of being afloat, he had gotten used to the erratic tendencies of the sea.

Tyrule's boat had three cabins, occupied by Adam, Tyrule, and Leira, and a hold where Talan slept. Although the rooms were rather cramped, the thrill of adventure kept their spirits relatively high.

Adam welcomed the solace of the morning. At long last, it seemed that a moment of quiet had found him. For the first time in several weeks, he was free at last. None of the prince's men could find him now unless Mustafo decided to reveal the truth. At the very least, Adam was glad to be free of the old man's gnarled clutches.

He realized that he was dwelling on the negative, and he shook his head as if to dispel these shadowy thoughts. He thought it best to leave the cabin and get a breath of fresh air. Slowly, Adam lifted his head and rose from the tiny bed. He walked straight for the creaky, wooden door and ascended the stairs at a leisurely pace.

The scent of the sea overwhelmed Adam with its intensity as he walked out onto the deck. The briny aroma stung his nostrils, and he wrinkled his face. Looking up to the sky, he noted that the clouds had not disappeared since the events that had transpired the night before. The clouds cast a thin veil between the sun and the sea. The glimmering jewel of the sky shone gently through the misty curtain.

Adam looked toward the front of the boat. His sharp vision pierced through the splashing water that cascaded along the sides of the boat, and he spotted Tyrule and Leira standing next to each other at the very edge of the vessel.

He hesitated for a moment, for he did not want to become the awkward third wheel in their delicately budding relationship. Adam knew better than to interrupt, but then again, what was he supposed to do all by himself? He slowly walked forward and took extra precautions not to make too much noise. When the other two did not acknowledge his presence, he stood behind them and coughed softly. Leira whirled around first.

"Oh, hello Adam!" she peeped happily.

Tyrule turned around with a smile. "Hello there, old friend."

Adam smiled back and waved sheepishly.

"You slept for a long time," Tyrule noted.

"Well, these last few days have been rough. And *old friend?*" Adam said with a shrug. He scratched his head.

Leira looked at him with a concerned expression. He knew all too well what she was about to say. "Adam, I think you need to tell us something," she said gravely.

Adam smirked to himself for guessing correctly. "You want to know what happened at the ceremony."

"We would all like to hear," Talan's voice spoke from behind him.

Both Tyrule and Leira nodded in agreement. Without turning to face Talan, Adam remarked, "I hate it when you do that."

"Maybe I should do it more often," Talan replied.

A smirk lingered on Adam's face for a brief moment, but it was soon replaced by a very serious expression. He looked at Tyrule, and then to Leira. He felt nervous about revealing everything.

"All right. But before I begin, you've got to understand something," he said quietly.

Leira nodded.

"What you're about to hear is unlike anything you've ever heard before. Trust me when I say that this seems like quite a stretch. I'm not planning on telling the whole world this, but you're my friends, and you have a right to know, especially if you've made the risk to join me."

And so Adam launched into his colorful tale about the events since their separation. Leira, Tyrule, and Talan listened closely to every word as he explained. The only time any of them interrupted was when Tyrule informed Adam that Prince Nicolas had been crowned king. Apparently, the story seemed convincing.

One thing bothered Leira, though. "But Adam, how did you do it?"

He took a deep breath. "Magic," he said dramatically.

He waited a moment for their reactions. Tyrule appeared a bit confused, but Leira had a fascinated twinkle in her eye. "Magic? But it doesn't exist. It's just not possible."

"That's where you're wrong. You, Tyrule, and everyone else have been led to believe that magic is not real because your new king has tricked all of you," Adam said.

Tyrule was still having difficulty grasping this information. "Hold on a minute. If you did the *magic*, what does that make you?"

"Okay, this is the part that is the most unbelievable. When I was running from the knights, I sort of *attacked* them."

"Attacked? How?" Tyrule asked.

"It's really hard to explain, but something like fire shot out of my hand. Well, it wasn't really fire, you know. Looked like lightning, too. Kind of like a weird mix between the two."

There was another long period of silence as Adam waited patiently for Tyrule and Leira to process the information.

Finally, Leira broke the silence. "Adam, what does that mean, then?"

"It means," Adam said, "that I've got to control and contain this power. We are travelling now to the mysterious Reximen Heights, where there are supposedly others with powers like mine. Now you know why Mustafo wants me. The Razorwolf, which is what they call me, is the reason I can hear things from so far away. That's why I heard your conversation last night. That's why—"

"You heard that?" Tyrule blurted out, turning a slight shade of pink.

"Couldn't help it. You honestly think I want to hear you two babble on? That's why I can see so much better and why my sense of smell is so much sharper. I'm even stronger now. Look, I know this is a lot to take in, but right now, you're the only ones I've got."

Leira and Tyrule stared at Adam for a moment, making him uncomfortable. He shuffled his feet nervously. Suddenly, there was a small rumble of thunder.

In a split second, Tyrule's head faced skyward. Leira looked up slowly. But Adam had already looked up at the great dome of the sky before the noise had even registered to the other two. The clouds had grown much darker since he first walked out on deck. He looked toward the water and saw the waves up ahead churning restlessly. Talan leaned against a mast in amusement. "You have yet to explain something to us, Adam. Tell us about the information you got from Mustafo."

"Oh, I almost forgot. Thanks for the reminder. That storm is no ordinary storm. It's part of the curse Prince—King, sorry—Nicolas placed over Roddington, the one that makes you oblivious to magic. Now, we have to sail through it. So don't even try to get around it. We will pass through safely, because, according to Mustafo, I am the key to this curse. Now then, who's with me?" he asked.

Tyrule looked back at Adam gravely. "All right, Adam. I'll help you. You'd do the same for me. Right now, though, we've got a storm coming."

Adam nodded back. "Just tell me what you need me to do."

"Me too," Leira said.

Talan stood up straight. "A little rain has never stopped me."

Tyrule bore a slightly mischievous grin. He looked out toward the growing storm and then back at his three-person crew. "All right. Adam, you get the mainsail. If you have gotten stronger because of this Razorwolf thing, then I reckon handling the sail won't be a problem. You'll just have to pull when I say so."

Adam nodded in full agreement and ran over to the mast. He looked back at Tyrule for further instruction.

"Adam, this boat is not designed for rough waters. I trust you know that! Now, I need you on the helm! Understand?" Tyrule shouted.

"Got it!"

Tyrule then turned to Leira, who waited nervously for her orders. "Leira, there are some things we can't afford to lose! Try to keep the food supply onboard! If we need to toss stuff off, I'll tell you! Understand?" he said loudly.

Leira nodded briskly and scampered towards the cabin, but Talan stepped firmly in her way. Adam and Tyrule exchanged confused glances.

"I'm afraid I can't allow you to do that. I'll keep the food onboard. You must stay safe," Talan said.

Leira glared at him. "Look, just because I'm a girl doesn't mean that I'm just going to sit around and be useless! If you would like to come help me, then I'm all for it."

Talan said nothing in reply as he led Leira inside of the cabin, much to Adam's amusement. Tyrule ran to the stern and climbed up onto the helm. A flash of lightning illuminated the sharp look of determination on his face.

The lonely boat moved closer and closer to the formidable storm. Adam spotted a powerful bolt of lightning blast from the sky to some distant point on the horizon. A loud thunderclap roared, as if to declare the hunger of the titans. Far out in the distance, Adam's keen sight discerned what appeared to be land. If they made it through the storm unscathed, then dry ground would be their refuge. They just had to keep holding on.

Nature played the first card of the precarious game, and the rain began to fall. Harder and harder, it fell upon them, obscuring their vision. Even Adam had a difficult time making out the faraway shore.

"Tyrule! Go port!" Adam yelled through the rain.

Tyrule followed Adam's instructions and veered slightly to the left. The wind whistled and howled furiously as it rushed against them. The sail got swallowed up in the gale, and the boat begin to veer a little too far to the right as if the wind were trying to prevent them from reaching their destination.

"Adam, hard starboard!" Tyrule shouted.

Adam pulled with all of his might at the ropes connected to the large white sail. Slowly but surely, the boat began to slide over to the left. The wind caused the waves to rise up in colossal crests; the boat quaked violently with each and every furious wave.

There was a clamor from under the deck, and Adam knew that Leira must have fallen over because of the unstable foundation beneath her feet.

Talan was far too experienced to make such a blunder. He turned and saw Tyrule, who had not lost that expression of fierce determination as he threw the steering wheel back and forth.

Lightning illuminated the sky with a titanic vengeance, and the thunder roared viciously in reply. The two mighty forces of lightning and thunder were in fierce combat in the heavens above, and the clouds hurled the icy water down to the earth.

The boat was being tossed about like a toy in the hand of a small child. With every forceful wave, the wooden structure of the boat groaned loudly. Adam and Tyrule were thoroughly soaked, but they had much bigger problems to contend with.

A loud shriek came from down below, and a quick glance at Tyrule told Adam that he was worried about Leira.

"Adam, tell Leira to come up here with me! At this point, we just need to survive!" Tyrule shouted.

Adam looked back at him and called, "Are you sure? What if she falls? Talan's down there, too!"

"She won't! And if she does, I'll save her!"

Adam let go of the sail immediately and ran toward the cabin entrance. As he drew closer, he suddenly slipped on the water sloshing around on the deck. He let out a yelp as he rapidly slid off the boat toward the thrashing jaws of the angry sea. Adam barely had the time to reach out and grab the edge of the boat.

"*Adam!*" Tyrule cried.

Adam fought to hold on, but doing so proved incredibly difficult. Several waves slammed his body against the hull with brute force, and he could hardly breathe. As the boat lurched, many times the lower half of his body was submerged in the water, and the force threatened to drag him under. For a split second, he thought he was about to let go.

"Hold on!" Tyrule screamed.

Adam struggled to clutch the side. "I can't—hold—on—much longer!" he yelled back.

Squinting, he saw a large mass off in the distance. Suddenly, it became alarmingly clear that what they were headed for was not land. Right before them was a formidable-looking rock.

"Tyrule! Watch out for that rock!" Adam screamed.

His words, however, proved to be useless, as the rain pounded too hard, and the thunder blasted all too loudly.

The frame of the boat shuddered as another wave came crashing into the hull. The impact of the blow would have caused Adam to fall had he not managed to keep a tenacious grip on the edge with one hand. He grimaced as he swung his other arm back to the edge of the boat.

Adam watched as Leira and Talan bolted out of the cabin and into the rain, their clothes drenched from the flooding waters. Failing to notice Adam dangling dangerously before the furious waters, she ran as fast as she could to Tyrule.

"Where's Adam?" she yelled.

"Down there! Help him!" Talan shouted and leapt towards him.

Tyrule watched as Leira looked around, and her jaw dropped in an expression of horror. She ran toward towards Adam, but another wave came and smashed against the hull of the boat. The impact tossed her into the air like a rag doll. Her head struck the wooden floor beneath her, and her body became immobile.

"Leira!" Adam bellowed.

Tyrule saw this and hurriedly jumped off the steering platform.

"No, Tyrule!" Adam cried.

Several times, Tyrule nearly slipped and fell; however, he was stronger and fitter than Leira and better able to avoid her fate. Adam watched fearfully as Tyrule abandoned his post. Talan jumped to his feet and ran towards the mainsail.

"Hurry, Tyrule! We're about to hit a rock!" Adam yelled.

"*What?*" he called back as he quickly scooped up the unconscious Leira.

"*WE'RE ABOUT TO HIT A ROCK!*" Adam shouted at the top of his lungs.

Horrified, he turned his head and saw the rock, which was now nearly upon them. If he did not climb up immediately, he would sink to the bottom of the sea in a matter of seconds.

"*Hurry, Tyrule!*"

Tyrule ran as fast as he could, but Adam knew it would not be fast enough. He looked again at the rock, paralyzed by fear. All of the sudden, he felt a strange sensation jolting his entire body.

The Razorwolf! Adam thought.

Even though the rain was hurling down from the heavens with cruel intensity, the sensation within him felt like a live wire. Adam felt his arms grow stronger than ever before. With a loud, inhuman grunt, he slowly pulled himself up on deck. When he finally clambered aboard, he waited for a minute to let the feeling subside; however, it only grew stronger.

Adam knew this was it. All of the tension of the battle against the forces of nature had culminated in the beast coming forth. The moment was only seconds away, and he could feel the magical vibrations within his very bones. To distance himself from the others, he sprinted for the bow of the boat.

"*Adam!*" Tyrule shouted from behind him.

Adam quickly turned his head and saw Tyrule standing helplessly at the steering platform. He opened his mouth to reply, but only a low growl issued from clenched teeth. He turned back and rushed forward.

At once, Adam fell on all fours as the sensations became overwhelming. He squinted at his arms. The worn clothes that Mustafo had given him were starting to bulge. Then, with a loud rip, the sleeves split open, and Adam saw bristly fur protruding. Unable to move, he watched as the fur seemed to sprout, travelling down his arm and to his hands. It was silvery-grey in color with the outsides of his arms being the darkest. The undersides, as well as his palms, turned white. His fingernails stretched to a sharp point and faded black.

Soon, the shirt Adam was wearing became so tight that it was strangling him. With a loud roar, he ripped it off with a clawed hand. His well-muscled torso was covered in pure white fur. The fur continued its way down along his legs and to his feet, all of which were the same dark silvery color as his arms. He could even feel the unnatural presence of a tail.

The worst part was when Adam felt a fiery pain erupt from his gums. He felt each of his teeth curved into sharp fangs. Crossing his eyes, Adam watched his nose elongate. He could see the dark fur cover the long bridge that was now clearly visible. His ears stretched up and out so that they resembled a wolf's ears. The hair on his head morphed into that dark-colored fur, and Adam could see white fur below his eyes.

With a snarl, the Razorwolf threw its head back and released a mighty howl. He stood up and faced the distant horizon. Clad only in his own fur, the monster looked to the land and growled.

"Adam!" Talan shouted from nearby.

The Razorwolf whipped its head towards the voice's owner. For the first time, Talan's eyes widened in fear.

Tyrule must have heard the howl, for he looked toward the bow. In the torrential downpour, all he would have been able to make out was the silhouette of what appeared to be a tall, muscular human with an oddly shaped head.

Before he would have been able to discern any other details, an earsplitting crack sounded from the side of the boat. The impact of the shock sent

Tyrule to the ground. When he looked back up, he saw that the boat had been split in two. Keeping a careful grip on Leira, he looked out to the other side.

"*Adam!*" he screamed.

No answer came except for the rush of icy water. Looking numb after the frigid shock, Tyrule reached out and grabbed a large piece of wood with one hand and held Leira with the other. A forceful wave crashed into the front half of the boat, and the force violently slammed Talan into the waters.

The Razorwolf, too, felt the shock when the boat split in half and looked away from Talan; however, he did not fall. Instead, he landed nimbly on all four clawed feet on the sinking fragment and peered directly forward through the heavy rain. A flash of lightning illuminated the land far away. After the mighty blast of thunder, the Razorwolf stood up and faced forward coolly.

From the far corners of his mind, Adam felt as if some powerful force were pressing against his consciousness. The monster resisted him with ease, and he viewed the events that were unfolding before his eyes with acute perception. With a mighty bound, the Razorwolf leaped off the bow and dove into the cold waters. The water felt unbelievably frigid, but the beast kept on going as if he was invincible. With powerful strokes, the Razorwolf came up to the surface for air. He felt white and grey fur plastered to his face as he looked for the shore. From the corner of his eye, he spotted Talan's head sink below the surface. With a great gulp of air, the Razorwolf dove beneath the waves and snatched away Talan's unconscious form. In a matter of seconds, he broke the water's surface and glared forward.

Through the haze of rain, land would have been hardly visible to the human eye. The Razorwolf, however, was not human. With extremely keen vision, he spotted the shoreline. With one arm, the titan propelled himself forward with potent strokes. In the other, Talan barely clung to life.

CHAPTER NINE

Closer and closer he came to the shoreline. Soon, it became nearly impossible to miss the sight of land, as it increasingly took up a great portion of the horizon. Finally, when the water was shallow enough for his feet to touch the sand, the Razorwolf walked upright toward the shore, cradling Talan in his arms.

His long strides were slowed down by his water-soaked fur. And the continuous hammering of the rain worsened his predicament. Even with the burden of Talan, the Razorwolf kept taking one powerful step after another.

At last, the water reached only his furry ankles. He took a few more steps forward and then remained still. Looking at the land before him, he spotted a couple of palm trees billowing violently in the wind. *Shelter*, his instinct told him.

Slowly, the incredible beast walked to the trees before turning back to face the water. The boat had sunk, and Tyrule and Leira were nowhere in sight. Exhausted by the swim to the safe ground, the Razorwolf lay Talan's body under the protection of a tall tree before leaning against another one nearby.

No longer did the rain bother him. No longer did the wind cause him discomfort. The flashes of lighting became commonplace, and the roars of thunder became like music to his tired ears. He closed his eyes slowly. Listening to the sounds of the rain and sea, the powerful Razorwolf let everything float away, and the world around him dissolved in a soft haze.

CHAPTER TEN

OUT OF THE DARKNESS

A cool breeze tickled the side of Adam's serene face, and he rolled over to hide his face from it. All of the sudden, he tasted something bland and gritty. Confused by this unwelcoming texture, Adam inhaled sharply and sucked in more of the foreign material. He coughed loudly and rolled over so that he lay face up. There was more of it on his face, so he raised a hand and wiped it away. The gritty stuff still remained in his mouth, and it felt as disgusting as ever.

Slowly, he sat upright and spat whatever it was out of his mouth. When his eyes flew open, his vision became flooded by the dazzling sunlight reflecting off a glassy surface. Adam recoiled and rubbed his eyes. Slowly, the clear blue sky came into focus. Right below the colossal dome lay the complacent sea, undulating slowly in the slight breezes that rode toward the land on the backs of small waves. Adam suddenly became aware that he was sitting on a beach. He realized that the odd, gritty substance in his mouth was sand. He gazed upward and saw the large, billowing leaves of two palm trees swaying in the breeze.

He looked down at himself and saw that his shirt was gone, and the only thing he had on was a rather tattered pair of pants. He stood up and looked around at the new landscape. The pristine beach seemed to extend infinitely in both directions. Behind Adam was a dense copse of trees. He could barely make out the shape of a titanic mountain, way off in the distance. Other than these marvels of nature, he was completely alone.

"*Fallador*," he breathed.

He remembered setting sail two nights ago with Tyrule and Leira, but they were nowhere to be seen. The memories of the following day quickly rushed back to his mind, as fast as a rogue strike of lightning. There had been disaster on the now serene waters. He remembered the fall, and he remembered the storm. He remembered Tyrule assumed the role as captain, and he remembered that Leira had slipped and fallen. More importantly, however, Adam remembered the Razorwolf.

The occurrence felt unreal. At long last, Adam had finally had a real glimpse of his true power. The mighty Razorwolf had come forth in a time of need. It was curious, though, because Adam's conscious stream of thought was but a feeble whisper against the overbearing instinct of the noble warrior. He knew that he had lost total control and that the monster had a will of its own that he was no match for.

Adam looked down at his own hands as if to verify their reality. For several moments, he stared at his outstretched palms in amazement. The power had felt unbelievably thrilling, but what good did it do him when he could not willingly transform himself or exert even the slightest bit of self-control? His mission to reach Reximen Heights was quickly becoming more imperative than ever before.

Still, he felt the absence of Tyrule and Leira. Had they disappeared in the storm? Were they—?

No.

Adam could not even bring himself to complete the awful thought. They must have survived, he told himself. He was no fool, but he sought to convince himself by repeating the statement over and over again.

Tyrule and Leira had left behind all that they had to help him, and now they were missing. He felt his heart sink at this woeful thought. Suddenly, he remembered hauling Talan to safety during the previous night. Adam glanced over at the nearby trees and saw that the rogue had vanished.

The next step in his quest suddenly became obvious. He would forgo the journey to the Heights momentarily. Talan could not have gone far in his injured state, and Adam desperately needed his guidance. He realized that venturing out after him could be very dangerous, but searching for his friends was, he believed, the only way he could survive the trip to find the Heights. Without them, Adam felt he was nothing.

With that, he rose slowly to his feet and peered out toward the horizon, the mysterious place where the sky touched the sparkling blue water in ancient union. After a good stretch, he looked out to the left and the right; the beach sprawled out endlessly in either direction. Sooner or later, he would have to choose the way.

An idea occurred to Adam. He walked away from the shore and left noticeable footprints behind him. That way, he could go either way without getting hopelessly lost. If he went in one direction until the sun began to get lower in the sky, he could easily turn back and find his starting point. The next day, he could resume his search in the other direction.

With this in mind, Adam abruptly decided to take the path on the right. Before leaving, he walked out to the fringes of the clear water. He paused for a moment and let the small waves tickle his toes. It was hard to imagine that he had emerged from the water mere hours ago as such an extraordinary marvel as the Razorwolf.

CHAPTER TEN

At least I know what it looks like now, Adam thought, as the water began to ebb back toward the open sea from whence it came.

He kept walking in the wet sand as he began the search for Talan, Tyrule, and Leira. As he looked at the awe-inspiring sights of this new landscape, there was something about it that he just could not place his finger on. The land itself seemed to exude a special kind of aura that seemed to call Adam further into the interior, the domain of the unknown.

His trek was a magnificent spectacle. He felt incredibly tiny walking along the vast beach all alone. He wondered whether anyone even lived on this curious island. Sometimes, Adam would walk near the water to cool his feet. Every now and then, the water would come and wash them away, as if to conceal the traces of his former life. For a teenage boy, he possessed a remarkable amount of inner strength. He prided himself on this, and this thought propelled him, step after step.

As he travelled along the beach, Adam could not help but notice the awe-inspiring sight of the two mountains looming distantly toward the heart of the land. He knew that they were the mountains of which Mustafo spoke. Their allure was sorely tempting, but he remained fiercely committed to finding his friends.

The noonday sun hung high in the sky. Adam had been searching for several hours to no avail. He wondered why he was not extremely hungry or thirsty yet, but he also thought it wise to leave well enough alone. If he was not hungry or thirsty yet, there was no point in getting sidetracked to look for food.

As he kept walking, a strange thing occurred to him. He was still wearing pants after the Razorwolf episode. It was curious, he thought, because he had lost his shirt, yet his pants, tattered as they were, had remained intact. Adam supposed that the fabric had simply become one with him when the change happened. Of course, he had no objection to his pants having survived.

He looked ahead and saw that the shoreline curved in a series of snaky turns. With no other choice, he followed this route, hoping for an end to the beach on the other side. When at last he made the turn, he was dismayed to see another expanse of sand and water.

Several hours under the heat had oppressed Adam's spirits. The sun burned his pale skin, and he staggered forward with his mouth wide open. His eyes drooped with exhaustion. At last, he had enough. Even he was not afraid to admit that he had reached his limits. Suddenly, his acute ears detected a weak groan from nearby.

Adam hurried away from the water's edge and to the sound of the noise. As sand faded into grass, he could make out a dark lump lying motionless in an open plain. The messy black hair was a blatant giveaway.

"Talan!" Adam cried and sprinted over to the body.

At a closer glance, Adam saw that Talan lay on his side, his face away from the sun. Adam knelt beside him and shook Talan's body gently.

"Talan, wake up!" he shouted.

A wispy groan escaped from his feeble lips, and his eyes drooped sadly. Adam shook him harder to dispel the languor. "Come on, Talan! We have to find the others!"

Again, Talan did not move, but his eyelids slipped closed, and he did not stir. Fearfully, Adam tilted his head towards Talan's mouth and heard the faint sound of breath. He was barely alive, but he desperately needed help. Glancing at Talan's motionless body, Adam spotted several ghastly wounds along his arms and sides. The events of the previous night took a fierce toll on the rogue. As fast as he could managed, Adam grabbed Talan's arms and heaved him over his shoulder. It took him a moment to adjust the weight, but he staggered forward once the unconscious man was secured.

Their journey stung painfully, but Adam kept reminding himself to place one foot in front of the other. Together, they slowly covered more ground as the day grew hotter. Several hours later, Adam panted heavily and lay Talan upon the sand for a moment. The sun did little to make matters easier, and Adam's temper was beginning to bake. No sign of intelligent life made its presence known, which infuriated him.

Finally, he glared up to the sky in frustration. "Is anyone here at all?" he shouted to the heavens.

He stared down at the ground. The pearly white sand remained as still as ever, and the only sound that answered him was the soft waves. In rage, Adam knelt down and punched the ground as hard as he could, leaving a deep impression in the earth. Gradually, another sound faded into existence, an unusual noise. Several muffled thumps cut across the landscape, and Adam looked forward just in time to see a horse and its rider racing towards him.

Snatching Talan from the ground, Adam turned around and ran towards the waters, but by the time his feet touched the surface, it was too late.

"Stop!" a gruff voice shouted from behind him.

Reluctantly, Adam turned around and faced the rider. The black horse the stranger rode was so massive that Adam nearly fell over.

"Who are you?" The rider asked.

"I'm Adam," he answered. "I need help."

The man regarded him in silence. The sunlight reflected brightly through his blonde hair, yet he appeared to be unusually small for his steed. He wore a baggy, orange garment that draped about his countenance like a robe. "That depends. Who are you, Adam?"

"You have got to be kidding me. There is an unconscious man over my shoulder, and you want to hear who I am?" Adam asked.

"Maybe you can start by explaining *why* there is an unconscious man over your shoulder," the man said flatly.

"Er—yeah," he answered. "I found him lying on the sand a few hours ago."

"And you just picked him up? Do you normally pick up strangers?" the man asked.

"Well, of course not. He just looked like he really needed help," Adam lied.

"So you're the heroic type. We need people like that around here. Name's Leon," he said and extended a hand.

Hesitantly, Adam reached out and shook it. Leon smiled warmly and leapt down from the horse.

"Nice to meet you," Adam said.

At ground level, he towered over Leon. The comical observation amused him, but he managed to suppress the grin that tugged at his lips.

"You're not from around here, are you?" he asked.

Shaking his head, Adam replied, "No. What gave it away?"

Leon shrugged. "Lucky guess?"

"As much as I'd love to stay and chat, my friend here is only getting weaker. Can you please help us? We mean you no harm," Adam said.

Leon thought it over for a moment and nodded prominently. "I can help you. Let's put him on the saddle, and together we'll walk him back home."

"Home?"

"I live in a small village called Tahvokia. We really should get you acquainted with Fallador later this evening," Leon said.

Together, Adam and Leon lifted Talan onto the saddle, where he slumped forward pitifully. Leon guided the horse with a rope, and Adam walked on the other side to keep Talan from falling over.

"So, how long have ye been here?" Leon asked.

"Not even a whole day, I suppose."

"Did you ride in on that storm?"

"You could say that," Adam answered carefully.

CHAPTER TEN

Leon paused for a moment. Adam could tell that the gears in his mind were turning. "Well, there were two others that came by. Asked for directions to the strangest of places."

Adam's heart skipped a beat. "Two others? Who were they?" he asked in quickly.

"I don't know. One was a boy, other was a girl, and they didn't say much. Why? Do they mean something to you?" Leon answered plainly.

"Yes. They're friends of mine. Did they say where they were going?"

"They mentioned something about Reximen Heights."

A feeling of relief washed over Adam. They were alive!

"Do you know which way they went?" Adam asked.

"Well that's simple. The only way to Reximen Heights is through the Forest of Belliteth! I also told them to watch out for the river."

"The river?" Adam said quickly.

"Slow down! But yes, the River of Thanatos can be quite mysterious when it wants to be," Leon said, as if it were the simplest fact in the world.

"Well, I guess there's a lot to learn," Adam said to the small man.

"You remind me of some people in Asarmina. Is that where you're from?" Leon asked.

"I think so. I hit my head pretty hard during the accident."

Through nervous eyes, Leon glanced at Adam. "The accident?"

Adam answered, "We didn't get far when the storm reared up and made life miserable. There was a giant rock sticking out of the water, but we saw it too late. The boat smashed against it, and we were separated. I think they landed in the water, but I smacked my head on the floor of the boat, and I woke up on the shore this morning."

"You're lucky to have survived."

"Very lucky," he said.

"And you met another unconscious stranger as you wandered aimlessly along the shore? What are the odds?" Leon inquired.

"Oh, normally I wouldn't do anything like that. But after experiencing this last episode, I knew how it felt, so I wanted to help," Adam lied.

"I see. I wonder how he got all of those wounds."

"Maybe he can tell us when he wakes up."

"Hopefully he won't attack us," Leon said seriously.

Adam paused for a moment. "I have a weird feeling that he won't. After all, we saved him, right?"

Leon nodded.

"I suppose I'll have to try and look for the others," Adam said bravely.

"Listen. I know this place like the back of my own hand. Come stay at my house for the night. I'll help you get to your friends tomorrow. I'd hate for anything bad to happen, and there's some pretty dangerous stuff out there. You seem like a good kid when you're not shooting out those remarks of yours."

Adam hesitated for a moment. Another choice, it seemed, had wandered willingly into his midst. He did not want to risk further separation from Tyrule and Leira. Then again, Adam noted gravely, he did not want to be separated from his own body.

"Okay. I'll stay, but only one night."

"That's all we'll need. Follow me," Leon walked toward the forest.

Adam did as he was told and walked alongside the horse. Talan lazily drifted towards Adam, who had to hop in order to push him back in position. As Adam and Leon covered more and more ground, the sand beneath their feet diminished, and soft grass gradually appeared to replace it. For a split second, Adam thought they were going to enter the mouth of the forest that waited straight ahead. But Leon surprised him by making a quick left turn, thus dodging the forest completely. Adam let out a small sigh of relief and obediently followed his savior. The mouth of the forest was not an inviting sight by any standards.

CHAPTER TEN

Leon led him around several palm trees. After rounding one particularly thick one, Adam spotted in the distance what appeared to be a tiny shack. He wondered how it would be possible to share such a small space with Leon, let alone accommodate the unconscious Talan, as it would be a truly awkward experience.

When they arrived at the front of the shack, Adam noticed that the front door was made of a very thick kind of wood. Leon stopped abruptly.

"All right, let me just check if anyone's in here," he turned and told Adam.

Adam could not fathom the idea that anyone else could possibly fit inside the tiny living space. Regardless of Adam's thoughts, Leon knocked thrice on the door.

"Leon, is that you?" a windy voice called.

"Yes, it's me. Who else? Well, actually, I've also got someone else. Two people, actually," Leon answered.

"All right. Come on in!" the voice shouted.

Together, Adam and Leon carefully removed Talan from the saddle. They placed him gently on the ground while Leon went to tie his impressive horse to a nearby pole. When he returned, Leon swung the door wide open and entered. Adam lifted Talan on his shoulder once more and followed his host inside quietly. When he poked his head through the small doorway, he blinked in astonishment, for there was no one inside.

CHAPTER ELEVEN

THE KREVVLER'S SECRET

Adam carried Talan on his shoulder and followed Leon into the house slowly. Certainly, he thought, there was another person inside, but all he saw was what resembled a living room. Two chairs sat at a small table in the center of the room, and a turquoise carpet extended from the front door all the way to the back wall. There were shelves filled with books of different shapes and sizes mounted along the walls. Other than that, Adam noticed that there was not a door in sight.

"Er—Leon?" he asked.

"Yes?" said Leon, who had walked over to the table and picked up a cup.

"Didn't you hear someone?"

"Of course I did. He's somewhere around here," he said, after taking a sip from the bubbly green substance in the porcelain cup.

"But there's no one inside but us!"

Leon set the drink down. "Don't be silly. Of course someone else is inside of here. It's a full-sized house."

Adam looked at him incredulously. Surely this man had lost his mind. "Who then? The invisible ghost?"

Leon chortled. "No, he's not invisible. He's Seth, my brother," he replied with a half-grin.

"Your brother?" Adam repeated.

"Yes, my one and only."

Adam was still terribly confused. "Then how come we can't see him?"

"He's in the other room."

"Leon, there is no other room," Adam stated flatly.

"Sure there is!"

Adam raised an eyebrow. "Leon, there aren't any doors anywhere in this room. This is all."

"Well, there would be if you closed it all the way," Leon said. He looked at the front door.

Adam turned around and saw that the front door was indeed not completely closed. After placing Talan down gently, he reached out and pulled the handle. With a small creak, it clicked shut. He also noticed something peculiar on the door. Right in the center was an odd-looking object that appeared to be made out of stone. It was hexagonal, with each corner pointing to minuscule words.

"Now, kindly turn the knob to where it says 'Seth's Room'," Leon said.

Adam turned around. "You mean turn that rock thing? What good will that do?"

"Just do it."

Feeling slightly awkward, Adam turned back to the door. He looked at the odd object and noticed that one of its corners extended further out than the others. He brought his face closer so that he could read the tiny writing.

The corners were inscribed with the names of rooms. Adam saw that the longest corner pointed to *Living Room*. The other corners had written markers: *Leon's Bedroom*, *Wash Room*, *Spare Room*, *Dining Room*, and *Seth's Room*.

Hesitantly, Adam placed his hand on the raised stone and looked at *Seth's Room*. With careful deliberation, he turned the rock until the largest corner pointed directly at the words. When he withdrew his hand, there was a sudden *whoosh!* sound, and he stepped back quickly. "Leon, what did I just do?"

"You just opened Seth's room," he answered in his low voice.

Leon stepped forward and placed his hand (which seemed rather large considering how short he was) on the door handle. With a small grunt, he pushed the door open.

With an arched eyebrow, Adam watched Leon. He had expected to see palm trees and sunlight when the door flew open. Instead, his skepticism was reduced to ash when he saw that the doorway led into another room. Not thinking much of it, Leon stepped into the room and looked around. Adam, on the other hand, took a small step forward, his mouth agape with astonishment.

"Seth, where are you?" he called.

Adam walked out from behind Leon. A small bed was situated in one of the far corners. A small, disheveled dresser sat at the opposite end, and several books were strewn across the floor. The messy bed itself was littered with several pages and complicated diagrams.

"I'm right here!"

Adam looked around to see where the voice had come from. The ends of the blanket that had been draped from the bed to the floor wiggled briefly. He was surprised when he saw a little hand reach out from under the bed.

"Ah, Leon, might I have a hand?"

Leon walked over to him and grabbed his outstretched hand. With a yank, the other boy slid out along the floor. Leon let go of him and took a step back. He stood up and brushed the dust off of him.

"Impeccable timing," he said with a wide grin.

Adam looked and closely noted the resemblance between Leon and his twin. Seth, Adam supposed his name was, had blonde hair like Leon's except it was a bit shorter and neater. He had shining blue eyes hidden behind a pair of spectacles that gleamed in a way that gave him an air of ambition. Unlike Leon, he favored a green garment of sorts.

"Well, I aim to please," Leon said.

"Ah, Leon, who is your friend? I should very much like to meet him!" his twin said excitedly.

Leon turned his head toward Adam for a second. "Oh, this is Adam. Adam, this is my brother, Seth."

Seth stepped forward enthusiastically with an outstretched hand. "Such a pleasure it is to meet you! Say, what brings you here?" he asked in a lively voice.

"The feeling's mutual. What brings me here? Coincidence, I guess," Adam replied quietly and gripped his hand.

Seth shook it with such a firm grip that Adam nearly winced in surprise.

"Probably," Leon added.

"I don't believe in coincidence. How can it be that a mere accident dramatically changes history? No, it is fate. Fate brought you to us, Adam," Seth said as he released Adam's hand.

He noticed how much more polished Seth's speech was than Leon's. "Well, either way, I'm glad to be out of the storm."

"*The storm?*" Seth said with wide eyes. He looked at Leon, who merely nodded.

"You were stuck in that storm? Oh my, how frightening!"

"Trust me, it was."

Seth chortled at this remark. "Well then, I'm sure neither of you two would enjoy staying in this mess I call my bedroom, so shall we venture into the dining room?"

"You two go ahead. I'm going to take care of our other visitor," Leon answered.

"Well, where is he?" Seth asked.

"We left him in the living room. He's had a rough day, to put it plainly," Adam answered.

Seth looked at the door, then back to Leon. "I suppose supper can wait. After all, if he needs help, then we ought to make him our first priority, wouldn't you think?"

Nodding, Leon answered. "I agree. Let's hurry now."

Leon turned around and walked over to the door. He pulled it closed tightly. After that, he grasped the stone on the door. With a quick flick of the wrist, he spun the device. As soon as he removed his hand, the door made the *whoosh!* sound again. Adam was still a little jolted by the sound because he was not as used to this strange mode of travel as Leon and Seth undoubtedly were. Seth, who was standing at Adam's side while Leon opened the door, noticed Adam's reaction.

"Have you never heard of this kind of thing before?" he asked.

"Heard of what?" Adam looked at Seth.

"The thing on the door. Do you know what it does?"

"I suppose it changes the rooms, but I have no idea how," Adam admitted.

Seth nodded. "It certainly does. It's a magical stone, that is. It's called a Krevvler."

"A Krever?"

"A *Krevvler*."

CHAPTER ELEVEN

Leon opened the door and stepped through. Adam and Seth followed, still engaged in conversation.

Adam was intrigued. "How does it work?"

"Well, the Krevvler, you see, is an interesting artifact I spotted while up in the mountains once. When it is attached to a door, it learns the rooms of the house. When we first got it, it acted terribly confused. One time, I told it to send me to my room, and it spat me back out in the wash room."

"It learned the rooms of your house?" Adam asked skeptically.

"Oh yes. It took a while, but now it works just fine. Be careful not to insult it, or it will put you in the wrong room and lock you out! Leon found that out the hard way, didn't you?"

Leon looked back at them and nodded. "One time, when I was in a mood, I shouted 'open up, you stupid old rock and let me into my bedroom', and it answered my request. The only problem was that I was locked in my room for a whole day. I think I just hurt its feelings."

Adam looked at the door behind him. He certainly had no intention of insulting any stone, magical or not.

"Oh, and it doesn't like it when you throw rocks. It has some spooky way of knowing," Seth added.

"I guess I won't be throwing any rocks, then," Adam said quietly.

Adam looked past Seth and saw that they were back in the living room. Talan lay pitifully on the turquoise carpet, and Seth ran to his side immediately. Leon and Adam watched as he examined Talan's body.

"Adam found him earlier today," Leon said.

"You found some stranger in this condition?" Seth asked incredulously.

Nodding, Adam replied, "Yeah. I wasn't just going to leave him there. He looked pretty bad. You'll be able to help him, won't you?"

166

"Definitely. Help me get him into the spare room so we can tend to him. Once he's all taken care of, we can hurry up with dinner," Seth said. "Could you turn us to the spare room, Adam?"

"Sure," Adam said and stepped back to the door. He spun the mark over the label *Spare Room* and waited for the gush of air, which startled him again. Holding the door open, Adam watched as Seth and Leon carried Talan's unconscious form into the spare room. From the doorway, he watched them place Talan on one of two beds. Seth said something to Leon, who ran out of the doorway.

"Excuse me, Adam. I need to get some things. I'll be back in a flash," he said as he placed his hand on the Krevvler.

Before Adam could so much as breathe, Leon twisted the knob disappeared behind the doorway. Seconds later, he reemerged with an armful of bandages and rags. Looking around the room, an unsettling expression formed on his face. "Confound it! I forgot that we were in the spare room. Well, that's alright. You can come along then and see for yourself."

Leon turned them to the spare room, and Adam followed him to Talan's bed. Seth stood with a hand on the victim's forehead. When he spotted Adam and Leon, he gestured quickly for them to bring the supplies. "Hurry!"

Both of them hurried and handed Seth the bandages and a damp rag.

"Will he be alright?" Adam asked quickly.

"Like I said earlier, definitely," Seth answered as he carefully removed Talan's shirt.

After several minutes, Talan's well-muscled body was covered by fabric bandages, and Seth placed the damp rag over his eyes. When they were finished, Seth walked past Seth and Leon and placed a hand on the Krevvler, turning them to the point labeled *Dining Room*. As they all stepped out, Adam saw a large table in the center of the new room with two plates at either end. There were only four chairs, with one on each side. Forks and knives were placed neatly on napkins beside the plates.

"Leon, go get our friend here a plate and some cutlery," Seth said.

Leon nodded and went over to one of the cupboards along the walls. He rummaged through one for a few seconds, and then he produced another white plate and the necessary cutlery.

"Adam, you can go ahead and sit down. It's Leon's turn to make dinner," Seth said as he took a seat in one of the chairs.

Adam did as he was told and took a seat to the left of Seth. He waited patiently as Leon placed the plate in front of him and arranged the fork, knife, and napkin.

"So, Adam, where are you from?" Seth asked.

Remembering the name of the town Leon used earlier, Adam lied. "I'm from Asarmina."

"You're not very good at lying," Seth said flatly.

"What?" Adam asked nervously.

"If you're from Asarmina like you say, then you of all people should know what a Krevvler is. Also, I saw the wounds on the man in the spare room. Sure, you may be the rescuer type, but someone like that doesn't coincidentally appear on the beach," Leon answered.

Feeling the color rising in his cheeks, Adam said, "But he needed help."

"I might have bought that if you didn't say anything about Reximen Heights," Leon continued.

"But I didn't say anything."

"You said your friends were seeking it, and from the looks of it, you were in a hurry to get there yourself. No one just takes a stroll to Reximen Heights. It's not a place for the weak. I consider myself to be good at reading people, Adam, and I know that you're not bad. If you were, I might not have rescued you. Now, can you please tell us what's really going on?" Leon asked.

Adam nodded. "We sailed from Roddington in search of Reximen Heights. I can't tell you why, which makes me feel uneasy. Keeping secrets from others is not right. I didn't want to admit that I have secrets."

"Adam," Seth began. "Not all secrets are evil. You can keep a secret for the right reasons, and I know you keep yours for that purpose."

Nodding, Adam shivered in the cool air.

"Oh, how insensitive of me!" Seth ran over to the Krevvler. He spun the dial, and let go. Quickly, he disappeared behind the door. Adam saw Leon give him an odd look.

A brief silence was followed by the familiar whoosh! noise, and out came Seth with some fabric in his hand.

"I can't believe we didn't give you proper clothes earlier! Here, take this!" Seth said quickly, handing him a red shirt.

"Now, I'm sure you're aware of our small size, but we have frequent visitors, so we happen to have something that appears to fit you," Seth said.

Adam gratefully accepted the shirt and pulled it over his head. The material draped comfortably over his shoulders. It was quite soft and smooth. "Thank you."

"Oh, you're welcome. I feel foolish for forgetting that! I mean, it was obvious, after all!" Seth burst.

"It's all right."

"Leon, how come you didn't do anything about it? You've been with him longer than I have!" Seth snapped.

As he stirred a pot, Leon merely looked up at the other end of the room. "Seth, it's a bit warm outside. He hasn't even been here that long."

Adam could see a reply forming on Seth's lips.

"Really, I'm fine," Adam insisted. He heard Leon grating cheese in the background.

"All right, then. Surely you have plans?" Seth switched the subject.

"Actually, I'm still working on that part. I have no idea how to get to Reximen Heights. From what Leon told me about the forest and the river, it sounds difficult. I need to wait for Talan to come back around," Adam said.

"So that's his name," Seth remarked.

Adam said, "Yes. If it weren't for him, I would be dead by now."

"Friends like that are valuable. Well then, if both of you are strangers to Fallador, then it only makes sense that we help you get there. We do a lot of traveling up to the mountains. I might have already mentioned this, but I found the Krevvler up in those mountains. We can make the journey again, and our experience would be something useful to have in those parts," Leon said.

"It wouldn't be too much trouble, would it?" Adam asked innocently.

"Not at all. Besides, you'll need us to help you in case we have to travel along the River of Thanatos," Seth said.

Adam was about to ask what was so dangerous about the river when Leon stood up to his full height. "Dinner's ready."

"Oh, brilliant," Seth said happily.

Leon placed before Seth a steamy bowl of soup. A couple of seconds later, Leon placed an equally warm bowl in front of Adam. Seth chuckled to himself.

"What?" Leon asked.

"Silly me for thinking we needed forks. Spoons are better for eating soup, don't you agree?" Seth rose from the table.

Leon sat down to the right of Adam and across from where Seth was sitting. A minute later, Seth hurried back to his seat and passed spoons to Adam and Leon.

"That's better. Now, let us enjoy this fine meal," Seth said.

Simultaneously, all three picked up their spoons and dipped them into their bowls. Leon and Seth each placed a spoonful in their mouths and went for another. Adam, however, put a spoonful in his mouth and felt searing heat.

"Oh!" Adam exclaimed, his hands flailing about.

Leon and Seth looked at him oddly.

"What's the matter, Adam?" Seth asked.

"It's really, really hot! Might I get some water?"

Seth looked at Adam's bowl and then back to Adam. "Well, that's odd. I've never found any of Leon's soups to be too hot."

"That's probably because we've grown so used to it," Leon said with a shrug.

"Probably. You know, Leon makes the best soup I've ever tasted. One time, when it was my turn to make dinner, I asked him how to make this kind of soup. Toblesque, That's what it's called. I swear I followed his instructions word for word, but it didn't come out nearly as well as his usually does. I think Leon's got a skill in cooking that managed to skip me," Seth said.

"Thank you," Leon said.

Adam tried another spoonful, but it was still incredibly hot. He wondered if the new sensitivity of the Razorwolf senses were to blame. As he waited for it to cool down, he watched Leon and Seth eat theirs. Leon ate quickly, but Seth ate slowly, savoring it, as if he were enjoying the experience. Adam felt a bit awkward sitting and doing nothing.

Adam waited until Leon was finished before trying one more spoonful. It was still hot, but he felt that he could tolerate it. He finished his soup faster than Seth, so he and Leon waited patiently for him to finish.

When Seth finally swallowed the last bit of soup, he exhaled sharply and looked at Leon. "Well, that was as good as always," he said cheerfully.

"Thank you again, brother."

"Oh, sorry I forgot to ask this earlier, but where are we? I mean, what's this place called?" Adam asked.

"You mean the village? Tahvokia," Seth answered.

"I didn't see a village when I was walking by."

"Well, that's because I found you outside of the boundaries before. We live on the very edge," Leon said.

"That's a shame you didn't see the village. It's really quite delightful. Everyone has huts all over the beach. One person, a friend of ours named Sorah-Kown, has her house on the water! It's brilliant!" Seth chirped happily.

"Wow! Might we take a look before we go?" Adam asked hopefully.

Seth turned to Adam. "Actually, we might have to. We'll need supplies, and we only own one horse."

Adam nodded in reply.

"Excellent," Leon said. "Now, Adam, go ahead and visit the wash room. You'll probably enjoy feeling clean again after that nasty ordeal. After that, just go to the spare bedroom, as that's where you'll stay."

"Seth, if I use the Krevvler, will it still work for you?"

"Yes, of course. It's still like an actual house. Multiple rooms can be accessed by multiple people. It's so efficient. In fact, if you're nice to it, it might surprise you and even make the room clean. It's done that a few times for me."

"All right, then. Thank you." Adam rose from the table.

He walked over to the door and peered at the words. Once he found *Wash Room*, he grasped the stone firmly and turned it in the proper direction. When he released it, the familiar noise could be heard, and this time it did not bother him. Once the sound had subsided, he admitted himself into the room.

He ended up taking a nice, warm bath for what felt like an hour. He washed himself very carefully, as he had not enjoyed the luxury of a bath for a while. When he was finished, he dried himself off and put the red shirt and a nice pair of dark blue pants on. He returned to the Krevvler and unlocked the spare bedroom, just like Seth had told him. In fact, Adam was careful to use words such as *please* and *thank you* so that he might convince the stone to be kind in return.

When he set foot in the spare room, it was impeccably clean, and he knew at once that the Krevvler had taken his politeness into consideration. The arrangement of the furniture in the spare bedroom was nearly identical to that of Seth's room, except that books and things were in their proper places.

On one side of the room, Talan lay still on his bed, eyes covered. On the other side, a fresh bed waited for Adam. As he moved over to it, Talan stirred.

"Talan?" Adam asked and hurried to the other bed.

"Adam, it's—it's…you," he answered heavily.

Talan tried to move his hand to remove the damp rag, but Adam stopped him. "No, keep that where it is. It's going to make you feel better."

"Adam, you…you saved…me."

"I guess we're even."

"No…no…you saved me…twice," he breathed.

"And you would do the same for me, Talan."

"Adam, I have…to tell you something …my…secret."

Listening carefully, Adam answered. "What is it, Talan?"

"I—I—I am," Talan began, but his speech drifted away.

"That's alright. You need your rest," Adam said and returned to the other side of the room.

Adam climbed up on the bed in the corner and slipped under the soft covers. For a moment, he stared at the ceiling. Closing his eyes, he wondered what Tyrule and Leira were doing now. They were also probably trying to sleep too, he realized. He also thought about what the journey ahead would be like. In a land of magic, any number of things could happen. Several fantasies floated about in his head, the most illustrious being of dragons, castles, and fair maidens. One thing disturbed him.

What was Talan's secret?

CHAPTER TWELVE

THE SHADOW OF FEAR

"A dam, you need to get up now."

With the discomfort associated with the early morning, Adam's eyes blinked open and a white ceiling slowly came into focus. He turned his head lazily toward the door.

Seth stood in the doorway with a strap over his shoulder. Adam stared blankly at him, his eyes full of sleep. He sat upright and said nothing. Seth knew that his guest was getting up, so he hurried away.

With heavy eyes, Adam watched the wall intently as if it was about to perform a magic trick. He blinked, and suddenly he remembered the world around him. He rubbed his eyes and ran a hand through his extremely messy hair. He removed the covers and turned so that his legs hung over the edge of the bed, the tips of his toes on the floor. With a tiny groan, he stood up, stretched his arms widely, and let out a long yawn. Looking at the bed on the other side of the room, Adam saw that Talan was gone.

Adam took his time crossing the room and reaching the door. He raised a hand to grab the Krevvler, but it was not there. He blinked in astonishment.

"The Krevvler's gone!"

"Just knock on the door. It'll come back!" Seth called from outside the room.

Adam did as he was told. Quietly, he knocked twice. Sure enough, the piece of stone materialized on the door. He looked at it for a moment before reaching out to touch it. When he placed his hand on its cold surface, he brought his face close to the small writing and turned the dial to *Living Room*. As soon as he removed his hand, the loud sound of rushing air from behind the door jolted any remaining languor from him.

The door clicked, and Adam pulled the handle to admit himself into the room where Leon and Seth stood hunched over a table. He closed the door behind him and made his way over to them.

He noticed that several items were sprawled all over the table. Some of these items included swords, pouches, and odd little contraptions that Adam had never seen before. Leon noted with satisfaction that their guest had finally joined them.

"Good morrow," he said.

"What?" Adam replied groggily.

"It means good morning," Seth told him.

Adam blinked. "Oh. Where's Talan?"

"He's outside taking a stroll. He recovered remarkably well. You know what we're doing? We're getting our things ready for the journey," Leon said, engaged in the task sorting object into piles.

Adam noticed the swords with a sense of alarm. "Will we really need those? The swords?"

"You never know what you'll find in the Forest of Belliteth," Seth answered mysteriously.

Adam said nothing in return. Seth divided the items into four equal piles. After this task was completed, he shoved each pile into the four pouches. Seth stood up to his full height, which was not very impressive at all, and he handed Adam a pouch, which was rather large; it really seemed to be more like a backpack. Seth gave another to Leon, and he kept the last for himself.

"Right then. Adam, you have the supplies needed to make the journey to the mountains. Inside that bag, you'll find everything you need: food, clothes, and the other essentials. Oh, you asked about the swords? Yes, I keep mine hanging off of the side. Keeping it readily accessible is not a bad idea," Seth said.

Adam nodded and turned his bag over. Sure enough, there was a sword hanging loosely from a strap. Wide-eyed, he gaped at the scabbard. Making swords was one thing, but actually using them to kill was an entirely different beast. He turned the bag back over again, and Leon stepped forward. "Well, I think it's about time, wouldn't you agree, Seth?"

"Yes, we really should get going. Oh, Adam. Take this," Seth said. He tossed Adam something bright.

With open hands, Adam caught the object and saw that he had been given a fruit of some sort. It was an extremely vibrant shade of violet. Trusting Seth, he slowly brought it up to his mouth and slowly took a bite. He was expecting a sweet, fruity taste. Instead, he tasted the zest of salt. The fruit was not bad at all; in fact, it tasted delicious. Adam quickly finished it and wiped the purple juice off his mouth.

"What was that?" he asked in amazement.

"A scaradula? You've still got much to learn," Leon answered.

"Well then, off we go!" Seth said excitedly.

Seth hurried over to the door and spun the Krevvler around in a complete circle three times. As soon as the third spin was completed, the *whoosh!*

noise sounded clearly. He removed his hand from the peculiar device and reached for the door handle. With a forceful push, he opened the door to reveal the bright beach landscape.

When the familiar image of the palm trees greeted him, Adam reminded himself that this was not the time for sightseeing. He waited outside as Seth and Leon exited the house. Seth walked over to Adam and turned on the spot to watch his brother. Leon shut the door with enough force to close it properly. Adam wondered what the Krevvler would do if one decided to slam the door shut. Leon quickly went over and unfastened his massive horse from its pole. When he reached Adam and Seth, he looked up them with one eye squinted against the sunlight.

"Right then. Are we ready?" Leon asked.

"Wait for me," a tired voice called from nearby.

Turning their heads, Adam, Seth, and Leon spotted the figure of Talan emerge from behind the house. Slowly, he walked to the group and apologized for not coming sooner.

"I'm glad you're alright," Adam said.

Talan smiled grimly. "Thank you."

"Well, now that we're all here, I'd say that we are ready! Come, Adam! Our quest begins!" Seth said in a squeaky voice.

Leon walked past Adam and Seth, not stopping to wait for them. Rather, he turned right, and the other two followed him obediently. They were approaching the mouth of the same forest Adam had seen when Leon first led him to their humble abode.

When they finally stood before the great entrance, Leon stopped. He turned directly to Adam, who watched, his confusion no doubt showing on his face. As Leon and Seth walked ahead, Adam walked close to Talan.

"Talan, you were trying to tell me something the other night. Do you remember what it was?" he whispered.

"Remind me."

"You thanked me for saving your life, which was unnecessary because of all that you've done for me. Then you mentioned something about a secret."

Talan's complexion darkened. "That," he began, "is something we will discuss later in private."

Adam blinked in surprise. "Why not now?"

"We are not alone."

Suddenly, there was a rustle nearby, and they all turned their heads. A tall figure approached them slowly with her hands dangling complacently at her sides. Seth stepped forward to greet the visitor with a bright expression. Leon also stepped forward, but his face was devoid of excitement.

"Sorah-Kown! What brings you here at this early hour?" Seth asked happily.

The woman stopped before them with a dignified expression. Her long black hair was drawn back, and the sun shone softly upon her dark skin. She paused for a moment, and then she returned Seth's warm smile.

"I heard you were leaving," she said in a regal voice.

"And how," Seth mused, "could you have known that?"

"I have my ways as far as you know."

Adam raised an eyebrow at Sorah-Kown's cryptic response.

Leon stepped closer to her. "Sorah-Kown, do you think we could borrow three of your horses."

She smiled through perfect white teeth. "I thought you'd never ask." Sorah-Kown whistled shrilly, and three young stallions leapt out from the foliage behind her. Two of them were black, and the smallest one was white. Seth and Talan hurried forward and claimed the black ones for their own. The white one regarded Adam with youthful eyes. Slowly, Adam walked over to the creature and gingerly placed his hand on its long face. The horse remained perfectly still. Smiling, he stroked the horse's snowy mane.

"Well, if you must know, Sorah-Kown, we are headed to the Reximen Heights," Seth said.

"You and who else?"

"Seth, Adam, Talan, and me," Leon said huffily.

"Adam? Is that him?" she asked, pointing to Adam.

With some discomfort, Adam slowly stepped forward. Leon and Seth both exchanged confused glances in response to Sorah-Kown's interest in him. A breeze ruffled Sorah-Kown's sky-blue robes, and the white embroidery on the shiny material resembled clouds. Adam noticed that she wore a silver chain around her slender neck, and a seashell of many colors hung loosely from it. The mysterious woman smiled as she regarded him.

"Hello. I am Sorah-Kown. My dwelling place is here in the village of Tahvokia. It is I who lives on the waters. And who, pray tell, are you?"

"I'm Adam from Roddington," he replied quietly.

The mysterious grin on her copper-colored face widened. "Seth, Leon," she said to the twins. "Might I have a word with the boy alone?"

Silently, they stepped away and turned their backs to Adam and Sorah-Kown. When they were far enough away that no one could hear them, the tall woman bent over closer to him, her eyes sparkling with a keen interest.

"You are more than just a boy from Roddington. I know what you are, Adam Crescent," she said softly.

Adam's eyes widened in shock. "You do?"

She hushed him. "How is not important. I have been waiting many years for you to come."

"You've been waiting for me? How can that be?" He shook his head in disbelief.

"This land has many secrets. I trust you'll learn that very soon. Tell me, Adam, why do you seek the guidance of the Pentacular Reximen?"

Shuffling his feet, he looked up at Sorah-Kown. "I want to master my powers," he replied honestly.

"And rightly so. This is the first of many steps in your great journey. I commend you for your valiance," she said brightly.

"Er—thank you."

"Do you know what awaits you at the Reximen Heights?"

He shook his head in reply. "Do you?"

Sorah-Kown laughed softly. "Even if I did, it would not be fair to tell."

"What of my friends, then?"

"Oh, Adam. What good would it do to reveal the ending when the story has only just begun? Find out for yourself."

He nodded in reply, and another thought occurred to him. "Then what *can* you tell me?"

Sorah-Kown's expression darkened, which caught Adam off guard. He gasped softly and blinked as if to dispel the sight.

"Only this. This is not our last meeting, Adam Crescent. There will come a time where you shall return here to Tahvokia, and you will be at your most vulnerable. All will seem lost, and your hope will nearly be shattered. You will be alone in the world. When this happens, you must come find me. Do not breathe a word of this to anyone else, for this is secret knowledge. Only you and I may share it."

Her words perturbed Adam greatly. He opened his mouth to speak, but the woman quickly placed a slender finger on his lips. "This is all I wish to discuss. Return to the others. We are finished."

He remained motionless as Sorah-Kown called Seth and Leon back. Adam was deeply troubled by her mysterious claims. *What*, he so desperately wondered, *could break my spirit like that?*

When Seth and Leon stood on either side of him, Sorah-Kown spoke softly to them. "Now then, I feel that your trip into the village is no longer required. Go now and make haste to the Reximen Heights."

Leon and Seth nodded in agreement. Sorah-Kown smiled kindly and wished good fortune upon them. With that she bade them farewell and headed to the beach. Before the esteemed woman disappeared, she turned her head and looked at Adam with a curious expression. He lowered his gaze to the ground, and a chill traveled down his spine. When he looked up, she was nowhere in sight.

"What was that all about?" Seth asked.

Adam remained still as Sorah-Kown's words floated through his mind.

"Adam?" Seth persisted.

"I don't even know, really," Adam murmured. He turned to the leafy forest entrance.

"Well, sorry we're not going to the village anymore, but perhaps one day you'll get the chance. Go ahead and get a good luck at this place. You won't be seeing much light where we're going," Leon said with a grim expression.

Adam turned his head around to look upon the calm beach landscape for one last time. The wind blew softly, and in their motion the waves and the palm trees seemed to be offering him one last farewell before he ventured onward. When he turned around, he looked Leon squarely in the eyes and nodded.

"Then it's time," he said and turned to face the entrance.

With that, Leon mounted his horse, and the other three did likewise. Together, they marched boldly through the entrance to the Forest of Belliteth. Seth followed suit, and Adam and Talan trailed behind him. The sound of the ever-moving sea gradually faded away. The gentle rustle of the palm leaves eventually disappeared as well.

The second Adam's horse stepped foot into the woody expanse, he felt that things had reversed to become the opposite of what he had just known. In an instant, the dazzling sunlight was snuffed out and replaced by a dim, eerie glow. Any sound that had once existed became choked by the heavy silence. The ground beneath the creature's feet was no longer soft, but was replaced with hard, coarse dirt. The only noises he heard were the horses' heavy stomps. His brightest thoughts were snuffed out like a candle in a cyclone.

Seth seemed to sense the growing physical distance between them. "Stay close," he said quietly.

Gingerly, Adam gently tapped his legs against his horse's side, and they moved quickly toward Seth. Leon did not look back at all, as he seemed determined to reach the end of the journey as soon as possible.

Adam could not help but draw an important conclusion about the twins. Seth radiated brilliance and ambition, but Leon's resolve went much deeper. On the surface, Leon appeared to be an average man. At first glance, Adam thought he was one of those people who took life one day at a time with no thought to the future. A closer look at Leon revealed incredible determination. Seth always knew what to do, but Leon possessed something more. When given a task, he would apply every ounce of his effort. Leon was a driven individual, and Adam greatly admired that quality.

Talan continued at the rear of the group wordlessly, and Adam could only wonder what sort of mysterious thoughts snaked through his mind. Adam's stream of thought suddenly disintegrated when he heard rustling noise. Leon stopped abruptly, and Seth's poor horse nearly ran into the beast in front of it. Everyone fell deathly silent and listened for any further signs of movement. After several moments of standing as still, Leon eased his horse forward and began moving along.

"We've got our swords," Adam heard him murmur.

Slowly, Adam's sharp eyes began to adjust to the darkness, yet they never quite reached the sharpness he had grown accustomed to. Gradually, the colors of the many trees began to stand out, and Adam was surprised at how many different hues a tree trunk could be. The colors varied from dark brown to rustic scarlet. It was almost as if an artist had strolled along the narrow trail and splashed a wide assortment of woodsy colors on the trunks. The canopy was dense with leaves that were the colors of life. The faint rays of sun that actually managed to reach the earth cast a hazy green glow over the forest.

Seth noticed Adam walking along behind them, so he waited for him to catch up. Adam was a bit nervous about traveling in such a dark place. He felt as if he were trapped in a woodland prison. A few seconds later, he walked right next to Seth.

"Are you nervous?" Seth whispered.

"A little."

Seth nodded with a knowing grin. "I remember my first time. I was scared, too. Sure, it's dark and creepy, but I think the worst part about the trip to the mountains is that your fears seem to follow you."

"It really seems that way."

They traveled a little further in silence. From what Adam could see, the trail spiraled on and on into the dark unknown. He envied Leon's bold demeanor as he led them further and further.

"I had to get him to lead me through the first time as well," Seth said.

"Did he ever go by himself?"

"Yes. I don't know how he did it, though. Leon's a brave one. Sometimes, I wish I had half of the guts he has."

Adam took some comfort in knowing that he was following a fearless leader. "These trees are kind of spooky."

"Yeah, you're telling me. You want to know something interesting, though?" Seth asked.

"Sure."

"In the stories, these trees can talk."

"Like you and me?" Adam asked incredulously.

"Supposedly. Leon swears he heard them whisper once."

"Do you believe him?"

Seth shrugged and offered a small smile. "I don't really know. I've never heard the slightest whisper come out of one of those things. Maybe Leon's ears were playing tricks on him."

"They could do it, right? I mean, isn't it possible?"

"Oh, sure. All sorts of things are possible in this place. I'm just saying this might be a rumor or an old wives' tale. That's all."

Suddenly, a fantastic thought occurred to Adam. "Are there going to be dragons?" he asked hopefully.

Leon and Seth made eye contact, and then they suddenly burst out laughing. Even Talan could not hide his quiet laughter. This was not at all the reaction Adam expected.

"What's so funny?"

"*Are there dragons?* What does this look like to you? A fairy tale?" Seth hooted.

"Oh." Adam frowned.

They walked further into the labyrinthine forest. Twigs and leaves crunched beneath their feet. Adam and Seth kept whispering to one another, and Leon continued forward as if he were surrounded by complete silence. Adam supposed he either did not care about what was being said or that he was too focused on the trail ahead. Either way, he was thankful for Seth's company because it took his mind off of their gloomy surroundings.

"The Forest of Belliteth is the first part. After this, we get to travel upriver, and we'll end up right at the base of the mountain," Seth said.

Adam remembered hearing something about the river in one of the many conversations they'd had the previous day. "What's so special about the river, Seth?"

"The River of Thanatos? Oh, it—Leon, what are you doing?" Seth hissed.

Leon did not bother to turn around. Adam noticed that he had decided to veer off the beaten track.

"I'm leading the way, aren't I?" he said gruffly.

"Well, yes," Seth said.

"Then let's keep it that way."

No one opened his mouth to argue as the group walked in between two particularly close trees. Adam looked up and saw several branches spiraling off in many different directions. The ends of the branches looked like curled fingers clutching at the air, a sight that repulsed him. The roots that they stepped over were thick and gnarled. The wide shadows cast by the trees blended ominously into the darkness. The air was certainly colder, Adam noted. A very disheartening thought slowly occurred to him.

"Seth, you don't think anyone has died in here, do you?" he asked quickly.

"I'm sure people have died here before," Seth answered plainly.

Adam looked at him in shock.

Seth raised an eyebrow. "What? It happens," he said with a shrug.

Adam was at a loss for words. The forest suddenly seemed to be much larger and darker than ever before. He gulped and looked ahead.

No one said anything for quite some time. Leon kept silent as he stared forward on horseback. After a while, a rumble of thunder echoed from the skies above.

Great, I'm stuck in the forest of doom, and now it's going to rain. Brilliant, Adam thought.

As if replying to this thought, Seth turned to Adam. "I know what you're thinking. Rain never comes down here. It always thunders, but rain never comes."

The false promise of rain was rather odd and unsettling, and it made the Forest of Belliteth seem even darker than before. The small bit of sunlight began to dwindle as the clouds gathered overhead and formed a large mass in the heavens above.

Adam heard several things in the span of mere seconds. Several birds hooted and squawked. He heard tiny feet skittering along the forest floor. The leaves rustled. The wind whistled once more, and a shiver ran down his spine.

Adam, a chilling voice whispered from nearby.

"Who's there?" Adam called.

Leon and Seth stared back at him with equally confused expressions. Talan watched him carefully. For a while, only silence ensued, and Adam opened his mouth to speak again. Before a sound could escape his lips, he heard the sound again.

Adam!

Suddenly, Adam's head erupted in pain and he rolled off of the horse, striking the ground painfully hard. Whispers surrounded him, and he pressed his hands tightly to his ears. Try as he might, nothing could silence the noise, for it was entering his mind.

Adam! Listen carefully, the hideous voice rasped. *Do not cross the bridge.*

In pain, Adam's eyes began to water as he writhed in agony.

The river. There is a bridge that allows safe passage across. Do not cross it. A trap awaits you there. The people claim to have what you want, what you desire most of all. You cannot give in. You must find another way.

Find another way...

The noise abruptly vanished, and the excruciating pain subsided immediately. Adam's face was drenched with sweat, and he breathed harshly. When he opened his eyes, he saw Seth, Leon, and Talan standing around him with concerned expressions.

"Did I pass out?" Adam whispered.

Talan shook his head. "No, you were with us the entire time. Tell us what happened."

Adam waited several moments before speaking. "There was a voice. It was inside of my head, and it warned me not to cross the river bridge. Someone has set a trap for us."

Seth and Leon exchanged nervous glances. "Are you sure it wasn't a trick?" Leon asked.

Shaking his head, Adam replied, "No. I've never heard of the voice before. The people waiting for us have something, an object, that I want. That's the trick."

"So you'd be willing to swim across the river?" Seth asked with an eyebrow raised.

Adam nodded. "Whatever it takes." With that, he slowly rolled over and climbed to his feet. Pausing for only a brief second, Adam boldly mounted his horse and stared forward. Leon nodded and pulled ahead, and the others followed suit until they all traveled in a line once more.

The forest grew blacker and more threatening as time slithered by. Sometimes Adam could only keep up with his companions by listening closely to the sound of their horses' feet against the ground. He began to worry that it would soon be too dark to continue traveling.

"Er—it's getting awfully dark. Perhaps we should think about finding a place to stay for the night," he suggested.

"No. Not here. Too risky," Leon grumbled.

Even though it did him little good in the dark forest, Adam swiveled his head this way and that to try to catch a glimpse of anything lurking in the shadows.

When it became very dark, the members of the group became committed to silence, as they needed to be able to hear each other's movements. The time spent in silence made Adam felt uneasy, and he tried desperately to get his mind off of his gloomy surroundings. At first, all he could think of was the string of incredible events that had occurred recently. But he realized he needed to remember something genuinely happy, something from his earlier days. He searched the corners of his mind for such a memory. Only one came to mind.

Seven years ago, when Adam was just an ordinary boy who had no knowledge of the Razorwolf and magic, he and Leira were walking about the town square because Gregor had decided that he had been good and deserved a break. The first place the two eager children visited was the market with all of its interesting wares. Apart from the usual goods, such as food, Adam took a particular interest in one vendor who sold all kinds of little animals.

The vendor, a kind man with a toothy grin, held before Adam and Leira a cage covered by a scarlet cloth. With a dramatic sense of mystery, he slipped the cloth off and revealed several tiny butterflies fluttering soundlessly in an ornately designed cage. These were not like ordinary butterflies, for their wings shone with all the colors of the rainbow. The children stared in awe at the beautiful creatures, and the merchant watched them with an amused grin. Leira whispered to him that she had been expecting something more dangerous, and Adam giggled. He caught sight of a butterfly that appeared to be more azure and violet than the others. This one genuinely interested him, for it seemed unique among the others.

His fascination with the tiny creatures suddenly disappeared when Gregor found him and Leira. Irritably, he sent Leira back to her mother, and he took Adam back home. He didn't say a word to the merchant as they left.

Gregor, unlike the children, did not approve of the merchant's ways, especially when it came to his selection of little creatures. He was never pleased when Adam excitedly gave him an account of the old man's wares. Gregor often told him that the man's activities were only sleight of hand tricks.

CHAPTER TWELVE

While Adam was learning how to fence properly, he could not erase the image of the butterfly from his mind. It was so different from the rest, and it seemed so special. He was so wrapped up in that thought that he forgot to lift his sword to defend himself. Gregor noticed this and somehow knew exactly what was going on in Adam's mind.

"Daydreams won't make us any better. We must dwell on what is real. Be real, Adam," he said.

Adam did as he was told, and he put all of his concentration back into the lesson. The next time he went out to the market, he looked all around for the merchant, but he was nowhere to be seen. For several visits, searching for the merchant became a sort of ritual, as Adam was so fascinated by him. The merchant, though, had closed up his small cart, and Adam quickly realized that he would never come back. One day, he could have sworn he saw a butterfly disappearing into the clear blue sky with a sparkle of azure and violet on its wings.

Suddenly, Adam's reminiscing was cut short when Leon and Seth came to an abrupt halt. He took a quick look around and saw that everything was nearly pitch-black. He could barely make out the small figures of Leon and Seth standing before him.

"Right then. This place is safe. We'll rest here for the night. Tie your horses to a tree, a *sturdy* tree. We don't want another repeat of last time, Seth," Leon said.

Seth scowled indignantly as he hopped off of his horse and tied it to a nearby tree. When Adam turned around to catch a glimpse of Talan, he saw that the rogue's horse lay peacefully on the ground. Talan marched over to Adam and helped him secure the white horse. While Talan worked on fastening a fat knot, Adam could not help but ask, "Do your wounds hurt?"

Talan looked back at him. "At first. These are nothing compared to what I've lived through before. You know the old saying 'what doesn't kill you makes you stronger'? Well, let's just say that I've found that to be true."

Nodding slowly, Adam said nothing in reply. When the knot was tight and secure, Adam, Seth, and Talan waited for a couple of minutes as Leon sifted through his pack and removed a fat candle and a piece of flint. Leon placed the candle on the ground and broke the piece of metal in two. Kneeling before the candle, he struck the two shards together and produced sparks. When one of the sparks finally managed to ignite the candlewick, Adam and Talan placed their packs on the ground and removed their mats. Seth already started unfurling his.

When they had unrolled their mats, they wasted no time in lying down. Adam looked to the canopy above and wondered what could have possibly happened to the butterfly in his memories. Gregor's words echoed faintly within his mind: *Daydreams won't make us any better. We must dwell on what is real. Be real, Adam.*

He mouthed the last few words and closed his eyes. Leon snored softly close by, and Adam could detect Seth's soft breathing with his sensitive ears. He closed his eyes and hummed softly. This time, sleep did not come as easily as it had the previous night. After several minutes, Adam fell into a light and uncomfortable slumber.

CHAPTER THIRTEEN

GHOSTS OF THE MIST

*T*he forest was illuminated by a strange green aura. All was visible, yet
Seth, Leon, and Talan were nowhere in sight. Something crackled nearby,
and Adam whirled around to face the noise. Sorah-Kown stepped out from
behind a tree with a solemn expression. He tried to move toward her, but she held out
a hand, rendering him immobile. She whispered things Adam could not understand.
Suddenly, a loud scream came from behind him. He fought Sorah-Kown's tenacious
hold, but he was too weak to escape, and she easily slipped the ropes over his hands
and feet. Leira moaned hideously from far away, but there was no sign of Tyrule
anywhere. Try as he might to scream, Adam opened his mouth, but the words would
not come. Sorah-Kown frowned sadly, and she disappeared in a puff of scarlet smoke.
In her place stood Mustafo, his countenance alight with ghastly pleasure. Sorah-
Kown's bonds suddenly vanished, but it was far too late to escape. The old man
stretched out a hand at Adam. Before he could leap away, Mustafo's palm glowed

a violent shade of scarlet. A jagged flame smote Adam across the chest. As his vision faded into blackness, he could hear the sound of shrieking metal.

No.

It was the sound of wicked laughter.

You must get to him first.

Adam snapped awake instantly. In one swift movement, he sat bolt upright. His breathing was harsh and ragged, and he could feel the tiny beads of sweat on his brow. His eyes flickered manically, and he felt as if he were still trying to locate Mustafo lurking in the darkness. Adam continued looking around for several seconds. When it became apparent that no one was hiding, his gaze shifted to his own feet, which were illuminated dully by the beams of moonlight that passed through the dense foliage above.

He had an odd suspicion that Mustafo somehow knew exactly where he was. The thought made him uneasy, and his goal to find Leira and Tyrule seemed much more urgent than ever before. He could not shake off the sound of Leira's terrible scream. Adam was startled when he heard a soft rustling noise from nearby. He quickly swiveled his head toward the noise and saw a small silhouette move.

"Adam, are you awake?" Seth whispered.

"Yes."

Adam's heavy breathing must have disturbed Seth. He felt a twinge of guilt, but at the same time, he did not want to draw any more unwanted attention to himself.

"I can't sleep either," Seth said.

Adam listened carefully and heard the sound of Leon's irregular snores. At least one of them was sleeping soundly through the night. He looked around at the dark surroundings, wondering why his superior vision had not kicked in.

"Seth?"

"Yes?"

"Do you think this forest is creepy?"

"Didn't you ask me that already?"

"Did I? Oh, well I'm sorry."

"Actually, there's a sort of rumor about this forest," Seth said.

"Yeah?"

"Well, there was a lot of magic at one point, and apparently this forest is *enchanted*, as one would say, to nullify certain types of magic."

"That explains a lot," Adam murmured irritably.

"I'm sorry?"

"Er—nothing. We're crossing a river, right?" Adam quickly changed the subject.

"Yes. Yes we are. Why?"

"Well, I always hear you and Leon talking about the river as if it's a bad thing. What's so bad about a river?"

"Interesting you should ask. The River of Thanatos is unlike others you have seen, I'm guessing. The ones you're used to flow in one direction, do they not?" Seth asked with a hint of amusement in his voice.

"Yes, they do, but I don't see how that's really important. All rivers do."

"All rivers except for this one, which does *not* flow in one direction. It changes all the time."

Adam paused for a moment. "How is that even possible?"

"Well, the river is cursed," Seth answered with a wicked grin.

"Cursed? How so?"

"It is cursed. The water deters you from reaching the end of your journey."

"So, if I wanted to go north, it would try to push me south?" Adam asked.

"Well, it would push you in any other direction *but* north, but you have the right idea."

Adam scratched his head in confusion. Apparently, he still had a lot to learn about magic and its mysterious ways.

"Well, why not just walk along the bank?" Adam asked.

"Ah, that won't exactly work. All credit to you, that's a sound idea," Seth remarked. "If you were to try and step in the sand, your feet would sink, and the sand around you would turn into stone."

"And how long would you stay that way? Could the sand spit you out?" asked Adam with wide eyes.

"Of course it would eventually. Once you had forgotten your quest, your goal, you'd be free. Apparently someone wanted very much to make sure that no one could reach the end, whatever it was," Seth said.

"Have you actually crossed the River of Thanatos before?" Adam asked.

"Yes, a couple of times. It wasn't easy, but we fought through the current. It was exhausting."

"Oh, great."

Seth chuckled softly. "You sound excited."

"What gave it away?" Adam replied with equal sarcasm.

Leon let out another loud snore, and both of them quickly looked over in his direction, startled by the sudden disruption.

"Is there anything else that I should be warned about?" Adam asked, slowly looking back to Seth.

"I think that's it. I just like the story behind it all. It's quite interesting."

Adam tilted his head, interested. "There's a story behind it?"

"Of course there is. There's a story behind nearly everything."

"Oh, right. I should have known. Well, what's so special about this one?" Adam asked.

Seth noticed how intrigued he sounded and smirked. "This one is something of a love story."

"Oh, I hope it's not one of those clichéd tales."

"Oh, no. This one's different."

"Well then, let's hear it."

"Well, it's about a girl," Seth began.

"Aren't they all?" Adam asked with a shrug.

"It was you who asked for the story, not I. Do you still want to hear it or not?" Seth said crossly.

"Yes, yes, yes. Sorry," Adam replied quickly.

"Well, in the early days of the land when magic flourished, there lived a king. This king was unwed, and many princesses from faraway kingdoms came to his castle every day for a chance to win his hand. Of course, none of the women struck his fancy.

"The king waited and waited for someone to find him, but the right woman never showed up at his castle doors. One day, he was out riding his favorite stallion in a vast field when he caught a glimpse of *her*. She was walking by, and he saw her fair face and night-black hair. His heart fluttered the very moment his eyes found her. He was so enchanted by her presence that he fell off of his horse and was knocked unconscious.

"When he woke up in his personal chamber, he demanded to know who the woman was. Not even his closest advisors knew anything about her. They thought he had been terribly mistaken, but the king refused to give in to such nonsense. He knew exactly what he saw, and he intended to find her.

"Several days later, when he was sprightly and well once more, he went with a group of knights to check on the province. By this time, the king was beginning to doubt the woman's existence himself. When all of his subjects bowed to him as he rode on horseback, the king looked straight ahead. A glint of green fabric caught his eye, and he turned his head and saw her. The woman stood looking at him calmly, but the king felt like his heart was about to hammer its way out of his chest.

"He immediately leapt off of his stallion and made his way through the crowd to find her. When at last he stood before her, the woman smiled serenely at him. He smiled back and held out his hand. The knights called for him to return to the procession, and both the king and the woman frowned. He did not want to be separated from her, nor did she want to see him leave. Before the king went back, he whispered in her ear to meet him at the castle gates at midnight. When she promised him that she would, he ran back to his horse and rejoined the procession.

"Well, the day certainly went by slowly for the king. Everything seemed so boring and dull, which only increased his restlessness. Even the tailor noticed that the king was anticipating something. When at last nightfall came, the king waited for the inhabitants of the castle to rest. He snuck into his wardrobe and removed an outfit designed to imitate the garb of an ordinary townsperson.

"The king managed to leave the castle without attracting any attention at all, and he had to fight hard to keep himself from running to the gates to meet the woman. From behind the castle gates, he saw the dark figure standing still on the other side. He quickened his step, and at last he stood before her, separated only by the curved wrought iron of the gates. Quickly, the king managed to slip through the gates and right before her. She smiled kindly at him and beckoned him to follow her.

"They walked along the outskirts of their town and took care so that no one would spot them, not even the most perceptive watchdog. They found a shortcut that allowed them to avoid the long and harrowing journey through the mountains. They passed through a meadow and a lovely looking forest before they heard the sound of gently flowing water.

"When at last they stood at one end of the riverbank, the woman turned to the king. She had a secret, and their passage across the river demanded its revelation because they could not hope to cross without it. For a long time, she was hesitant to reveal the truth, but she knew if the king really loved her, he would accept any truth.

"She told the king that she had a secret. He laughed and admitted that he had very few interesting secrets of his own. The woman confessed that she had magical abilities, and she expected him to become afraid; however, the king found this to be marvelous, and he asked for a small demonstration. She was somewhat surprised at this reaction, but she did as he wished. She faced the flowing river and held her arms out wide in the cool, night air. From her fingertips issued a silver mist that fell upon the water. The mist caused the water to freeze and form a bridge that she intended for them to cross. When the creation was complete, she lowered her hands and looked to the king.

"He had a look of awe in his eyes, but he was nervous about crossing. She smiled at him and took his hand. Gently, she led him across the magical chasm to the other side of the riverbed. On the other side was a beautiful shore with colorful flowers and snow-white sand.

"They both sat down to watch the calm river, and the king declared that he was in love with her. After a while, though, they knew the time had come for them to return. They remained together until they arrived back at the castle gates, where they were reluctant to part ways. He gave her a kiss, and made her promise to meet him the following night. At last, the two lovers bade each other a sad farewell.

"The next day, the king was tired, and one of his advisors noticed this. When nightfall came again, the advisor did not go to his quarters for sleep. Instead, he watched from a lofty window as the king exited the castle gates. The advisor became suspicious about the king's activities with the dark figure he walked away with. When the king returned the following morning, the advisor said nothing and acted as though he had been asleep all night.

"When the king retired in his personal chambers, the advisor went and summoned a select number of knights. He ordered that they follow the king and this mysterious person to their destination. The advisor told them that when they had cornered the king and his companion, they were to kill the companion. The advisor sought only to keep the king safe and in good order, and he believed that the nocturnal visitor was a distraction.

"So when the night fell upon the land for the third time since the king had met the woman, the knights followed them quietly. When she stopped to freeze the bridge, they were both amazed and terrified of the display. Still, they had a mission, and they would not fail.

"The knights waited for them to cross the bridge. Now that they knew that the king was with a lover capable of the most extraordinary magic, they came to the conclusion that she had bewitched his mind. Silently, one knight took his bow and nocked an arrow. Pulling back on the string, he aimed closely at the woman. Suddenly, a rustle came from a nearby bush, and the knight was so alarmed that he released the arrow.

"The arrow flew between the faces of the two lovers. They both whirled around and saw the shocked faces of the other knights. Realizing the error, the other knights nocked their arrows and fired at the woman. The king grabbed her and dove away from the attack. The knights could not see their target very well in the dark, so they used a piece of flint to light a torch, and they set several arrows aflame.

"The knights found the arrows were easier to see, but the lovers also saw the fiery projectiles hurtling toward them. The king tried to shout and call them off, but they did not obey. They still believed the magical woman had a hold on his mind, and they were determined to free him.

"One knight nocked another flaming arrow, which he aimed precisely at the woman. She was far enough away from the king that he would not be endangered. When the king saw the arrow cut through the air, he threw himself before her to protect her.

"When he hit the ground, his breath became shallow and ragged. He lay on the white sand, breathing heavily. He looked down at his chest and saw the smoldering tip of the arrow that had pierced his heart. He looked up at his lover, who let out an awful scream upon seeing him.

"The knights realized their grave loss, and they immediately tried to rush across the frozen bridge. In absolute fury, the woman waved her hands wildly, and the bridge shattered in a fierce explosion. Several knights were sent soaring into the air. Still, when the remaining knights began to try and swim across the river, she grew angrier.

"She shouted out an ancient spell into the heavens. The once peaceful waters of the river grew frenzied and monstrous. The wind swept about like an angry giant. She watched coldly as more of the knights were dragged beneath the furious waters. One knight managed to fight his way across the river, but the woman would not tolerate his presence. She placed a curse over the sands that he walked upon. In an instant, his feet sank deep within the wet sand. The ground upon which he stood turned to stone right before his very eyes. He pleaded for mercy, but she showed him none. She turned the stone into sand once more, but she sent a fierce gust of wind at him and hurled him back into the wild river, where he was swept away like the others. One knight on the other side of the river turned and ran back to the castle.

"When the waters had fallen still again, the woman wept and knelt beside the fallen king. He was barely alive, and he looked upon her with sadness. She cradled his head in her lap and it seemed as though her stream of tears would never end. She bent down and softly kissed him once more. Despite his terrible pain, he managed to smile gently at her. Then, he looked at her one last time, and he closed his eyes slowly. The king was gone.

"She turned her face to the full moon and screamed out in anguish. For several hours, she wept bitterly for her fallen lover. Before daybreak, she used a spell to lift him, and she buried him gently in a tomb made with her own magic.

"When the tomb was sealed and hidden, she returned to the shore-line and watched the river flow by quickly. She cried once more and watched as her tears mingled with the water. The river slowly stopped moving forward; instead, it moved in the reverse direction. Noticing this, the woman placed a curse on the river and the edges of the shore that would prevent anyone from disturbing her in her inconsolable sadness. Shortly after, the knights named the river after their fallen king, Thanatos. Thereafter, no one ever saw the woman, now known as the River Queen, again."

Adam sat silently and let the tragedy sink in. Seth waited for him to say something, but he couldn't find any words for several moments. When at last he decided to speak, he looked up at Seth with a curious expression.

"Whatever happened to her, the woman?"

"Some say she died. Others say she became a spirit. I think she eventually had to move on."

Adam nodded quietly. "Well, that's really sad. But where's the bridge now?"

"It is a sad story, but it's only a story to explain the odd nature of the river. It might not even be true at all. As for the bridge, someone took the liberty of making one out of ropes and planks. It wobbles when you move along it," Seth said.

"How can you tell whether the stories about this place are true or not?"

"I guess there's really no way to know for sure. Believe what you want," Seth answered with a shrug. Adam yawned and stretched his arms.

"Sounds like good advice."

"If you don't mind me asking, what do you think these people at the bridge have of yours?"

Adam paused for a moment. "I have no idea. I have nothing. I brought nothing here to Fallador. Every object I've ever owned is somewhere in Roddington."

Seth stroked his chin. "Perhaps it's more than some object. Maybe it's your fortune."

"They already took that," Adam said.

"If I wanted to force someone my way, I'd steal something really valuable. Something that would cost more than pocket change," Seth said.

"But what would be so—," Adam stopped midsentence.

"Adam, are you alright? You look a bit pale. Maybe you should rest."

"I'm fine. Rest? Rest sounds good, really good," he answered quickly.

Seth lay back down. "Well, I suppose we'd better try to get some more sleep before we actually try to cross the river."

Adam followed suit and stared blankly at the darkness overhead. He closed his eyes and let his mind wander. For a moment, he envisioned the woman weeping over her lost lover, the white sands stained scarlet. Unlike Seth, though, Adam felt the Queen's pain, for the stakes had just escalated to terrible heights.

CHAPTER FOURTEEN

A DARK VENGEANCE

When all was deathly still, Adam got up from his mat and extinguished the candle. Even in the darkness, he knew where his three companions slept. With deliberate footsteps, Adam tiptoed past Seth and Leon's snoring forms. At last, when he stood over Talan, he crouched to the ground and shook him gently. Talan's eyes opened instantly, and he blindly searched for a tangible person.

"Who is it?" he whispered.

"It's me," Adam answered.

Talan sat upright and stared blankly towards the sound of his voice. "What are you doing up so early?"

"I need your help, but we can't wake Seth and Leon."

"And why would we do that?" he asked.

"We have to go find the bridge. They won't be willing to lead us that way, especially since we were warned not to go there."

CHAPTERFOURTEEN

"You mean you were warned. Let's avoid the trouble and go back to sleep," Talan muttered irritably.

Adam stood his ground. "They have Tyrule and Leira."

Talan understood and nodded. "I see. And you need my help to rescue them?"

"Yes."

Neither of them said anything for a while, but Talan quickly rose to his feet. "I'll help you. Let's gather the horses, but quietly."

Together, they crept towards the sleeping horses, taking extra caution not to startle them. Adam's white stallion was easily visible in the darkness, but finding Talan's took several minutes. When both of them found their horses, they quietly led them away from the campsite. From the dense canopy above, Adam spotted the moon's pale glow.

"It must not be far from here," he said.

For a while, the two of them guided their horses in silence. Every now and then, a stray leaf would crunch, or a twig would snap, but they knew that Seth and Leon would not notice. When they were outside of hearing range, Talan whispered, "I owe you an explanation, Adam."

"Right now?" Adam asked.

Talan nodded solemnly. "It's about my past."

Adam fidgeted uncomfortably. "Look, I really appreciate it, and I'd love to hear it, but I'm too nervous about what we're doing now to focus on anything else."

"Understood," Talan said stoically. "I think we're far enough to mount."

"Me too."

They mounted the horses simultaneously and waited a moment before moving any further. In the moonlight, they could clearly see each other's features. Talan bore an expression of extreme determination. Adam hoped that his face would not betray the fears that spiraled within. Noticing Adam's hesitancy, Talan asked, "Are you sure you want to do this?"

"Positive," Adam answered through clenched teeth and jammed his heels into the horse's side.

At once, the still landscape around him became a blur, and the wind whipped angrily at his face. Narrowing his eyes, Adam imagined that he must have resembled an angry, yet determined warrior. From behind, he heard Talan trying to keep up. As they covered more and more ground, Adam could feel the oppressive enchantment of the forest growing weaker and weaker, and his heightened senses gradually returned. The path before him became more obvious, and the definition looked sharper than ever. Even through the sound of hammering hooves, he heard the sounds of the creatures in the night.

A few hours passed, and the Forest of Belliteth did not spring any nasty surprises on the travelers. Adam was expecting to hear the sound of moving waters soon, and he also expected to see the beginnings of a sandy shoreline. He remembered what Seth had said about the sand and how it ensnared those who tried to step upon it.

"If anything bad happens, whatever you do," Adam warned him, "do not step on the sand by the river."

"Why?" Talan asked.

"You'll be stuck there forever. It's cursed."

"So many curses," Talan remarked.

"You have no idea," Adam muttered.

They continued onward without much conversation except for the occasional grumble and small talk. Adam noticed that the forest seemed to look lighter and lighter with each and every step. Earlier, it had seemed unfair that the forest had nullified his heightened Razorwolf senses. On reflection, though, he realized that it was nice to feel truly normal for the first time in several days.

Normal. What is normal? he thought.

His thoughts were cut short when the sound of rushing water entered his auditory range. Stopping his horse, Adam leapt off of his saddle and landed quietly upon the ground. Talan did likewise, but he regarded Adam with a confused expression.

"We need to be on our guard," Adam whispered and withdrew his sword from his pack.

"Have you ever used a sword before?" Talan asked.

"Several times."

Talan led the horses over to a thick tree and secured them before rejoining Adam. Both of them moved quietly towards the sound of the water, and glistening, white sand came into view. On the shore, a lone boat lay on its side. Far off, both of them spotted the bridge in the distance, and the moonlight revealed two figures in the middle.

"That's them," Adam whispered and stepped forward. Suddenly, there was a forceful jerk on his collar, and he fell back.

"What are you doing?" Talan hissed in his ear. "We have no clue who's out there."

"But we know who you are," a woman's voice sneered from behind them.

Adam and Talan whirled around and faced the owner of the voice. A tall woman stood before them wrapped in black clothes. A long, blonde ponytail with fine braids dangled from her head. Her ruby red lips curled in a dark grin, revealing perfect teeth. Adam pointed his sword at her chest. "There's only one of you and two of us," he growled.

"Oh, I beg to differ. Name's Zenia. I already know your name, and I don't care about your little friend. And speaking of friends, here they come," she said softly.

Two men leapt out from the shadows and flanked Zenia. The one on her left had dark features, and the other had a pale face and dark brown hair.

"Well done, sister," the pale-faced man said.

"I appreciate it. Now let's get down to business, boys. We've got Adam Crescent right where we want him, so Master will be most pleased," she said.

The dark-skinned man spoke, "Look at how they point their weapons at us. Silly toys." He waved his hand, and the swords flew from their hands and onto the ground. Adam glared at him.

"What do you want with me?"

"Heart of a lion. I like it, kid. Here's the rundown: you can either come quietly with us, and your friends will be safe. The other option is to put up a fight and be killed. You've got ten seconds," Zenia remarked and examined her red nails.

"If I go with you, will you let them go?" Adam asked.

"Your friends are of no consequence to us. Once you come with us, we'll turn them loose," the man on the right said.

"Just like he said. Make it snappy. We don't have all day, you know," Zenia said.

"Do I have your word?" he insisted.

Zenia rolled her eyes. "What are you, a child? Yes, yes, I promise they'll go."

"You won't," Talan said quickly and dove at the dark-skinned man.

As Talan brawled with the other man, Zenia and her brother advanced towards Adam. "Your friend made the foolish error of challenging a Shadowlord. I'd hope you'd show more wisdom," she sneered.

"Nope," Adam remarked and delivered a powerful punch to the man's jaw.

Zenia snarled and released a violet spell, blasting Adam backwards into a tree. As he struggled to get up, Zenia marched over to him quickly and clutched his neck tightly. Adam squirmed to break free from her iron grip, and she laughed darkly in his face.

"How pathetic," she cooed.

Her taunt irritated Adam, and he allowed his anger to build from within. With a strong hand, he grabbed her arm and forcefully removed her grip. A flash of fear flitted across her eyes for a brief moment, but it quickly turned back into rage. Before she could attack Adam again, he held out a glowing hand and blasted her aside. Without hesitating, he ran towards Talan, who was losing the fight against the other Shadowlords.

"Adam, do it again!" Talan shouted mid-punch.

Before he could make another move, Zenia's brother leapt at him and struck him in the face. The blow knocked Adam off of his feet, and his body thundered against the ground. In the blink of an eye, he rolled over and narrowly dodged the follow-up body slam. The man swore in anger, and Adam landed a swift kick to his face.

Howling with rage, Adam's attacker clutched his face in anguish. Adam looked over his shoulder and watched as Talan delivered a devastating punch into the other man's gut. Looking back towards the water, Adam sprinted to the bridge, kicking Zenia's brother in the side as he sped forward. Suddenly, he felt something powerful ram into the side of his head, causing him to drop to the ground. Rolling over, he saw the Zenia's enraged face hovering over him.

"You think you can stop me with some little fireworks? You've got nerve, kid," she growled.

"They seemed to do a nice job of tossing you on your face. You might want to work on your falls, Grace," Adam retorted.

Zenia snarled and slapped him in the face. The blow stung, but it was not nearly as heavy as a punch.

"You're all talk Zenia, but you can't throw a proper punch? You give evil a bad wrap."

She glared at him and slammed her fist into his face. "You like that one?"

Adam forced a laugh. "You call that a punch?"

As she swung another fist at his face, Adam grabbed her arm, and she shouted in surprise. He wagged a finger in her face. "You've had three chances. You failed at every one of them. Now watch and——."

A fiery pain suddenly erupted in Adam's side. Blinking the flash from his eyes, he saw that Zenia and her brother towered over him.

"Now how about your kick?" Zenia's brother shouted and swung his foot.

Adam rolled on his side, and his chest absorbed the impact, knocking the breath from his lungs. As they prepared to finish him off, he heard the sound of hooves against the earth. Zenia and her brother whirled around, which gave Adam plenty of time to escape. Looking over his shoulder, he spotted Seth and Leon charge onto the scene. Using the distraction, Adam located their swords lying on the ground. In a swift motion, he swooped down and snatched them up.

"Talan!" he shouted and threw one towards his ally.

Talan kicked his opponent squarely in the chest, sending him flying against a tree. A loud shriek erupted behind Adam, and he turned just in time to see Zenia rush towards him, ruby claws outstretched. Deliberately, he pointed his palm towards her and released a flash of azure energy, and she screamed violently as the surge threw her on the riverbank. The force of the magic whipped the sword from Adam's hand and into the forest. Adam watched in terror as Zenia attempted to rise from the sand.

A silver flash cut through the air, and she threw her head back and howled to the night sky. The handle of a sword clearly protruded from her side, and the sand trapped her feet. As the vindictive light left her eyes, her feet slipped free from the cursed ground, and she toppled back into the river. In a split second, the current carried her lifeless body away.

When Adam turned around, he saw Zenia's brother regard him with a furious snarl upon his face before raising an arm to strike him with a deadly spell. Suddenly, the small figure of Seth appeared out of nowhere and tackled Adam's attacker to the ground.

"Go! Save your friends!" he shouted.

Adam did not need to be told twice, and he spun around and bolted for the bridge. With careful footing, he dashed along the wobbling planks and headed for the middle, where the bound and gagged forms of Tyrule and Leira squirmed with fear. Coming upon Tyrule first, Adam reached out and tore the fabric from his mouth.

"Adam, you should not have come! It's a trap!" he panted.

"Duly noted," was his reply.

In a matter of seconds, Adam worked his way through Tyrule's bonds. As Tyrule leapt up on his feet, Adam turned and watched as he saw Seth and Leon try to subdue Zenia's brother. At his distance, things did not look good. Moving past Tyrule, Adam swiped his hand downward and ripped another cloth free from Leira's lips.

"Adam!" she cried.

"Listen to me," he said urgently. "I have to go back and fight. You two need to run to the other end of the bridge. Look for the mountains, and we'll meet up there. Tyrule, you need to free Leira. Hurry!"

Tyrule nodded, and Adam raced back to the foot of the bridge. Without so much as a backwards glance, he leapt towards Zenia's brother and drove an elbow directly into his chest. Seth ducked quickly as the man swung a last-ditch punch his way.

"Thanks!" he huffed.

"Don't mention it. We've gotta get out of here," Adam ordered.

"The river," Seth said quickly as he kicked Zenia's brother again, "is our best chance at losing them."

"Then we'll take the river!" Adam agreed and ran towards Talan.

Once more, the dark-skinned man advanced towards Talan with a murderous stare. As Talan pulled an arm back to defend himself, Adam barreled forward and flicked his wrist. A single bead of light leapt from his finger-tips and hit the man in the face, causing him to fall to the ground. Talan kicked his attacker lightly, and he did not stir.

"Unconscious," Talan breathed, wiping blood from his lip.

"You know, I think I'm beginning to get the hang of this magic business," Adam remarked.

"That would have been useful five minutes ago. What's the plan?" Talan asked.

Adam nodded and pointed to the boat at the edge of the sand. "We need that."

"You can't be serious!"

"Try me."

Talan said no more, and together he and Adam ran towards the shiny boat, taking extra caution not to touch the sand. When they flipped the boat over, three paddles tumbled out and landed at their feet.

"Lucky us," Adam mused.

Hastily, they shoved the paddles back inside of the boat and grabbed opposite ends. Adam held the bow, and Talan managed the stern. Zenia's brother saw them and rose quickly to stop them. Despite their best efforts to resist, Seth and Leon lay facedown on the ground.

"Use the boat! Knock them down!" Talan cried.

Slowing down, Adam gave Talan a chance to run next to him, and the boat hung between them. With wide eyes, Zenia's brother tried to move out of the way, but it was too late. The metal struck him in the face and knocked him off his feet with a resounding *clang!*

"Seth, Leon! C'mon! We've got to get to the bridge! We have to get to the river!" Adam shouted as Talan corrected his position towards the rear.

Within seconds, Leon and Seth reappeared at Adam's side as they all hurried to the bridge. As they ran along the bridge, Adam noted with relief that Tyrule and Leira were out of sight.

"Let's run to the other end!" Talan called forward.

"No! Don't forget, there's still one of them left. The river will make it impossible for him to find us!" Adam replied.

When the only thing beneath their feet was water, Adam and Talan placed the boat down. "Everyone in!" Adam ordered. Seth, Leon, and Talan clambered into the craft, but Adam remained outside.

"What are you doing?" Leon asked.

"I'm going to push us off!"

Suddenly, a scream of rage shattered the night, and Adam turned to see Zenia's brother running madly towards them. Adam inhaled sharply and pushed on the boat with all of his might. From the corner of his eye, he spotted a vivid, scarlet flash rush towards them. Suddenly, fire everywhere in sight, and the planks on the bridge splintered into the air. The ground beneath Adam's feet vanished in the explosion, and he fell downward without a sound. In a swift motion, he corrected himself midair and plunged towards the inside of the boat, his features emotionless as he watched the fearful faces of Seth and Leon.

Adam felt the rush of adrenaline course through his body as the air around him swirled during the descent. Even with his eyes tightly closed, he knew that they were spiraling downward. The descent seemed slow, but Adam knew that in a matter of seconds, he would feel an impact of some kind. He wished desperately for the bottom of the boat to land neatly on the water.

Suddenly, there was a resounding smack, and Adam lurched forward as he felt his feet slam against the metal floor. Once he realized he was alive and unharmed, his eyes snapped open, and he saw the fierce waters charging at them from every possible direction. Now he understood exactly what Seth had described the night before.

Before he could even do so much as blink, the boat began to spin in rapid circles. Adam clutched tightly to the edges of the boat, his fingers like claws, as they kept moving.

"*Hold on!*" Leon shouted.

Adam needed no further instruction about this. He maintained the tightest of death grips on the edges and watched as the world around him swirled together like a dizzying kaleidoscope. He wanted to shut his eyes once more, but the sunrise seeped through his closed eyelids. Adam saw Leon stab the water's violent surface with his paddle. Leon grunted and winced with tremendous effort as he tried to counter the spinning. Soon enough, much to Adam's great relief, their erratic rotations began to slow down.

When at last the boat floated in one direction, Leon lifted his paddle from the water. His breathing was harsh and ragged from strain, and Adam found he was having difficulty breathing as well. All four of the passengers took the moment of stillness to catch their breath. Adam felt hopeful and released a weary sigh.

Leon glanced back at him and noticed the look on his face. "This part doesn't last long," he said in a raspy voice.

Upon hearing these words, Adam's heart sank deeper than the still water below. They waited for a moment for something to happen. The boat was floating in the center of the river. The current suddenly disappeared, and the water was absolutely still, its surface like smooth glass. Adam opened his mouth to say something, but a sudden jerk of the boat clamped his mouth shut. Once more, the forces of the cursed River of Thanatos were at work against them. Even Talan's face was darkened with fear.

"*Paddle against the current! Paddle against the current! Head for the rapids!*" Leon yelled.

Adam, who was barely able to snatch up his paddle from the bottom of the boat, thought Leon's instructions were absolutely absurd, for deliberately heading for the rapids had to be madness. He realized staying around a trio of evil warriors was madness. With all the muscle he could muster, he shoved the paddle in the water and pulled as hard as possible. The combined efforts of all of them forced the boat to turn completely around. Looking ahead, Adam saw dangerous-looking rapids.

Banishing common sense to the far corners of his mind, Adam did as he was told and joined his companions in the battle against the current. Their strokes were long and arduous, and advancing toward the rapids was a cruelly slow process. Despite the daunting circumstances, they remained determined to reach their destination.

As they inched closer and closer to the rapids, Adam sharply drew in a breath. The boat slammed into several protruding rocks, and several times, Adam was nearly thrown from the vessel.

Just once, I'd like to travel on the water in peace!

The boat struck the rapids, quaking formidably. Every time the hull made contact with a stone or a boulder, the vessel was knocked askew, and they were already having enough trouble as it was keeping the boat traveling upstream. One set of rapids dealt a particularly powerful blow to the side of the boat, and Adam could see the dent clearly from the interior. Seth did his best to avoid colliding with the rocks, but the wild nature of the river made it very difficult to manage such a feat.

Talan, who did not have a paddle, shouted fiercely against the current, "What would you have me do?"

"Stay alive!" Seth replied.

When the end of the rapids was in sight, Adam's heart leapt. Just one large boulder remained in their way. For a moment, he thought he saw a pentagonal mark on the eroded surface. It was probably damaged by another passing boat, he thought. Suddenly, a stray current taunted them and threw the boat toward the boulder, and he was forced to look away. They tried their hardest to paddle away, but clearly time was not on their side. The side of the boat screeched as it scraped against the boulder, and the boat leaned precariously to one side. Adam, Talan, and Leon held on for dear life and screamed during the clamor. Seth, unfortunately, suffered a fate different from that of the other three.

With a yelp, he tumbled out of the boat and into the vicious waters. Adam's eyes widened, and he shouted in dismay as Seth began disappearing below. The river was fast, but Adam was faster. In one swift movement, he leapt to the rear of the boat and snatched Seth's hand as the river dragged him under. Adam felt the icy cold waters splash his hands and he winced. He could feel Seth's erratic shivers travel though him.

"*Get him!*" Leon roared.

"*Got him!*"

Leon lashed out against the water with powerful strokes, and Adam struggled to maintain a proper hold on Seth. Thankful that the rapids were now behind them, he felt his enhanced strength pulsating. With Talan's help, he managed to lift Seth's freezing body from the depths. Seth slid into the boat quickly with his paddle clenched tightly in one hand. Gasping for breath, he clambered back into his seat and jammed the paddle in the water once more to help his brother. Adam nearly tripped over Seth while hurrying back to his seat.

There was little time to celebrate the rescue, for one look ahead caused Adam's eyes to widen once more. The sight of swirling water suddenly made tackling the rapids seem like child's play. The current ahead swelled menacingly. Adam looked forward at the back of Leon's head as if it held the answer to his frantic question.

"*What do we do about this one?*"

"*Don't let go!*"

Adam did a double take at Leon's vague instructions. He was hoping for more specific instructions, as they always made him feel much safer. "Don't let go" only increased his panic. Still, Adam fought against the current with all the strength that he could muster. *If we ever get out of this one*, he thought, *I think I deserve some kind of medal.*

Before he could think of anything else, Adam felt the mighty force of the whirlpool snatch up the boat. It was unlike the spinning they had experienced before. Adam could not help but let out a terrified yell. Leon kept his eye on a fixed point in the distance. A quick glance back at Seth told Adam that he was not the only one who was scared out of his wits. Talan gave him a subtle nod, demonstrating his trust in Leon's judgment.

"*On my signal, paddle backwards!*" Leon shouted.

"*W—w—what?*" Seth stammered.

"*Paddle backwards when he says!*" Adam shouted back at him.

Seth nodded frantically and waited for the signal. The spinning was making Adam dizzy, and he knew that if he closed his eyes, the sensation would only get worse. As they swirled closer to the heart of the monstrous whirlpool, Adam tried to focus on Leon's instructions.

"*Now!*" Leon called suddenly.

Automatically, Adam jammed the paddle in the water and pushed forward, along with Leon and Seth. The boat hopped back from the vortex with a small jerk. Adam allowed himself to smile at their small success.

"*Wait!*" Leon shouted.

Adam and Seth sat bolt upright and anticipated the next command with a growing sense of trepidation. After one complete trip in which they'd skirted the whirlpool's center, they listened intently for Leon's call, as their lives might depend on it.

"*Now!*"

With a sudden jolt, they struggled to paddle forward. Once more, the vessel jerked backwards. This time, Adam looked behind him and saw where the whirlpool ended. A couple of more times, he figured, and Leon would free them.

"*Now!*" Leon shouted once more.

"It's working!" Talan announced jubilantly.

Again, the boat went back even further. The tenacious grip of the titanic whirlpool was growing weaker and weaker, and their strokes became easier. Leon waited half a second longer, which set Adam's teeth on edge.

"*Now!*" he yelled.

This time, when they forced all their effort into their strokes, the small craft jolted backwards and out of the whirlpool. When the boat was facing forward, Adam was pleased to find that no rapids or whirlpool stood in their way. At the moment, it seemed like a fair fight, as the surface of the water was finally still.

Paddling on the calm waters seemed like the only break they would ever catch. Adam looked over his shoulder and saw a trembling Seth out of the corner of his eye. Smoothly, he turned to shift his attention back to the waters in case some other threat had yet to make itself known.

"Seth, you alright?" Leon asked.

"Y—y—y—yes!" he called feebly.

"Tha's good. I think tha's the last o' the traps."

Adam felt a wave of relief wash over him. This was quickly followed by a peculiar sense of foreboding because something seemed amiss. He listened closely to his surroundings. Apart from the noise of the rushing waves, another sound became increasingly distinct. A shiver traveled down his spine as the realization dawned on him.

"Leon, I don't think we're quite finished yet," Adam shouted.

"What do you mean?" Leon asked.

"I think there's a ..." Adam's voice trailed off as he listened more closely.

The sound was impossible to ignore. More water was rushing, but it made a much louder sound. Only one thing Adam could think of was capable of such a noise.

CHAPTER FOURTEEN

"What is it?" Leon demanded.

"A waterfall!"

Leon looked ahead and stared at the treacherous drop. "Well, this is new," he remarked.

Adam looked far ahead and saw the edge where the water seemed to thicken, and he felt any color left in his face drain instantly. Leon's fingers were curled tightly around his paddle.

Seth gasped in surprise.

"What do we do?" Talan asked loudly.

Leon turned his head slightly. "Looks like we're going down."

And with that, Leon paddled even harder. The other two did the same, but they lacked the wild spark of energy and determination that was in Leon's eyes. As they drew nearer to the edge, Adam saw the unmistakable shape of a mountain. At least after the drop, he reassured himself, they would be much closer to it.

Closer and closer they came to the terrifying precipice, but for some odd reason that Adam could not explain, his fears suddenly vanished upon seeing the monstrous waterfall ahead. Unlike Seth, he was ready to make the final descent. Only then, he realized, would he be one step closer to finding Tyrule and Leira.

All of them, save Talan, continued paddling with all the force they could muster until they felt the force of the rushing water pulling them ahead. Adam allowed his muscles a moment's rest. Slowly, the tip of the boat inched closer to the lofty edge. Adam closed his eyes and waited calmly for the inevitable.

The entire world around them slowed to a crawl. The tip of the boat projected into the air, teasing Adam as they began slipping over the edge with a cruel slowness. Once more, in the pit of his stomach, he felt the curious sensation of falling. He felt the boat slice through the cold air. He smelled the mist rolling off of the waterfall, the scent luscious and sooth-ing. The light drops of water splashing his face felt unbelievably refreshing.

Suddenly, he came crashing back to reality when the boat landed far below the precipice with an enormous splash. Adam's eyes flew open just in time to see two huge walls of water fly up on either side of the boat. The frigid water stung as it came crashing down upon them.

After the rush of water abated, Adam sucked in his breath sharply. Not too far off was the base of the mountain, a place where he knew it would be safe to step. He looked to the other side and saw more of the deadly white sand that Seth had mentioned in the story.

"Nearly there!" Leon shouted against the clamor of the waterfall.

Adam joined Leon in the rush to get to the rock slab. The current continually fought them, but the sight of their destination urged them on, enabling them to get past their exhaustion. As they slowly neared the edge of the slab, Leon stood on his feet, clutching a rope. Adam followed the cord with his eyes and saw that it was securely tied around the front of the boat. When at last they were close enough to touch the rock, Leon turned his head.

"I'll get out first. Then you three can help me pull in the boat!" he shouted.

With that, Leon clutched the rope in his hand. With a surprisingly large bound for such a small person, he leapt to dry land. Turning around to face the boat, he stumbled and tripped. Before falling to the ground, he released the rope, and the boat began to drift backwards.

Leon watched with wide eyes as Adam, Seth, and Talan floated farther and farther away. *"Paddle back! Paddle back!"*

Adam and Seth were terrified, yet Talan managed to remain calm. They thrust their paddles into the water and paddled erratically. Leon's absence made the effort extremely difficult, but luckily, they managed to start moving forward before the waterfall swallowed them. Using up the last remaining drops of his precious energy, Adam paddled harder and drew closer. Leon looked frantic as they moved toward the land.

"Throw the rope!"

Adam's heart dropped to his stomach as he leapt to the front and snatched the rope. He hurled it toward Leon, and it landed in the water pitifully. Adam hurried to snatch the rope out of the water.

"Hurry! I—can't—hold—much—longer!" Seth whimpered.

Finding the end of the rope, Adam tossed it once more. It bounced harmlessly off the edge of the rock slab, much to his dismay. Leon looked filled with dread. Adam rushed once more, using deft fingers to find the end of the rope. With a tremendous heave, he used his entire body to fling the rope, and it sailed high into the air. Seth gasped and dropped his paddle, watching helplessly as it floated away. Adam closed his eyes and waited for imminent doom to befall them.

Leon leapt into the air and snatched the rope with his bare hands. Realizing that he had not died yet, Adam opened his eyes and saw Leon standing triumphantly with the rope clutched securely in his fist. With Adam's help, he managed to pull the boat parallel to the rock slab. Adam and Talan jumped out as fast as they could, both of them eager to be free of the churning waves. Together, they held the boat steady so Seth, who shivered uncontrollably, could clamber upon the rocky ground. Once all of them were safely on land, Leon released the rope and fell backwards onto the stone ground. All four watched, breathing heavily as the current carried the metal boat into the gnashing jaws of the carnivorous waterfall.

Panting, Leon remained on the ground, and Adam heaved a heavy sigh of relief. His heart rate gradually returned to normal as he breathed softly. He looked to the sky and saw that the golden sun had begun its descent.

"What do we do now?" he asked after several minutes.

"We need to find a place to rest. It's about to get dark, and we need to get out of here before our friends come back," Leon answered.

Adam helped Seth and Leon up to their feet, and together they looked up at the spectacle of the great mountain. Making sure no one was watching him, Adam turned his head and glanced over his shoulder. Zenia's brother was nowhere to be found. One look at Talan's grim features, however, reminded him that they had yet to see the last of Shadowlords.

CHAPTER FIFTEEN

THE ROGUE'S TALE

The party of four did not get very far by any standards. The sun shrank behind the vast mountains ahead of them, and they trudged along slowly. They were exhausted beyond measure, yet Adam surprisingly possessed the most energy of the three. Leon's jaw sagged as he took step after step along the rugged ground, and Seth had not taken too well to the chilly weather. After his fall in the unruly river, his health seemed to decline. At first, Seth walked slowly and lagged considerably behind the other two as they ascended the large mountain. His predicament went downhill when he developed a loud, hacking cough. Things went from bad to worse when his coughing became interrupted by frequent sneezing.

Adam turned his head and stole a quick glance at Seth. He waddled forward and stared at the ground with puffy red eyes. Mostly, all he would do was sniff, and then every so often, he would launch into a percussive fit of coughing. His small frame shivered uncontrollably in the cold air. Only once did he look up at Adam as if to say please make it end. Talan walked quietly behind Seth, watching carefully for any unwanted surprises. Moved with pity for his friend, Adam hastened his step and drew closer to Leon.

"Leon, we ought to slow down for Seth. He looks awful."

Leon glanced back at Seth for a moment, and then he looked back to Adam. "He'll make it a bit further," he remarked gruffly.

This did not sit well with Adam, but he merely did as Leon insisted and kept walking along the nearly horizontal slope. In the distance, the great shape of the tall mountains loomed. Every once in a while, they passed sparse patches of trees. All of them were fairly tired, and Adam knew that, in their sopping wet misery, they each had a very short fuse. He was unhappy with Leon's decision to keep moving despite Seth's condition.

The rocky ground beneath their feet began to rise into a steep incline. Adam stayed behind with Seth to ensure his safety. Seth did not speak or make any unnecessary movements, as he barely had enough energy for the next step forward. When he began to slow down even more at the incline, Leon sensed the unfortunate lag.

"C'mon. Move faster. The sun's nearly gone," he insisted.

After spotting a nervous glance from Talan, Adam opened his mouth to protest, but closed it, biting back the words meant for Leon. It would do him no good to argue. In any event, he felt that an argument was almost inevitable under the circumstances, yet he wanted to avoid it for as long as he could. His temper simmered slightly, but he ignored it and kept close to Seth and Talan.

The fiery sun had indeed faded from a frenzied neon orange to a soft, luminous pink. Adam wished they had time to sit back and watch the sunset, always such a beautiful feat of nature. He forgot about the present for a moment and considered how tiny he was in the grand scheme of the universe. Frequently, he had wondered how it could be that he was meant to be great if he was so small, so insignificant. The wispy clouds rolled slowly across the crimson sky, as if to prepare the way for twilight.

Suddenly, he was drawn back into reality when Seth began wheezing loudly, and Talan immediately flew to his side. Before taking another step, he glanced at Leon and noticed him hesitate for a fraction of a second. He did not even bother to turn his head. Adam's temper flared hotly, and he stormed ahead of Seth. He placed one arm in front of Leon, and they both came to an abrupt halt.

"Leon, we have to stop," Adam said firmly.

"No, we have to go on," Leon growled.

"No. We stop now." Adam allowed some steel to enter his voice.

Leon stopped and turned to face Adam. Even though they were far apart, an infectious heat seemed to radiate off both of them.

"Adam, stand down."

Adam had no intention of standing down. Instead, he marched up right before Leon. He planted his feet on the ground with conviction and stood nose-to-nose with his adversary. Leon's eyes flickered with surprise, but his eyelids quickly narrowed. Both glared menacingly at the other.

"I will not," Adam said firmly.

"Back away, now," Leon insisted.

"No," Adam said in a low voice.

Leon raised an eyebrow. "You'd best stop acting bold and follow instructions, because I know what I'm doing, and you don't."

"I suggest that you get off your high horse." The words came easily to him.

Seth managed to waddle up to them, out of breath and red-faced. From a safe distance, the rogue watched as the tension unfolded.

"High horse? Who is it that rescued you from those fiends? Me!" Leon spat.

"Right, and the same person insists on dragging his sick brother even further. That same person intends to carry on and pretend he doesn't even notice!"

Seth's red eyes widened in worry. Both Adam and Leon ignored him and stared menacingly into each other's eyes.

"What could you possibly know that I don't? You said it yourself! You've never been past those waters on that beach! How can you sit here and tell me that I'm not doing things right?" Leon demanded.

"It doesn't take a genius," Adam commented.

"Oh, calling me stupid, are you?"

"Bravo. Now, are you going to leave me behind, too? At least let me know in advance," Adam retorted.

A wave of shock flitted across Leon's muscled face for a split second. "How dare you—"

"How dare I what? Speak the truth? Last I checked, I'm still allowed to do that."

Leon looked thoroughly incensed. "Why, you've got nerve!"

"Well spotted."

"Look at you! You're just a boy, a kid! Without me, you'd be left for dead by now!" Leon roared.

His words stung, and Adam knew he drew satisfaction from this fact.

"Please," Seth moaned quietly.

"You listen here! I may be a boy, but I know for a fact I've got more sense than you! You think you can understand what I've gone through?" Adam yelled.

"What makes you think you could even begin to tell me what to do? I've seen more than you could ever imagine!"

"*I've* seen more than *I* could ever imagine. So that makes two of us!"

"We've got only a couple of hours left, at best, and you're throwing the time away!"

"Is that all you really care about? Getting there on time?" Adam snapped.

"Of course not!"

"Then why haven't you stopped yet?"

"You're a fool, Adam Crescent!"

"Oh, stop dodging it! Give it up, Leon! We can afford to wait a bit longer!" Adam shouted.

Leon's fiery glare burned through Adam's vision. "Don't give me any grief about waiting when you have yet to find your own friends! If I was in your shoes, I'd have found them by now!"

The impact of this statement stung Adam with a sickening force. Nothing could have prepared him for such an icy remark.

"Fine! Why don't you go and finish your trip! I'll stay with Seth, your own brother!" Adam bellowed, trying to sting back.

"You wouldn't last a day!"

"How do you know?"

"Adam, you'd better stop before—"

"Enough!" Seth shouted in a raspy voice.

Adam and Leon stood fuming at each other. Simultaneously, they glared at Seth, who looked thoroughly spooked. Even Talan appeared impressed.

Now that Seth had their full attention, he stammered, "S—s—stop this fighting!"

Furious with each other, Adam and Leon remained silent.

Seth broke into a loud coughing fit. "I must rest," he said, wheezing.

Leon slammed his shoulder against Adam's as he stormed by. Adam did not bother to turn around. Defeated, Leon flung his pack to the ground in frustration. He fell to his knees and removed a large tent. Adam turned around and grudgingly offered him help, but Leon refused to accept the gesture from him.

Seth sat as close to the small fire as was humanly possible without getting burned. He was wrapped tightly in several layers of garments. His dripping clothes draped pitifully over a nearby rock. He watched the fire intently as if he expected it to speak. It looked as if, to Seth, the only real thing in the world was the crackling flame.

Leon leaned back against a boulder and watched with narrowed eyes as the flames licked the logs that he had been smart enough to pack. On the other side of Seth, Adam sat silently on the cold ground. Adam and Leon's faces must have contrasted sharply with each other. Leon's eyes still shimmered with anger, but Adam felt only remorse. From the shadows, Talan watched the fire thoughtfully.

Leon had single-handedly pitched the large tent that stood behind them. The fire cast three hazy shadows against the shabby white fabric. Adam turned his head around and watched the tall, motionless shadows. They seemed to tower above their real-life counterparts, and he felt as if the shadows lingered because of the deathly atmosphere. They seemed to be watching in the deafening silence.

The air was so quiet that even the smallest crackle of the fire resounded with the magnitude of the mightiest clap of thunder. Even the wind could be heard, fluttering with an unmistakable ruffling sound. The stars sparkled brightly in the clear sky, and the crescent moon hung gently, as if suspended by an invisible thread. Its light shimmered down upon them, mercifully offering them soft light for their weary eyes.

After another loud crackle, Adam tore his longing gaze away from the twilight heavens. He stared at the pile of flaming logs and saw that they had collapsed under the strain of several hours' burning. Smoke snaked its way from the tips of the flames and formed a puffy black cloud. Seth inhaled some of the serpentine smoke and coughed heavily. His lungs protested the air vigorously, his coughing growing more violent.

Leon stood up and fanned the flames. The fire did not rise any higher, but the smoke lazily drifted off in the opposite direction. Seth's loud hacking gradually ceased. He squinted and sneezed suddenly, sniffing pitifully as he continued watching the dying fire with somber eyes.

Adam felt sorry for him and wished that he could do more, but he felt that to do so would create another barrier between Leon and himself. Adam was quite glad, though, that Leon had risen to dispel the smoke for his brother.

Before long, Seth began to shiver again, which meant that the fire was no longer working as it should. Adam also knew they would need firewood. He realized that he would be the one sent to retrieve it; however, he did not want to volunteer for the task so that Leon might instead ask him and therefore reestablish communications. It was a childish sort of plan.

Seth pulled the numerous sheets around him even tighter. Quickly, Leon moved back inside the tent for a moment. Adam watched as the smoke continued to drift off into the night. Leon reappeared from the tent with a few extra pieces of wood, the last of his scanty supply.

After jogging over to the fire and meticulously placing the logs in a careful arrangement, Leon reluctantly turned to Adam, who knew what was coming, but he waited and acted as if he was completely oblivious.

"Adam."

"Yes, Leon," he said innocently.

"Could you go get some more wood? This little bit should last us two hours or so, but I want to have enough to keep him warm." Leon gestured toward the huddled figure of Seth.

"Anything you say," Adam said kindly.

"Thank you."

"Don't worry about it."

"You need a light?"

CHAPTER FIFTEEN

Adam thought it over for a moment. Deciding that the moonlight and his vision would be adequate, he shook his head in reply.

"Alright then. Well, the trees are scattered, I guess you could say," Leon said.

"Well then, I guess I'm off."

Talan stepped out from his dark sanctuary. "May I come, too?" he spoke for the first time in several hours.

"Of course," Adam replied.

He waited for Talan, then turned promptly and headed away from the warmth of the fire. They had set up camp on a flat area on the otherwise rugged surface of the mountain. After taking a few steps into the darkness, Adam felt the ground beneath him rise and fall in an unpredictable pattern.

As Adam traveled down a hilly incline, he could not help but think about his situation. He thought his response to Leon's request would mend the rift between them, and that it would seem as if their dispute had simply never happened, but it seemed as if he had taken only a tiny step in the right direction. Had he been foolish to think that acquiescing to Leon's wish would grant him a complete pardon? As with any friendship, he realized, significant and visible effort would have to be applied to make things right once more.

"Adam, I need to tell you something," Talan said softly, breaking Adam's train of thought.

"Go ahead. Sorry for cutting you off earlier. I was just nervous," Adam said.

Talan nodded. "That's alright. Now I see why, but I haven't been entirely honest with you."

Even in the dark, Adam could make out the lines of conflict etched within the rogues face. "How so?"

"I am not who you think I am. You may think I'm just a royal guard member gone wrong, but I was broken long before that. I used to be happy, but the prince took everything away from me," he said sadly.

"What happened?" Adam sidestepped to avoid a particularly dangerous-looking hole in the ground. After his experience earlier in the forest, Adam was immensely grateful for the guidance of the silvery moonlight. Having retained his exceptional sensory abilities was helpful as well.

"My father and I lived in Roddington a few years before you were born. He was a carpenter, and a good one at that. Like you, we knew that something was amiss in our lifeless city, so we looked for a means of escape. Together, we tried to set sail for the unknown world, but a storm trapped us, and we were thrown into prison. The prince had us both branded with a death sentence, and I—"

"I know who you are," Adam breathed and fell still.

Talan turned to him and looked him in the eyes. "Who?"

"You're Balian. You're Halbern's son."

The words hung in the air, and neither of them spoke for a while. Far off in the distance, Adam's sharp ears detected the sound of the moving river. Unlike the vicious force of nature he had witnessed earlier, the water seemed to be flowing in one consistent direction. He supposed this could be accounted for because no one was in the water trying to reach a certain destination.

"Yes. I am Balian, and Halbern was my father before he was murdered in cold blood," Talan said finally.

"Why didn't you tell me?"

"I was afraid that you would be afraid or resentful. I know that you befriended my father in those cells. He was good to you, and you were good to him. I couldn't bear the thought of ruining your friendship," Balian admitted.

"I understand, and I'm sorry you felt that way. Tell me how you escaped," Adam pressed.

Balian cleared his throat. "Unlike you or my father, I learned to resent the world outside of the bars. I sought vengeance against all who had wronged me, so I waited silently for the moment to come. One day, for evening meal, a lonely knight came down and gave me dinner. It was mutton. As he turned to leave, I began coughing as loud as I could. Being a boy no older than twelve, no one would question if I was lying or not. The knight unlocked the cell in a hurry to check on me, and I seized the moment. With one pound of my plate against his temple, I knocked him unconscious. Using his keys, I opened the door and dragged him into another cell with a raging murderer. My tracks, it appeared, were covered.

"I knew I wouldn't last long, but I remembered hearing the knights talking about an execution log of sorts, so I found it and marked myself dead. Of course, if I was dead, then so was my name. I looked back at the records from many years past, and I spotted the name I would assume. Talan. It was clean, and no one would ever connect it to a young boy named Balian. The prince really should consider recording names for the future, because I returned to the castle the following week and asked to serve as a page. King Philip allowed it, and I quickly went from a carpenter's son to a skilled warrior in several years. Long after my knighthood, which was founded on lies as well, I learned the deadly arts and went on secret missions for Prince Nicolas to gain his trust. For a while, I had blood on my hands.

"As I continued earning favor, I searched the prisons for my father to no avail. And then, out of nowhere, you show up and make a farce of the knights with your power. I watched as Prince Nicolas dealt you that blow to the head, and I heard what he said, which was, 'Take him down to the cell next to Halbern. Let's see if we can break him before he goes to die.'"

Adam stared at Balian in horror. "He said that?"

"Word for word. I found my chance, though. I followed the other knights and helped carry you to your cell. I never said anything to my father, but I could sense his presence somehow. For most of your stay, I dwelled in the shadows, listening to the two of you speak to one another. I envied you, Adam, and I wanted your place in the cell. In the beginning, it was my plan to save him, but then I heard Nicolas make his sick ultimatum. If he was willing to die for you, then you must have meant a lot to him, so I changed my plans to accommodate you.

"It was I who fired the arrow into the glass tank that day at the execution. My father was an honorable man who deserved an honorable death. Yet try as I might, a stray arrow ended his life, and I could not mourn. You see, Adam, I also made a vow that day. I vowed to help you do what was right to stop the prince."

Adam peered downward into a small cluster of trees. The moonlight illuminated their thin shapes and cast skeletal shadows of the trees against the weathered rock of the mountainside. He was amazed at how the trees could grow in such a peculiar pattern on the mountain. "I didn't know any of this. You have done so much, and you've come so far."

"That means a lot, really, but I don't deserve it. I had to plot and kill my way to safety. I even erased myself for many years. You, though, you're another story. You have not murdered anyone. I don't think you would do it the same way. Maybe in self-defense, but not like I did. You really are the hero our world needs. I've traveled alongside you over the past few weeks. You didn't have to save me, but you did. You didn't have to rescue Tyrule and Leira, but now they're somewhere safe on this mountain because of you. You may not realize it now, but you're becoming a real hero. To me, you're incorruptible, and I wish I could have the courage to do what you've done," Balian said.

Together, they continued the descent because Adam was also in a hurry to help Seth and to please Leon. In his haste, he nearly tripped over a protruding rock. Thankful that he did not take an unwanted tumble, he slowed his step to avoid the slightest possibility of injury.

"As you can see, my reflexes need work," Adam mused.

"That can be fixed in time."

At last, when Adam stood before the trees, he noticed that they were dead, and he recalled that dead wood made terrific firewood. Without a moment's delay, he seized one of the branches and began snapping the pieces limb from limb, and he tossed each fragment to the ground. In no time at all, he had created a large pile of firewood. Balian made the process much easier with his considerable strength.

When at last the trees stood completely bare, Adam and Balian smiled with satisfaction. Adam removed his pack from his shoulder and knelt on the ground. One by one, he shoved piece after piece in the bag until it could fit no more. When Leon had pitched the tent earlier that day, Adam had wisely placed all of his things in a corner to dry, so the pack had enough space to fit the firewood.

When he had finished stuffing a couple of more handfuls of twigs in his pack, he slung it over his shoulder. Balian carried as much wood in his bare hands as he could manage. After they stood up, a soft noise caught Adam unaware.

He became absolutely still and held his breath to listen. He could barely discern the sound of indistinct muttering. Very slowly, Adam stood up and peered in the direction of the noise. He stood on a ridge, but far off in the distance was an unmistakable shimmer of light.

Were there others out here? Adam wondered as he continued to stare at the light. *Who would be out here at this time of night? Why would they come?* He paused for a moment and considered his options. He realized that the people nearby could either be allies or adversaries; however, he knew that no one in this part of Fallador had ever laid eyes on him before. Understanding that he had anonymity on his side, he made up his mind to follow the light. The voices became quiet, yet Adam and Balian crept forward silently. He was quite surprised at how capable he was of stealth.

He was utterly mesmerized by the light. As he drew closer, it seemed as if all had fallen still except for the wavering glow and himself. After taking a couple of cautious steps, Adam saw the light waver. *Fire*, he thought.

Suddenly, he spotted a lone silhouette pass before the flames. He moved slightly faster now. Both of them regarded the other in surprise for a moment, but excitement quickly flooded into Adam's mind. The prospect of other people was too exciting for him to bear. After all, the whispers sounded friendly. He did not care what these people looked like. The novelty of finding someone in this new place was an adventure in itself.

From the passing shadow, he was unable to determine the strangers' identity. Adam wished the figure that had passed before the fire would speak. For some odd reason, he felt that if he could hear speech, he could develop a better mental image of the people. Despite this wish, no one spoke. Only the occasional snap of the large fire could be heard in the still air.

Curiosity got the better of him. He was already so close! He silently inched forward and stared directly at the dancing bonfire. Compared to this one, the fire at Adam's camp was a meager display of cloudy smoke and smoldering ash. Balian stayed back in case there were more people behind them.

Adam stopped before walking into the bright light. Safely enveloped by the shadows, he surveyed the scene for a moment to make sure that no one would unexpectedly jump out and catch him off-guard. He willed his feet forward and heard the sound of a twig splitting beneath his shoes. The snap was only a fraction of a second, but the sound sliced through the silence of the night.

With a small gasp, Adam's heart leapt to his throat. He waited, deathly still, for several moments. When no one rushed out to find him, he poked his head out from the shadows and quickly took a peek at the illuminated area. All that he could see was the fire. Quietly, he stood up to his full height and turned to leave. He only managed to take a small step away before a sound reached his ears.

"Adam?" a familiar voice whispered.

Adam inhaled sharply, stopping dead in his tracks. He knew that voice all too well.

CHAPTER SIXTEEN

A NIGHT WITHOUT SHADOWS

Adam turned and saw the silhouette standing firmly against the firelight. The figure was tall and well-muscled, and Adam did not know what to expect. He remained rooted to the spot and could not find the words to speak.

"Adam, is that you?" the voice repeated, even louder.

He knew that voice! Adam took an energetic step forward and let the firelight fall upon his features. He felt his mouth open in amazement as he ran closer to the shadowed figure.

"Tyrule! It's me!"

The unmistakable figure of Tyrule eagerly rushed forward. They embraced one other, and Tyrule clapped Adam on the back rather hard. Their excitement was enough to overpower any previous discomfort they had felt. When they stepped away from each other, Adam easily recognized his friend's familiar features. He looked exactly the same as before, except that his normally neat hair was quite a mess.

"Oh, Adam! It's wonderful to see you!" Tyrule nearly shouted.

"It's great to see you, too!"

Adam forgot about his quarrel with Leon at once and let the happiness of the moment wash over him. Tyrule stepped back quickly and tilted his head.

"Leira! Come quick! There's someone you might want to see!" he shouted jubilantly.

Adam's heart nearly skipped a beat when he thought about Leira, especially after what had happened to her during the voyage.

"Coming!" Adam heard her reply from far away.

Tyrule turned back to Adam with a wide smile.

"Is she all right? You know, after the—"Adam's voice trailed off.

"After the storm? It was just a bump on the head. That's all."

Adam heard the sound of light footsteps draw near. At last, Leira emerged from the shadows and took her place next to Tyrule. She brushed away a clump of wild hair and opened her mouth to speak.

"Water supply is nearly gone, but—*Great Scott!* Adam?" Leira gasped when she saw him.

Adam nodded, and she became so excited that she could hardly speak.

"Oh, Adam! We were so worried! We thought terrible things, and the forest, and—" she said in a squeaky voice.

"Take it easy. There's plenty of time to explain things. Look who came with me. Ba—er—Talan, would you mind stepping out? We're among friends," Adam said.

Balian moved out from the shadows and silently joined the gathering, shaking hands with Tyrule and accepting a hug from Leira. Relieved, she looked to Tyrule and smiled brightly. He returned the look with a smile of his own. Adam saw his hand clasp hers.

"You can't be serious," he moaned.

Tyrule and Leira nodded eagerly.

"Completely!" Leira said proudly.

"Well done," Adam said, and he clapped his hands quietly.

Leira beamed at him, and Tyrule nodded with a wide grin. They both looked at one another and smiled dreamily. It was absolutely fantastic to see them in good spirits after the storm, but Adam realized that their behavior would take a while to get used to. Tyrule watched Adam standing awkwardly by himself. Both Adam and Balian shuffled their feet as Tyrule and Leira guffawed at each other. Finally, Adam cleared his throat loudly.

"Come, Adam. It's a bit chilly. Let's gather around the fire and share our stories," Tyrule said.

"Brilliant idea," he remarked in reply.

Tyrule held onto Leira's hand as they walked closer to the blazing fire. Adam followed behind them and ignored their romantic gestures. They sat together next to the warm fire. Adam took a seat next to Leira, though he was not as close to her as Tyrule was. She leaned her head against Tyrule's shoulder and sat with her legs crisscrossed. Adam could tell from the shadow of a smile that lingered on his face that Tyrule enjoyed her display of dependence. Adam, too, sat with his legs loosely crisscrossed and tried to focus on the fire. As usual, Balian distanced himself from the others and sat opposite of Adam.

Noticing this, Adam called to him, "Come join me, friend."

The semblance of a grin appeared on Balian's face as he stood up. Once he was seated next to Adam, the discussions began.

"So, tell me what happened," Adam prompted.

Leira sat upright and faced him with an answer formed on her lips. "Well, after the storm, Tyrule rescued me and we managed to float on a piece of driftwood all the way to a beach. Of course, we had no clue where we were, so we walked around trying to gain some sense of direction. Not knowing what happened to you, we had a decision to make: wait around for you to show up, or try and find the tower. Knowing you, I figured you'd try and get to the tower. That was a good idea, by the way." Leira nodded toward him.

Adam felt himself turning slightly pink upon receiving this compliment. "Thanks."

"You're welcome. Now, after walking through all that sand, we came across a little man running about. We asked him if he lived here, and he said yes. I decided not to reveal our names just in case he was secretly dangerous. You know, like that old bloke who stands at the street corner near my house? Anyway, Tyrule asked for directions past the mountains and to the tower. This man pointed to the beginning of the forest—he called it the Forest of Belliteth—and told us that we needed to cross a river and scale the mountain. We thanked him and went on our way.

"I must tell you, the forest was quite scary. Oh, Adam, it was so dark! It reminded me of nightmares I had when I was little. While we were in there, *they* found us."

"They called themselves the Shadowlords," Tyrule said grimly.

"How did they find you?" Adam asked quietly.

Leira hesitated for a moment. "It wasn't pretty. We'd already been in the forest for several days, but one morning we heard that horrible laugh. Her laugh."

"Zenia," Balian growled.

Tyrule nodded.

"Yes, Talan, it was Zenia. We tried to run away, but they were just too fast. They grabbed Tyrule and me and held us hostage. Of course they made one mistake because they thought you were Tyrule. I hate to say this, but you're in trouble. They're after you," Leira warned.

Adam nodded. "I know. Did you catch any other names?"

She shook her head no. "Only Zenia. She pointed and said, 'you' when she wanted someone's attention. I could tell, though, that one of her followers had to be her brother, seeing as he was overly protective."

"Doesn't matter now. Zenia's dead. I killed her," Balian said.

"That was you? From what I saw, it looked like Adam threw her into the river. I really thought you beat her once and for all, Adam," Tyrule said.

Glancing at Tyrule with a dark expression, Adam said, "I won't kill unless I'm forced to."

"That sounds like the case with this episode," Tyrule remarked.

"Well, both of you should be worried about her brother," Leira whispered. "He's not going to forget your little scuffle at the bridge easily. I'd watch my back if I were you."

Balian and Adam looked at one another quickly. "Tell us more about the forest before they showed up," Adam said.

"Oh, I wouldn't have made it anywhere if it wasn't for Tyrule."

Tyrule beamed softly at her. Adam was genuinely surprised that his friend was capable of such a soft expression.

"I think you could have. Would you like me to tell some of the story? I know you hated that place," he said.

Leira nodded and leaned her head back on his shoulder.

"Well, she's right. The forest was a creepy place. There was hardly any light at all. We could only tell it was nighttime when it became totally dark. Sleeping on the forest floor was hard and uncomfortable. I didn't sleep much, but I kept watch so that Leira could sleep safely, if she actually managed to sleep at all.

"On the second day, we woke up early and waited for the light to come back. There was not much at all, but we had no choice. This next part is a bit embarrassing, so try not to judge me, Adam."

Adam chortled softly. "I promise."

"Right. Well, I managed to get us lost. Hey! I can see you smiling! Anyway, I suppose I took a wrong turn. That midget told us that we should see a river on the second day. Well, a lot of time passed, and I hadn't even heard a drop of water. We both got scared when the sun went down that night. I'll admit that I thought we were not going to make it. So, I told Leira the truth about how I felt about her, which was much easier than I expected. After that, she told me something quite similar. What was it you said?"

Leira smiled wryly. She sat upright once more and looked at Tyrule. "I said that I'd been feeling the exact same way about you, and that I'd felt that way for a long time. You knew that, though. You just wanted to hear me say it again, didn't you?"

Tyrule grinned at her. Adam felt slightly uncomfortable now that they were together. Balian rolled his eyes at the childish romance before him. Before Leira could make another flirty remark, Adam cleared his throat rather loudly. The noise produced the desired effect, as they both looked at him with vacant expressions.

"You were saying?" Adam said.

"Er—right. Anyway, we decided to keep going through the forest together. After all, it had to end sooner or later. Well, the next day we were really thirsty, so we couldn't go very fast. Luckily, we stumbled upon a spring. The water was nice and cold, and it was exactly what we needed. You know the feeling?" Tyrule said.

Adam nodded in reply.

"Yes, it was really refreshing. Honestly, that's the only encounter we had with water. We only heard moving water was when we came here. At the spring, we drank until we couldn't hold down anymore. We kept walking in a straight line. And you know, the Shadowlords got us. What you may not have known is that they dragged us along to the river and tied us up. The whole point was for you to see us on the bridge and come springing into action."

"Wow. That's quite a story, but Talan," the name sat uncomfortably on his tongue. "Talan and I are smarter than that."

"You still managed to spring the trap," Tyrule said, shrugging.

Adam opened his mouth to protest.

"So, where have you been?" Leira asked quickly, cutting him off.

Adam had waited patiently for the chance to tell his story. He and Balian wasted no time at all in relaying what had occurred over the last couple of days.

He began his account with the incident on the boat and described how the boat had split in two after colliding with the rock. He described the Razorwolf transformation and his silvery-gray and white appearance. Leira and Tyrule appeared to find his description fascinating.

Adam told them about the narrow escape and waking up on the same beach they had and how he rescued Balian on the beach. He explained to them the details of his trek with Seth and Leon. He spent a moment talking about the magical Krevvler door, which made Leira gasp in amazement.

The night at the twins' house was very comfortable, he told them. Out of respect to Balian, he omitted any reference to his friend's real identity. The trek through the forest, he realized, was just as dismal as Tyrule and Leira had found it earlier. Adam spoke only briefly about the forest because he really wanted to tell them about the River of Thanatos.

He quickly learned he was a good storyteller when he began to describe the fierce battle against the Shadowlords. Adam vastly enjoyed the account where the bridge went up in flames, and they plunged off the crumbling structure and into the water. He found himself making all sorts of exaggerated hand gestures as he described the wild, angry river. Watching Tyrule and Leira's reactions, he spoke even louder as he told them about the rapids, the whirlpool, and especially the great waterfall.

Adam described how he and Seth had almost got sucked back into the waterfall. He admitted that he and his new friends did not get far, but he acknowledged that they were safe. He chose to leave out his fiery argument with Leon. Adam explained how Seth had a cold and that he had just been sent to retrieve firewood.

"So, I heard a noise and saw the fire. Talan and I came over here to get a quick peek, but I never expected to find you two."

Leira and Tyrule stared at him with wide eyes. Adam was secretly satisfied with this reaction, but he tried not to show it.

"Wow. And you say the river was magical?" Leira said breathlessly.

"Yes. Cursed."

Leira stared at him in awe.

"So, where are you two going to sleep?" Adam asked, changing the subject.

"Well, we don't really have anything," Tyrule said.

"It's cold, though!" Adam remarked.

Tyrule shrugged. "Well, we've got a fire, don't we?"

"Yes, but what if something bad happens? What if they come back? Especially after what Leira said about Zenia's brother. Why wait until the morning when you can come with us now?" Adam asked.

"We won't let anything happen."

"That's foolish," Balian said.

This did not sit well with Adam at all. He fidgeted uncomfortably. He originally had intended to remain there for the entire night, but the image of poor Seth lingered feebly in his mind.

"Come with me to our camp," Adam finally said.

"Right now? Isn't it too late?" Leira asked.

"No. If I can get down to get firewood, I'm sure I can get back up. Besides, you're going to try to sleep on a mountain. Don't you think that will be a little uncomfortable?"

Leira thought it over, but Tyrule was not completely ready to commit to the idea. "Won't you be sleeping on the same mountain?"

"Of course, but we've got mats and blankets."

Tyrule turned to Leira. "Do you want to go?" he asked softly.

She nodded slowly.

"All right, Adam. We'll follow you back," Tyrule said.

Adam scrambled up to his feet and waited patiently for his friends. Tyrule rose slowly and helped Leira to her feet. Adam felt bad about leaving the fire ablaze, but was consoled when he realized that nothing flammable was in sight.

"Ready?"

"Ready," Leira and Tyrule replied simultaneously.

Adam and Balian then turned and walked out of the firelight and into the soft moonlight. The other two followed closely, with Adam growing steadily uncomfortable while listening to their intimate conversations. He reminded himself that his senses were probably sharper than theirs, so he said nothing and kept walking.

The fire disappeared behind them, and Adam knew that they were getting closer to the camp. Adam retraced his steps to the tree where he had found the firewood. He asked Tyrule to grab some, and Tyrule kindly obliged by grabbing a handful.

Adam turned and saw the faint outline of the summit against the night sky. They soon reached the natural incline of the mountain. He was thankful that they were able to keep climbing, unlike Seth who had barely managed to endure the ascent.

Several times, though, Adam and Balian had to stop and let both of them catch their breath. He could tell that his friends were very tired after their difficult excursion in the forest. Adam considered himself very lucky to be in the knowledgeable company of Balian, Seth, and Leon. He realized that if he had not, he would have been in the same position as his friends, or worse, dead.

"Adam, are you sure this is the right way?" Leira asked.

"I found you two, didn't I?" Adam retorted indignantly.

That was the only real exchange of words they shared on the way up. Adam felt that there was nothing more to be said, and the other two seemed too exhausted for further speech.

The incline rose a bit more, and Leira and Tyrule's pace slowed considerably. Adam waited patiently, but all he really wanted to do was get back up to the camp and sleep so that he could be on his way to the tower the following morning.

"A little faster," Balian whispered to Adam.

"What you see is what you get," he motioned to the other two.

When a tiny sparkle of flames became visible from afar, Adam knew that they were nearly there. Leira and Tyrule must have seen it as well, for they tried to speed up. They took long, heavy steps while Adam took light, quick ones. Adam nearly jumped out of his skin when he heard a small cry escape from Leira's lips.

He whirled around to check what was wrong. Wide-eyed, Leira sat on the rocky ground. One of her legs was caught in the small crevice that he had nearly stepped in only moments ago. Before he could move to assist her, Tyrule flew to her side and gently eased her foot out of the crevice. She smiled gratefully at her rescuer. Adam merely shrugged and turned to keep walking. For a moment, he felt a twinge of annoyance.

At last, the incline began to level out, and Adam could see Seth's small figure, still attracted to the dying fire like child to his toy. The hill evened out into a flat surface, and Adam heaved a sigh of relief when he found himself nearly at the camp. He looked over near the fire and watched as

Leon walked toward him from behind Seth. He stopped before Adam and looked him in the face.

"Did you get the wood?"

"Enough to last for days." Adam removed his misshapen pack to show him.

"Great! Adam, I need you to listen. Back there, you know, earlier today? Well, I didn't mean any of the things I said. We were all tired from the river escape." His voice trailed off, but Adam understood completely.

"Of course, Leon. We've been together for weeks now. We were bound to lose our heads eventually," Adam said with a small grin.

"Yes, that's what it was. I hope all will still be the same."

"Why wouldn't it be?" Adam asked kindly.

Leon gave Adam a look of gratitude. Their reconciliation was short-lived, for at that very moment, Leira and Tyrule clambered up behind Adam. Leon looked at them with wide eyes.

"Who are—"

"Leon, these are my friends. You met them before. This is Tyrule, and this is Leira," Adam said cordially.

Leira extended her hand. "How do you do?"

Leon scrutinized her for a second before grasping her hand. "Oh yes. I remember these two."

Tyrule offered his hand, and Leon accepted.

"Oh, and this is Leon, and over there is his twin brother, Seth," Adam said. He pointed to Seth, who sat by the fire, watching them with sad eyes.

Leon looked to Adam. "So, now that you've found your friends, do we go to the tower?" Adam nodded emphatically in reply.

"Well then, that's not far off. We'll probably get there by sunset tomorrow!"

Adam, Leira, and Tyrule all looked at each other in excitement. Finally, the end of their tedious journey was within reach!

"Excellent! Well, Tyrule and Leira, there are a couple of mats in the tent. Feel free." Adam gestured toward the large tent.

They looked at Adam gratefully before wandering over to the tent and disappearing inside. Once more, Adam looked at Leon. "I'll get the firewood. Go inside and rest. I'll sleep out here with Seth."

Leon nodded thankfully and followed the others toward the tent, but he paused before entering. He turned to Adam with a curious expression on his face.

"You know something, Adam? You're unlike anyone I've ever met before. You'd be a fine addition to the Pentacular Reximen."

"Thanks, Leon. It means a lot." Adam was grateful for the dim light that successfully hid his face, which he was sure was turning pink.

"Where's Talan?" he asked, looking around the camp.

Adam had his suspicions. "I think I know. Don't worry, I'll find him."

With a final wave, Leon turned and entered the tent. Adam walked over to the fire and removed a few logs from his bag. He tossed a couple on top of the fire and watched the tips of the flames extend into the air, and spotted Seth sitting hunched over in front of the fire. Seth must have enjoyed the heat, for he lay down and closed his eyes, cushioned by all of the layers of fabric surrounding him.

Peering beyond the fire, Adam spotted the silhouette of a figure watching the moon. Quietly, he moved into the darkness and sat next to Balian. The rogue regarded him with a solemn glance, then he returned his watchful eye to the moon.

"What's the matter?" Adam asked kindly.

Balian sighed. "I hope I'm doing the right thing."

"Of course you are. Why would you doubt it?"

"It's just that I can feel certain barriers melting away. You've probably noticed. I'm pretty standoffish. I'm just not too sure about all this," he said.

"That's because you're with friends."

Balian looked at him sadly. "A luxury I've never had."

Adam nodded. "You know, it's kind of funny how we've gone along these past few weeks. When I first met you, in the forest, we argued over stupid stuff. But look at us now. You've shared your past with me. And I will keep it safe, I promise. Here's what I think. I think you're trying too hard to be Talan, if you know what I mean. Balian's a great person, and more people could benefit from an honest person like you. Don't feel bad about the past anymore. You did what you had to do so you could save Halbern. You never had evil motives. That's what makes us different from the prince. That's the difference between a hero and a villain."

"I never thought of it that way," Balian said.

"Well, neither have I, but enjoy this night. I'm going to watch the fire with Seth, and you can do as you please. Good night, Balian."

"Good night, Adam."

Leaving Balian to his observations, Adam returned to the fire and sat with his arms around bent knees. He watched the flames dance in the night. In a day's time, he hoped he would be in a place where he could find some answers, which greatly reassured him. He continued staring at the blaze as the cool breeze fluttered by. Closing his eyes, Adam listened to the symphony of the world around him.

THE REALM OF DREAMS

That night seemed to last for what Adam felt like was an entire year. While all of the others slept comfortably, he stayed awake and tended to the fire, making sure that it was nice and hot for Seth and that it did not burn out of control, causing unwanted damage.

Adam did not complain at all about the night watch, for it was an excellent chance for him to clear his mind and really think for the first time in a while. He felt a mixture of both excitement and apprehension when he thought about the prospect of reaching Reximen Heights. Weeks ago, he would have thought such a quest was impossible. Now, it seemed completely realistic, even easy. After all he had experienced, Adam Crescent was a new person. The fact that they would arrive by the end of the day was absolutely astonishing to him. The only worry he had was that he would be an outsider among outsiders.

CHAPTER SEVENTEEN

After a while, the shimmering moon was no longer visible. Adam gazed at the summit. Golden rays of light were already starting to ripple along the side of the titanic mountain. Above the mountaintop, the sun rose, a marvelous ball of fiery intensity casting down its light upon the land.

As the last day of the journey dawned, he stood up and stretched. He yawned quietly and walked over to the tent. He did not enter, but he grabbed a handful of fabric and shook it gently, causing the tent to shake.

"Wake up, you lot."

A few grumbles and sighs from inside the tent told Adam that they had clearly understood the message. He turned and made his way over to Seth, who lay sleeping soundly next to the smoldering fire. He bent down and shook him gently.

"Seth, we need to get ready to go," he said quietly.

Seth's eyes slowly opened and he stared blankly at what was left of the fire. He let out a gaping yawn and rolled over on his back to face Adam.

"Morning," he groaned.

"Feeling better?"

"Loads."

"That's good. We'll need to get going soon if we are to make it before nightfall."

"Okay."

Seth rolled out of his cocoon of blankets and onto his stomach. He slowly clambered to his feet and stood up. He, too, stretched and remained standing in place. He appeared oddly thin without being shrouded in fabric. Adam turned to check on the others.

"Hey, Adam?"

"Yes?"

Seth walked over to him. "Thank you for trying to help me yesterday. I know that Leon can be a bit tough sometimes, but he's just trying to get us there as fast as he can. He means well."

Adam smiled back at Seth. "I know he does. Everything's fine. So can you travel today? I mean, are you feeling up to it?"

"I've got some minor sniffles, maybe a cough every now and then, but I think I'll be fine. We just need to rest in a proper place."

"Brilliant. Talan!" he called.

There came a rustling noise from behind him, and Adam turned just in time to spot Balian emerge from the tent. They exchanged a knowing glance before Leira tumbled out from the fabric. Her blonde hair was awry, and her eyes were rather droopy from lack of proper sleep. Tyrule followed her out and looked equally tired. His hair hung in his eyes, and he yawned widely as he walked out. Behind him was Leon, who appeared unnaturally sprightly in comparison to the other two. The party of six stood in an irregular circle. Leon stepped forward to say something.

"Right, just over the summit is the town of Setulptus, home of Reximen Heights. It's a day's walk with our numbers, but I imagine we'll get there all the same."

All of them nodded in reply.

"Well then. Gather your things. I'll take down the tent. We'll be ready in a few minutes," Leon said.

Leira, Tyrule, Seth, and Balian went inside quickly to gather their belongings. Adam, however, stayed outside with Leon.

"Leon," he said, walking over to him.   "Can I help you with the tent?"

"Adam, it's alright. You don't have to prove anything to me."

"I know, but I want to help out."

"Then by all means, let's take it down."

Together, they worked quickly to dismantle the large tent. At one point, the fabric fell over Leon, and Adam had a difficult time trying not to laugh. When the tent was safely stowed away, Adam looked and saw that

Leira had done him the kindness of packing his things for him. She walked over to Adam and handed him the bag. Accepting the thoughtful gesture, he smiled gratefully.

Everyone but Tyrule and Leira threw their packs over their shoulders and gazed up at the lofty summit. At last, they were ready to get moving. Leon wasted no time and started for the summit, followed closely by Balian. Adam and Seth followed directly from behind, and Tyrule and Leira walked at the rear.

Their trip along the mountain was quite arduous, but that was expected. It was not an easy business by any means. Several times, Leon stopped to allow Leira and Tyrule to catch up. Seth was holding up remarkably well; given the poor state he was in the previous day, he seemed to have recovered miraculously. Adam was slightly tired after the sleepless night, but his excitement far outweighed any feelings of fatigue. Had he been traveling alone, he might have nearly bolted up the slope. The only two who had a decent night's sleep were Leon and Balian, who looked brighter than usual.

The looming, titanic mountain obscured the lands beyond it. In the bright sunlight, the mountaintop had a cloudy hue. Adam had expected it to be topped with snow like the ones he saw in pictures. He could only wonder what the world beyond this great mountain looked like and felt as though he were about to open an immense gift; this idea amused him as he continued forward.

The way up twisted this way and that, and they often found themselves sidling along the mountainside when the path became too steep, yet no one complained about the trek. Adam found mountain climbing to be much more enjoyable than trekking through an ominous forest or paddling up a vicious river. Compared to the previous challenges, the journey up the mountain was a nice stroll in the park.

At one point, the incline was so sharp that all of the travelers had to scale the rocky wall to reach the next level surface. Leon allowed the others to pass before him. Adam and Balian were strong enough to hoist themselves up on the wall, but Leon formed a step with his hands to offer Leira, Seth, and an embarrassed Tyrule a boost. Once the others were fairly high up, Leon jumped and grabbed a protruding rock and began the long climb.

All of them climbed at a rather slow pace. Adam was very surprised when he noticed that he was high above the others. The heights did not scare him, and he recalled his rooftop adventures and realized how small they were in comparison. As he climbed, he engaged in light discussion with Balian. Tyrule, who gradually began climbing faster, grabbed rock after rock not far below them. Leira and Seth were quite a bit lower and climbed at the same level and pace. Leon was at the bottom, but he remained there to act as a safeguard.

Higher and higher they climbed. Adam turned his head around to get a glimpse of the ground below them. He gasped when he saw the rest of the mountain below. He saw the River of Thanatos, which extended as far as the eye could see. The grim Forest of Belliteth stood out like a sore thumb. Suddenly, his hand slipped from a crag, and he quickly turned around and focused on the mountain, taking extra care not to fall.

At last, he reached up to grab the top of the next ledge. With a small groan, he placed both hands on the surface and pulled himself up on the ledge so that his eyes cleared the top. When he had drawn himself up high enough, Adam saw that the mountain went no higher. He had reached the summit! He dragged himself up completely on the ledge. After lying facedown for a moment to make sure he would not fall, he cautiously rose to his feet.

Adam stood at the very tip of the mountain. He saw another great mountain just ahead. He looked to the clear, blue sky and marveled at how vast the world really was. A look on either side revealed much happier-looking forests and open expanses. Adam looked at the tip of the other mountain and followed with his eyes its magnificent ridge, all the way down to the ground. He was pleasantly surprised at what he saw.

The midday sun cast a brilliant light upon the other side of the mountain. Embedded within the rocky surface stood an enormous fortress, a colossus like no other. The black and gray walls rose and formed daunting towers that contrasted sharply against the azure sky. Unlike the castle in Roddington, this structure appeared to be ancient, which gave it an aura of enchantment. Adam's heart leapt at the sight of the bold Reximen Heights. A closer look at the land surrounding the tower revealed a large town. Many buildings were scattered across the valley; Adam felt as though he was looking at a child's collection of toy houses. From such a great distance, Adam could not distinguish much else about the town. He did notice, however, that the houses and shops were spaced out in amusing arrangements. Several clusters of buildings were gathered in circles, unlike Roddington, where the houses were arranged in neat rows.

Adam heard Balian grunt from behind him. He whirled around and watched as his friend clawed his way onto the face of the summit. Adam backed up and took a quick look at the ground upon which he stood. The summit floor extended to fit several normal-sized people. This observation made him a little more comfortable about moving on the top of the high mountain.

One by one, the others came up, too. After Tyrule came Leira, then Seth, and finally Leon. All five of them walked up and stood next to Adam as he gazed down at the city.

"It's amazing, isn't it?" Tyrule said breathlessly.

Adam kept his eyes glued to the landscape and merely nodded in reply. The view of the land beyond them was simply breathtaking. Fortunately, though, they were on a mission, and it was nearly complete.

"It's amazing, indeed, but we must finish what we started," Leon said.

"Is the descent harder than that last climb?" Leira asked.

Leon did not answer. Instead, he merely pointed forward. Adam noticed that his large finger was pointed to a small notch at the very edge of the summit. He cautiously walked over to the edge and stole a downward glance.

At first, the view from such dizzying heights was overwhelming. Adam quickly took a small step back and looked back down at the rocky summit floor. He was surprised to see that the single notch that Leon pointed to led to an indentation. After that one was another and another, as far as the eye could see—steps, as luck would have it.

With his eyes, Adam traced the steps carved into the mountain all the way down into the town. The trip down the mountain would be much faster than the climb up.

"Whoa! You have to see this!" Adam shouted at Tyrule and Leira.

They walked cautiously over to Adam and looked down. He watched with amusement when their eyes widened in shock.

"Will this take us all the way down to that town?" Tyrule asked.

"Yes. It's an extremely fast and convenient way," Seth piped up.

Balian allowed himself a laugh. "It's about time we found *something* on this trip that's easy."

Adam turned and smiled brightly. "Well then, what are we waiting for? Let's go!"

With quick and nimble footing, Adam began to hurry down the stone steps. He could hear the others trying to catch up, but his excitement knew no bounds. His feet began to match the rapid beating of his heart. He did not bother looking back, and he could practically feel himself gliding down the lofty slope. The summit of the mountain was quite far behind him, yet a great distance remained before he reached the town.

Adam ran down the steps with a vibrant gusto. The wind blew his hair back and he laughed in exhilaration. For so long had he longed to find this place, this fortress of legends. Now, it stood only moments away, and no one would stop him from getting there. Even the thought of Zenia and her cronies disappeared from his mind as the steps brought him closer to the town.

"Wait!" someone called from behind him.

Adam did not process the command, nor did he have any interest in finding out who had issued it. He was still running as fast as he could down the steps.

Suddenly, Adam stumbled and managed to catch himself quickly. He came to an abrupt halt and looked down from where he was. Although he was considerably lower than when he'd stood on the summit, the prospect of falling over the edge was still highly unappealing.

Even so, Adam allowed himself to walk briskly. The tower began to look even taller, and the buildings began to come into sharper focus. Adam could even make out the tiny moving dots that he assumed were people. As he continued to get closer, he was satisfied to see that his assumption was correct.

Several minutes later, he noticed that the steps had begun to become shallower, until they all but disappeared into an almost horizontal slope. Adam's heart hammered even faster when he saw that the end was in sight. Throwing caution to the wind, he sprinted down this last stretch.

When at last the gray steps met faded red cobblestones, Adam stopped running. Finally, he stood in the town that not long ago had seemed unreal to him. Weeks ago, he would have questioned its very existence. He had survived the quest! He had made it to the town of Setulptus, the dwelling place of the Pentacular Reximen!

Adam smiled delightedly, and he turned and saw the others hurrying down the steps as fast as they could. He remained standing at the end of the steps, but he turned his attention back to the town.

The buildings, he noticed, were grander and far more illustrious than the ones in Roddington. Each house and shop resembled the sort of old-fashioned buildings that one might expect to find in a fairy tale. The ground upon which he stood was of cobblestones. Rising high above the roofs of several buildings stood the majestic tower. Adam's fascination with the scene was cut short when another person walked by.

A girl passed him, and he turned to look at her. She had jet-black hair streaked with scarlet highlights. She wore loose-fitting brown clothes that flapped about her ankles and black closed-toe shoes.

"Excuse me!" Adam called out to her.

She did not notice this and merely kept going on.

"You there!"

The girl stopped and turned to him. Adam nodded once he realized she was looking straight at him. A few stray stands of hair fell over her pale face. A pair of scarlet eyes gazed into Adam's blue ones. He stood enchanted by the ruby eyes as she drew closer to him.

"Yes?" she said.

For a moment, Adam forgot how to speak intelligibly. "Doyoulivehere?" he blurted.

"What? I couldn't understand you," she replied.

"Oh," he laughed nervously. "Do you live here?"

"Yes, why?"

"Oh, I'm not from around here. Do you know how I might . . ."

Adam quickly realized that the girl was extremely pretty. For once, he empathized with Tyrule over his feelings for Leira.

"You were saying?" the girl reminded him politely.

"What? Oh yes. Do you know where a good place to stay might be?"

"Oh. There's an inn right around the corner. It's actually not that far at all. Walk past the old hat shop and you should see it."

"Er—thanks. What's your name?"

She smiled politely. "Selena. What's yours?"

"Adam."

"Well, Adam, I hope we will meet again soon," she said with a smile.

Adam froze for a second. Suddenly, his brain reminded him that he was in the presence of another human being. "Er—definitely! One more question!"

Selena nodded. "What is it?"

"I need to go to Reximen Heights."

Her eyes brightened and she answered, "Interesting. Well, you won't be interested in any inn, then. You'll have to stay at the Heights. Actually, you could just stay the night with your friends—you brought friends along, I'm assuming. From what I hear, it's not an easy trip from the other side of the mountain."

He nodded. "They're coming down now, those slowpokes. I think I'll go to the Heights after I see them off. Do you live there?"

"But of course. How else would I be able to direct you there?" she asked.

"Good point. Can I just see them off for now? I don't know if it'd be too much trouble, but could you send someone for me?" Adam inquired.

"Yeah, they do that kind of stuff all the time, especially if you're a newbie, which I gather you are."

"That would be me."

She smiled. "I'm a good guesser."

"Maybe you should guess where we go next."

"What?" she asked.

Adam turned scarlet. "Er—nothing. I said maybe you should guess where I go next."

"I'm not that good."

"Oh look," Adam said, changing the subject. "My friends are almost here. Thanks for the advice. Goodbye, Selena."

"Well, bye then." Selena walked off.

He watched as she disappeared into one of the many buildings adorning the streets. When she was gone, Adam cursed his luck.

Adam turned around and saw the other five come down the last stretch of steps. When they had made it down and stood next to him, they all panted heavily. Clearly, the rush to keep sight of him had them all out of breath.

Adam turned to them. "Good news. I just met this girl, and she told us where we can go rest!"

The news was music to their tired ears.

"Where?" Seth said, huffing and puffing.

"I'll show you! Follow me."

Balian drew up closer to him. "You met a girl?"

Turning red, Adam whispered, "It did not go well."

Laughing quietly in amusement, Balian walked at his side. Adam did as Selena had told him. He turned the corner, following the cobblestone path into another street. He walked slowly so that his friends could have a chance to catch their breath. When they turned the corner, he looked this way and that in search of a hat shop.

Adam finally spotted a large sign with a rather large and fluffy hat painted on it. He led the others toward the shop. It was difficult to keep focused in such an incredible new place. All sorts of things were happening, and all sorts of people were running all over the place. The many shops sold goods ranging from common things such as food, to unique things such as Teratid Scrolls, which were copies from ancient texts.

At last, they passed the hat shop and stood before a wide, well-kept building. The inn reminded Adam of the buildings of fantasy lore that he had seen in storybooks. The windows were round and wide. The door was bright red, and Adam could tell that many happy people paid the inn a frequent visit by the large number of friendly, smiling people coming in and out. He was about to climb up the few steps leading to the front door when he heard a familiar voice.

"Adam Crescent, is that you?" an older voice said from behind him.

He let the others pass him before turning to see who had called his name. He gasped at what he saw. There, right before his very eyes, was the mystical merchant from so long ago. He wore an emerald shirt, and his lips curled into the familiar smile from Adam's memories.

Adam's eyes widened in surprise. "The merchant! You're actually here! I thought you just—"

"Left? Well, I felt it was time to return home." The tall old man smiled brightly.

Adam walked over to him quickly. The others turned to him, and he told them to go ahead and find some rooms. He really wanted this moment to catch up with the merchant. Adam stood right before him.

The old man seemed to marvel at the sight of him. "Blimey, Adam. You've grown up quite a bit. Last time I saw you, why, you were no taller than the counter on my cart," he said with a laugh.

Adam laughed back and watched the hazel eyes sparkle with laughter of their own. The merchant pushed his grey hair back against his head.

"So, Merchant, do you still have those butterflies?"

"Adam, I've got a name. Flaugherty. And as for the butterflies? I've still got a few at home. They're doing well."

"Flaugherty," Adam said. He tasted the word on his tongue as if it were a food he had never tried before.

Flaugherty nodded and smiled kindly at him. "How old are you now? Last I remembered, you were waiting to turn seven."

"Oh, I'm fourteen now. But Flaugherty, do you live in this town?"

"Yes. Best place there is. I knew you'd come here one day. I could sense that you were special."

"You and everyone else, apparently," Adam muttered. "How'd you get back? Surely the prince stopped you."

"The prince isn't all powerful Adam. Even the mightiest spells have holes."

"Oh. Do you know what goes on in the fortress?"

Flaugherty looked at him with an amused twinkle in his eye. "The Reximen Heights? That's where those with special gifts are sent to learn," he said with a wink.

Adam understood exactly what he meant. "Well, I think I have a special gift."

"I'm sure you do, Adam. Otherwise you wouldn't be here now."

"Do you know anyone in the tower?"

"Why, of course! My own daughter lives there! But, to answer your question, yes I can talk to someone later, if you'd like. They're not exactly what I'd call teachers, but I'd be glad to."

"Really? You would do that for me?"

Flaugherty chuckled. "Of course, but he'll probably send for you during the nighttime. Is that all right?"

"Perfect, because I'm about to go to this inn and catch up on some sleep, so send him this way," Adam said, realizing that Selena would probably forget to do it anyway.

"Oh, I will. Well then, I ought to be letting you get some rest. You look exhausted. Goodbye, Adam. Hope to see you again soon."

"Same here!"

When the old man had walked away, Adam turned back to the stairs. After taking a couple of steps, Adam stood on the very last step and knocked thrice on the red door. He did not have to wait long because a kind-looking woman answered the door promptly.

CHAPTER SEVENTEEN

"What's your name?" she asked.

"Adam. I need a room. Any room will do."

"Not a problem, *Adam*. My name is Gliddela. Welcome to the inn! Your friend's room, Room 318 I believe, is just up the stairs, down the corridor, and on your left. Enjoy yourself!" Her voice rang out brightly.

Graciously, Adam thanked her and walked past. He traveled all the way down the winding corridor and stopped before the last room on his left. In large brass characters, the number 318 clearly adorned the neat wooden surface of the door.

Adam quickly turned the handle and opened the door. Inside the room was a neatly made bed and a washroom. He let himself inside the room and quickly shut the door behind him. He removed his pack, dropping it to the floor, and removed his shoes and tossed them to the floor. Adam spent a few precious minutes in the washroom. Once he was clean, he emerged in new, comfortable clothes provided by the inn.

At last, a bed! I almost forgot how nice it was to have one, he mused.

After leaving the washroom, he threw himself on the bed. He did not even bother slipping underneath the neatly pressed blankets. As long as his head was on the fluffy pillows, nothing else really mattered. He turned his head away from the window, which was letting the pale afternoon sunlight in. While he waited for someone to come get him, Adam closed his eyes and tried counting the days since he left Roddington. The only trouble was that he fell asleep before even reaching the number four.

THE DARKEST HOUR

*K*nock! Knock! Knock!

Adam groaned and rolled over in his bed, pressing his face tightly against the pillows. Everything went quiet, and he tried to fall asleep once more.

Knock! Knock! Knock!

"Adam Crescent, are you there?" a voice whispered from the other side of the door.

He rolled over and looked through the window. It was dark both inside and outside, but a few stray lights were visible outside.

The stranger knocked again.

This time, Adam slipped out of bed. He bent over to the ground and flipped over the shoes that he had tossed to the floor only hours ago. He trudged over to the door and pulled it open gently.

CHAPTER EIGHTEEN

In the doorway stood a tall man clothed in black. He wore shiny black boots, a smooth black cloak, and a high collar that obscured his neck. The man's, hands hidden in black gloves, adjusted the hood that shadowed his features.

"Who are you?"

"Flaugherty sent for me. Come. We must begin," the hooded man said.

Adam rubbed his eyes for a moment. "Why at this hour?"

Adam saw the hood tilt in one direction. "You must be tested. The hour is part of your test."

Adam nodded.

"We must hurry, then. We need to see what you can do."

"Listen, it's not—"

"We cannot talk here. Follow me." He turned down the corridor.

After snatching up his pack, Adam quickly ran out of the room and watched as the shadowy figure kept moving. He closed the door quietly behind him and walked briskly to catch up to the mysterious man. The innkeeper was not in the entrance hall. The man waited by the door for him to catch up.

When Adam finally managed to reach him, the man turned and swung the door open silently. He held it open for Adam, who quickly stepped outside. The man closed the door softly and walked out into the open.

Adam followed closely and watched as the stranger's black boots slapped against the pavement. They were moving so fast that Adam hardly had time to look anywhere. Out of the corner of his eye, he spotted several dim streetlights disappear behind them.

He tried to keep track of all the twists and turns he and his mysterious companion made. Soon, he gave up on this idea, as it was impossible to focus. He heard a rat's tiny feet skitter from somewhere in the darkness behind them.

The time must have been unusually late or early, for not a single shop was open. All of the houses' windows were completely dark. Adam wondered why in the world the man had insisted they travel at this time.

Finally, lit only by the torches outside it, the sprawling tower came into view. As they approached it, Adam's mouth fell open in awe of the enormous structure before him. Like the other buildings, no light shone from the several windows on the sides of it.

The man stopped before a set of large, oaken doors, and Adam nearly bumped into him. He watched with bated breath as the man removed one of his gloves. A pale, white hand contrasted sharply with the darkness. He placed his hand on the door, and a violet light issued forth from the door. Adam's eyes widened, and he gasped as the light grew brighter. Slowly, the mystic glow dissolved into the shadows, and the man removed his hand.

There was a loud click, and the door swung open. Neither Adam nor the man touched it, so Adam peered inside to see who could have opened it. As it happened, no one stood in the doorway. It was magic, as he had suspected.

After quickly slipping his glove back on, the man led Adam through the doors and into the tower. Adam glanced downward and saw an intricately tiled floor in a fantastic, radial pattern. He noticed several doors on the first floor. He followed the mysterious man over to a spiral staircase that attached itself to a large, round pillar. Several dim torches shed an eerie light on the stairs.

The man grabbed the iron rail and began to ascend the steps with lightning speed. Still sleepy, Adam had no hope of catching up to him. He passed door after door as he jogged hastily up the stairs. Even in the dim light, he could see that some of the doors were different colors.

The man was still visible against the soft glow of the torches, and he kept going higher and higher. Adam went as fast as he could to follow him, or at least he tried to keep him in sight. He kept up with this maddening game of sorts as he passed several floors and more doors. He was becoming increasingly tired, but he knew that he could not lose sight of the man.

At last, Adam looked up and saw that he had nearly reached the top of the stairs. Just above him, the steps merged into a landing. Adam struggled to cover more ground faster. At last, he took the last step and stood on the level floor. Directly in front of him stood the man clad in black, and behind him was a single door.

The door was flanked on either side by two dim torches that flickered every once in a while. When the man saw that Adam had arrived, he withdrew a tiny key from his pocket. He turned to the door and carefully slipped the minuscule key into the lock above the door handle. He turned the key sharply, and the door slowly creaked open. He dropped the key in his pocket and pushed the door open even further.

For the first time that evening, the man let him enter first. Adam thanked him quietly and admitted himself into the room. As he walked into the center of the room, he was confused when he saw that the room was completely empty. Nothing hung on the walls, and the floors were bare. There were no objects or furniture anywhere in sight. Adam realized that it was just the man and him.

The mysterious man stepped inside and walked over to Adam. He did not bother to close the door, which Adam thought was rather curious. When he stood face-to-face with Adam, he turned and held out a hand toward the door. With his palm stretched out, he flicked two fingers back, and the door squeaked and closed itself.

Adam watched the man with amazement. He let his hand drop and he looked back over to Adam, who stared back.

"How did you do that?" Adam asked incredulously.

"It's our gift, Adam." He spoke in a chilling voice.

Adam felt that something was not right. "Who are you?"

"Well, it depends who you ask. I am Rowtag."

"Rowtag, how did you find me again?" Adam asked softly.

"The one called Flaugherty told my superior. You were supposed to come tomorrow, but I needed you sooner."

Adam took a tiny step back. "Wait, *you* needed me? I thought it was the other way around."

"Oh yes, Adam. More than you know," he said with a small chuckle.

"I don't understand."

The hooded man faced Adam directly. "You have a power that many would die for. Are you not the Razorwolf, Adam Crescent?"

"How did you—?"

"I have my ways. I saw the escape you made at the ceremony. Legendary, I must say."

Adam issued a challenge. "Take off the garb. Show me who you really are."

"That won't be necessary."

"Take it off, or I leave," Adam insisted.

Rowtag did not move. Adam walked past him and headed for the door. The man raised his hand once more and snapped his fingers. Adam jumped backwards when a wall of flames suddenly stood between him and the door. He turned around angrily, and the man laughed coldly.

"You want to see me that badly? Fine, I'll give in to this one request."

Adam watched as both gloved hands reached up to the edge of the hood and slowly pulled it back. He had never seen the face before. Rowtag had long, dark brown hair that was pulled back. His sharp nose was pointed at Adam. What troubled Adam the most were his eyes. Unlike most other people he had seen, the man's irises were blood-red. A twisted grin formed on the Rowtag's pale face. Suddenly, the man's identity dawned on him.

"So this is your revenge?" Adam asked coolly.

Rowtag stepped closer to him. "You know exactly what I want."

"I didn't kill Zenia!" Adam protested.

"Oh yes. I saw the spell you inflicted upon her. You're no hero."

"And you were also the knight who gave me the commission for the sword."

"Correct. I never expected you to have any gift. You were just an easy means to dispose of that disgrace Phillip. All this time, we thought you were just a simpleton blacksmith, a useless boy. Getting you to make the sword was easy, especially after we added a little pressure."

Adam spoke casually. "You know, I find it really hard to believe that you picked me by coincidence. Yeah, you guys are powerful, but you're not too smart."

Rowtag smirked wickedly. "Adam, your sharp tongue has no use here." I hold power over you. Surely you can understand that," he said softly.

"No, all I understand is that you are a murderer and a manipulator!" Adam spat.

Rowtag made a tsk-tsk noise. "Adam, you're looking at this all wrong. Listen, I know you can't control that power. I can help you," he said calmly.

Adam hesitated for a moment. "You're wrong," he replied, though he did not entirely believe it.

Rowtag laughed softly. He looked at Adam with his red eyes. "Am I? Wouldn't you want to keep your friends safe? Imagine if you accidentally released your power, and ... oops," he said, taunting Adam.

Adam glared at him. He said nothing at first though, as the sinister man's words were true.

Finally, he said firmly, "No. Quite frankly, I'd die before I joined you."

"Well, that makes my job much easier. You see, Adam, if you were on our side, you could live. But since you're not, your very existence poses a threat. Shall I explain before you beg for mercy?" Rowtag laughed cruelly.

"You're going to explain anyway, so why even ask?" Adam asked bluntly.

Rowtag turned and faced the wall of fire. "You see, Adam, the Razorwolf and the Master of Shadows cannot hope to coexist unless united by a common force."

Adam silently placed a hand on his pack. "And why not?" he asked, keeping Rowtag occupied.

"Well, two superior forces are both attracted to and repelled by one another. Unless united, the clash between the two could be devastating. Many people would die. Innocent blood spilled. I'm sure you wouldn't want that."

"And who is the Master of Shadows? Prince Nicolas?"

"Someone you do not wish to cross. It is only a matter of time before all of Fallador is in his grasp."

Adam held the pack with one hand and slowly let his fingers search inside it. "So, what is your power?"

"I'll show you more."

The man snapped his fingers. A small scarlet flaming spark was suspended in the air. Adam watched intently despite his frantic search inside the bag. The spark twisted its way around Rowtag's hand in a helix shape. It traveled around his arm and across his torso. When it reached the other side of his body, Rowtag clamped his hand around it. When he finally opened his fingers, a small wisp of smoke issued forth from his outstretched palm.

Suddenly, Adam felt the cold metal handle of the dagger Leon had given him. With great care, he silently removed it from the pack and slowly placed the bag over his back once more. Adam took a step closer to Rowtag. Suddenly, several items in the pack shifted noisily.

Rowtag whirled around and looked directly at Adam, who stood rooted to the spot in fear. He flashed an evil smile at him. "Come now, Adam. That's not very nice."

CHAPTER EIGHTEEN

He swung an open palm out in the air in front of him. Adam gasped when the dagger tore itself from his grip. It dangled dangerously in the air as Rowtag walked closer to him. Adam quickly snatched the weapon from the air and gripped it tightly. When they stood nose-to-nose, Rowtag clutched his fingers in a steely fist. Adam felt the sword suddenly vanish, and he watched in horror as metallic dust fell through his fingers.

"Oh, Adam. You are far too predictable. Destroying you will be easy. Any last words?" he sneered.

Adam looked into his eyes with a fiery intensity. Blue met red, and the connection between them was unbreakable.

"You will lose," Adam said.

Rowtag laughed loudly. Suddenly, he swung his arm. In a flash, the back of his hand smacked the side of Adam's face so hard that he was thrown to the ground. Lying facedown on the cold floor, Adam winced and tasted blood. He heard Rowtag's footsteps draw nearer. A sudden searing pain erupted from his side. He rolled over on his back and saw Rowtag standing over him.

"You are weak, Adam Crescent, and you shall die," he said in disgust.

He snapped his fingers and a large sphere of fire appeared above his hand. Rowtag pulled his hand back and contorted his face. Adam quickly rolled over and scrambled to his feet. With a shout of rage, Rowtag hurled the fireball at Adam, who escaped by mere inches.

He ran all about the room as Rowtag hurled fireball after fireball. For a while, he was hopeful that he would survive the onslaught. Suddenly, he slipped and fell to the floor with a loud cry. Rowtag walked over to him slowly with a fireball suspended over his outstretched palm. He pulled his hand back to throw it.

Fearfully, Adam looked at him. "Wait!" he pleaded.

Rowtag hesitated.

"Why didn't you just wait for Mustafo? He had the chance! You could have easily taken me from him!" Adam yelled.

Rowtag threw back his head and laughed wickedly. He brought his gaze back down to meet Adam's eyes. "After all this time, you think it was Mustafo who wanted to use you as a bartering tool? What foolish notion is this?" he sneered.

"It has to be him! I saw the letter! He knew about everything! He could have stopped it!"

"You fool! Of course Mustafo knew about the king, but he was too late to save him! Mustafo is a mere shadow of the man he once was! Of course, what good could that have done? He has no powers!"

"No, that's impossible! He would have wanted me to become a Shadowlord! He was obsessed."

"Mustafo? A Shadowlord? You have been terribly misinformed! If anything, he would have died before taking on this great power. He is the epitome of weakness," he said coldly.

"But—"

"No more! This ends now!" Rowtag shouted.

He went right for Adam and grabbed him by the neck. With incredible strength, Rowtag held Adam out far and up high. The iron grip the murderer possessed was too much for him. He tried desperately to claw his way free, but Rowtag would not relent. He only gripped his throat even tighter. He laughed cruelly as Adam kicked and struggled for air.

"Now you will die!" Rowtag cried.

Adam fought fiercely to resist. Suddenly, Rowtag threw him backwards, and Adam's body pummeled through the stone wall. In another vacant room, Adam struggled to get up, but Rowtag cast the wreckage upon him. Buried under the stone, Adam's breathing was shallowand ragged. His life flickered feebly.

CHAPTER EIGHTEEN

"As I said earlier, you are no hero. Is this how the mighty Razorwolf dies? A crushing death? You're weakness," Rowtag remarked scathingly.

Try as he might, Adam could not speak.

"This could have been so much simpler if you went with us in the first place. You could have lived. But now that my sister is dead, your fate will be to join her. That's not my Master's decision. That's mine. After that, I'm going to take this city apart brick by brick. I'll start with your friend Balian. Oh yes, I know who he is. I'll see to it personally that your companions die in absolute pain one by one. And does it matter? You'll be dead!" he continued.

Suddenly, a wild impulse raced through Adam's mind. With the strength of a fully-grown man, he forced himself onto his feet. The stone that buried him fell to the ground noisily as he stood upright. Even through a black eye and a cut lip, the glare he shot at Rowtag was fierce.

"No, Rowtag. You're not going to touch any of those people," he rasped.

Fearfully, Rowtag stared at his young adversary. Slowly, Adam stepped forward, one foot in front of the other. He broke into a run, then a full sprint as he headed directly for Rowtag's body.

Zenia's brother reacted too slow. Adam dove at him and slammed him to the ground. Before Rowtag could so much as protest, Adam delivered punch after punch to his formerly smug face. He tried to strike back, but Adam batted his attempts back and hit even harder.

Rowtag wheezed fearfully. *"Please! I surrender! I surrender!"*

Adam pushed himself off of the ground using Rowtag's chest. He stood over the pathetic Shadowlord in disgust. "Like I said before. You will lose."

"Are you going to kill me like you killed her?" Rowtag snarled.

"I don't kill," Adam answered. "Now, release the door. I'm leaving."

Rowtag nodded quickly and snapped his fingers. The flames around the door dissolved into smoke, and Adam was free to leave his enemy to wallow in his misery. As he stepped towards the door, a terrible laugh rose from behind him.

"Did you think it would be that easy? I'll give you this, you fight well with your fists. But this is a land of magic, and I have the advantage," Rowtag's voice said cruelly.

Adam turned towards him and asked, "Do you?"

Rowtag extended a hand towards Adam, but he was too late. Adam responded quickly by holding both hands out and sending a massive wave of light towards his adversary. The force smashed Rowtag's body into the wall, and he scowled in pain. As he slowly rose from the floor, he eyed Adam madly. "That's all you can manage? The Razorwolf? I expected more. It will take more than that to stop me!" Rowtag cackled.

Suddenly, there was a loud slam followed by the sound of clattering debris, and Adam heard Rowtag curse in pain. He opened his eyes and saw his attacker on the floor surrounded by shards of wood. In the doorway, Adam saw an older man who bore a particularly fierce expression with an open palm outstretched.

The older man waited patiently for Rowtag to get up once more. When he did, Rowtag looked at him in disgust.

"Oh, it's you. Well, your death can be arranged as well!" Rowtag said, and he charged at him.

The other man held out his hands, and a white streak bolted from his fingertips and struck Rowtag's chest. Rowtag staggered momentarily, but quickly retaliated.

"I'm stronger than you too!" Rowtag screamed. He blasted a stream of fire at his opponent.

The man held out one arm and extinguished the fire with an airborne stream of water. Both fire and water met with a vicious hiss, and a cloud of steam hung in midair. When Rowtag drew closer, the man curled his hand into a fist and swung it directly at the scoundrel's face.

Rowtag fell to the floor with a muffled thud. His opponent flicked both of his wrists, and Rowtag's arms and legs snapped together and were held there by a white cylinder of water. He twitched angrily on the floor and tried to free himself.

"Get it off me, you scoundrel!" he spat.

The man walked over to him calmly. "Not until you're safely stowed away, Rowtag," he said coolly.

Adam watched with great interest as the man bent down close to the furious Rowtag until their faces were mere inches apart.

"You may have got me now, but this is only temporary!" Rowtag screamed.

"Not under my watch. You will threaten us no more!"

Rowtag laughed bitterly and looked into the man's eyes, his own eyes wide with madness. "You think this is over?"

"I think your efforts are wasted."

Rowtag laughed madly once more. "You're wrong! You are blinded by arrogance! You and the boy! The Shadowlords will rise again, and we will be more powerful than ever before! Mark my words! The Master of Shadows, the greatest being, will be the death of the Pentacular Reximen! He lives! You will all perish! Not even the Razorwolf can save you!" Rowtag said violently.

"Even if they were to come back, it's a pity because you'll be locked away," the older man said casually.

Adam watched as the man looked to the doorway and gestured for others to join him, but he never saw anyone else. He stood up and looked at the doorway. Suddenly, his pain and fatigue caught up with him. The room around him spun out of control, and all of the color faded away. Adam's head felt unbelievably heavy, and he teetered precariously. He felt his knees buckle, and his body sagged heavily. A feeling of weightlessness overcame him as he descended to the floor. He felt no pain, for his eyes closed upon the impact, and he knew no more.

CHAPTER NINETEEN

THE PENTACULAR REXIMEN

The first thing Adam heard was a gentle tinkling from nearby. Initially, the soft metallic sound seemed like a random noise. As he became more and more aware of it, the tinkling seemed to become a chain of serene notes. The music was soft and slow, but Adam felt its peaceful presence as an invitation to life.

He opened his eyes, and everything was a blur. He sat up very slowly and looked straight ahead. He blinked over and over again until the blur dissolved. When all was clear once more, Adam noticed that he was not in his room at the inn. Looking to the left, he saw a large window that overlooked the town.

The sound of the music registered once more in Adam's ears. He looked beside his bed and saw a shiny creature perched on the bedside table. On closer inspection, he saw that it was a silver bird. The bird continued singing its wondrous notes but tilted its head to look at Adam. It stared innocently at him with little beady black eyes. A smile formed on his face.

Adam noticed that the bird was standing on a piece of paper. He cautiously reached out so as not to scare the tiny creature. It hopped backwards, and Adam gently picked up the paper.

The paper was completely blank. Adam flipped it over and saw that there was a note meant for him. In curly, ornate handwriting, it read the following:

Adam,

If you are feeling better, meet me in the back grounds. Just follow the stairs and head out the doors directly across from the entrance hall. We have much to talk about—your journey and the events of last night.

Acacius

P.S. A friend of yours by the name of Flaugherty left you a gift.

Blinking sleep from his eyes, Adam leapt out of the bed and to his feet. He became aware that he was wearing light-blue pajamas, but he wanted nothing more than to pay a visit to this Acacius. The silver bird warbled a long note as Adam ran to the door. He turned back and saw that the bird was pointing its beak at a crisp roll of bread on the same table.

"Oh, I'm fine, really. You can have it if you like."

He watched as the bird hopped toward the roll and picked gingerly at it. Adam turned quickly and burst through the door. Faster than lightning, he flew down the stairs. Although there were others walking down the stairs, Adam took enough care not to knock them over. When at last he arrived on the first-floor landing, he turned and looked at the closed door that he and Rowtag had hurried through during the events of the previous night.

He walked briskly across the room to a set of doors at the rear of the first floor. With a gentle push, the doors creaked open, and Adam's eyes met a blaze of sunlight.

Squinting, he slowly headed out into the light and looked around for someone he might recognize. Several others were walking about on the neat, stone walkways. Dozens of benches lined the edges where stone met green grass. A majestic tree stood in the center of the courtyard. Adam looked all around. Finally, he spotted the man who had defeated Rowtag.

Adam hurried over to the bench where he sat. He was engaged in a lively conversation with the very same girl Adam had met the previous day.

"Selena?" Adam asked.

She swung her mesmerizing black hair as she turned to look at him. "Adam?"

They both looked at the man. He chuckled softly to himself. "Well, I see you two know each other."

"We just met yesterday. I had no idea I'd see him here, though," Selena said.

Adam looked at her once more.

"It is strange when our smallest expectations become the truth. Now, Selena, not to seem rude, but I need to have a word with Adam here," he said kindly.

"Of course, sir." Selena walked off.

Adam looked at the man.

"By all means, sit down," he said, gesturing to the empty space beside him.

Adam slowly took a seat on the stone bench and looked into the man's soft brown eyes. In this light, Adam had a better opportunity to examine his features. His graying brown hair glinted in the sunlight. He wore gray clothes similar to those of Rowtag, except that he had wide sleeves, no gloves, and his kind face was exposed. The corners of his smile wrinkled his face, but his eyes were aglow with a youthful luster.

"I suppose you have several questions."

Adam nodded.

"Well then, don't be shy. Ask, and I shall answer."

"Okay. For starters, what am I to call you?"

"Oh, did I really forget to introduce myself? I really should observe the niceties, shouldn't I? Well, I am called Acacius. To you, I shall be known as Master Acacius."

Adam mouthed the words *Master Acacius*. They seemed genuinely benevolent.

"Well, Master Acacius, I just need to know something."

"Anything."

"Why do the Shadowlords want me?"

Acacius paused for a moment. "You see, Adam, you possess a special ability that has only been seen once in the entire span of history. Do you know what this is?"

"The Razorwolf."

"Correct. I trust you know this, especially after the events of last night, but you have tremendous power. The ability to transform and the ability to perform near limitless magic makes you quite an asset to those who seek power."

Adam paused to think about his words. Then, he remembered something. "I knew a man named Mustafo. He said I was special, too. I thought he wanted to help me, but then I saw a letter, and I ran."

"I, too, knew the Mustafo of whom you speak. He was a great man, and it is a shame that you didn't confess your doubts. Nonetheless, you are here, and that is what matters."

"So, Mustafo was on my side the whole time?" Adam asked.

"Yes. He has always been on our side, but Mustafo's history is not our concern at the moment."

"Sorry."

"Don't be. You're merely curious, and that's fine."

"Do you know of Sorah-Kown?"

"Who?" Acacius asked.

"Never mind," he said quietly.

Acacius smiled softly at him, and Adam thought of the words Rowtag screamed before he had passed out.

"The Shadowlords," Adam continued.

"What about them?"

"Rowtag said that they would come back. Is it true?"

Acacius sighed and looked to the skies as if a simple answer was inscribed upon the clouds. He peered once more into Adam's blue eyes. "Some would claim it to be impossible. However, given the demonstration of last night, I'd say those people are wrong. I'm afraid, Adam, that it seems they are mounting a return," Acacius said softly.

"What makes them so terrible?"

"You and I have special abilities, Adam," Acacius said. "Yours are just now manifesting themselves. My powers are not nearly as strong as yours. To answer your question, everyone like us has different powers. The Shadowlords are not exempt from this. They have unique abilities. Some, like Rowtag, can manipulate things like fire. Others have much more dangerous powers like shape-shifting and mind inhibition. Trust me. The list goes on and on."

"Why do they want me so badly, though?" Adam persisted.

"They believe that your power can make them truly unstoppable. They will stop at nothing to acquire the highest powers."

"And they're going to keep searching until they find me, or until I'm no longer a threat," Adam said grimly.

"Sadly, yes."

Neither of them said anything for a while. Acacius merely sat and looked up at the cloudy sky. Adam stared for a long time at the ground in front of him.

"So, what do I do, then?" he asked, without looking up.

"You make the choice," Acacius said simply.

Adam raised his head and looked at him. "Choice? There's a choice?"

Acacius looked back at him. "Of course there's a choice. There's always a choice. Even the Razorwolf has a choice, Adam."

"What are my choices then?"

"Well, the way I see it, you can go one of two ways. You can continue to run from the Shadowlords and ultimately yourself, or you can remain here to learn to control what lives within you so that you can face them when the time comes. Your pick."

"Why do I have to be the Razorwolf? I mean, I'm just a blacksmith's apprentice!" Adam protested.

Acacius smiled. "You *were* a blacksmith's apprentice. Now you are one of the noble Pentacular Reximen. You know something about fate? It works in mystical ways. Sometimes, we must all ask ourselves, 'Why me?' You see, fate rarely calls upon us at the moment of our choice. Why? We will never know. What we do know is that we can choose to ignore it and live a life of despair, or we can embrace it and come to know fulfillment."

Adam nodded.

"So, what do you think?"

"I know I can't hide forever. I also know I need to learn how to control it."

"So what is your choice?"

"I think we both know what I'll say. I accept the Razorwolf destiny, no matter where it leads me. I will keep going until the Shadowlords cannot harm anyone ever again," Adam said firmly.

"That is an awfully large commitment."

"Fate is a large commitment."

There came a loud slam from the back door to the fortress, and a tall, bristling woman hurried towards Acacius. Adam could tell something was wrong by the look in her worried eyes.

"Acacius, we have a problem," the woman said in a regal voice.

Scratching his head, Acacius answered, "Go ahead, Cosma."

She eyed Adam hesitantly. "What about the boy?"

"I suppose you're right." Acacius smiled at him. "Well said. Now, I believe that is all. Why don't you go and find your friends?" he said warmly.

He and Adam stood up at the same time. Acacius reached out a slender hand. Adam reached out and shook it with a firm grip.

"Well then, hurry back tomorrow, and your training will begin," Acacius said.

As Adam walked away, his sensitive ears picked up the conversation between Cosma and Acacius.

"It's about Rowtag," Cosma said darkly.

"What about him?" Acacius asked.

"We found him."

"Where?"

"Dead."

Acacius paused for a moment. "You mean to say that he killed—"

"No. His powers were neutralized, and there was no possible weapon," Cosma interrupted.

"No loose ends," Acacius whispered.

Adam hurried to the back doors. He walked slowly and pondered the conversation he just heard. The small twinge of guilt he felt about accusing Mustafo of unsavory motives vanished on the spot. Someone killed Rowtag to ensure his silence, and the highest authority of Reximen Heights had virtually no idea who could have committed the deed. Now Rowtag could never reveal the secrets of the Shadowlords. Adam thought of what Acacius said only moments ago.

No loose ends.

Shaking the thought from his mind, he found his way into the entrance hall once more, and his eyes found the staircase. Unlike the first time he ascended, he walked up the stairs slowly until he reached his room. When he got inside, he found his pack and his regular clothes hanging up on a wall. After grabbing them, he strode to the door to leave. From behind him, he heard a sharp chirp.

He whirled around in surprise and saw the shiny bird staring at him with a half-eaten roll of bread beside it. Adam held out an open palm and looked to the bird. It stretched its silver wings out and propelled itself into the air. He watched with amazement as the tiny creature landed in his outstretched palm. He laughed softly at this miraculous feat.

"You need a name, don't you?" Adam said.

The bird cheeped in reply.

"Hmmm ... what about ... Silver?" Adam asked, feeling rather uncreative.

The bird seemed to nod in approval. Adam smiled once more.

"Well then, Silver it is," he said as he turned to leave.

Adam quickly left the fortress and walked out in good spirits. He traveled all over the town square trying to find the inn. He enjoyed the walk with Silver because of the air of awe and magic that seemed to emanate from the whole town.

In full daylight, the town was incredible in its liveliness. People wandered all over, chattering happily with one another. The windows in the buildings, unlike during the previous night, were aglow with vibrant life and motion. Adam smiled brightly and walked further.

He fought the urge to enter several of the colorful shops that he passed on his way back to the inn. Many people waved at him and his new pet, and he waved back gleefully. The town called Setulptus gave Adam a rush of hope and happiness that he had never known in Roddington. For once in his life, Adam felt as if he were more than the lowly son of the blacksmith. He felt important, like a hero. Acacius's words about the Shadowlords' faded away in his happiness.

When Adam turned a corner, he was both surprised and delighted at what he saw. Uninhibited, he ran, and Silver fluttered at his side. When he stopped, he breathed heavily and looked right into the shiny eyes of the one he longed to see the most.

"Why, hello there, Adam! I see you have a new friend," Flaugherty said kindly.

"Thanks, he's great," Adam said, huffing and puffing.

"Adam," Flaugherty said in a softer voice. "I want to apologize."

Adam looked at him curiously. "For what?"

"I told him about you. I didn't know what he really was, I promise."

Adam smiled back at him. "Flaugherty, it's not your fault. I know you wouldn't do anything like that. You're a good person."

A warm smile came to Flaugherty's face. "Oh, Adam. You may be older, but deep down inside, you're still that curious and good-hearted little boy."

Adam ran up to him and gave him a hug. Flaugherty appeared to be a little surprised, but he wrapped his arms around Adam as well. When they stood apart, both of them grinned at the other.

"So, are you going to leave?" Flaugherty asked.

"No, I'm staying right here."

"That's good. Maybe you'll meet my daughter. I'd love to chat some more, but you should probably go see your friends," Flaugherty said. He pointed to the red door of the inn.

Adam took a step to leave, but he quickly remembered something. "Flaugherty?"

CHAPTER NINETEEN

"Yes?"

"Where are those butterflies?"

"Oh," he replied with a laugh. "They're around here somewhere. All you have to do is look."

"Thanks. Just curious. Well, I'll be going then," Adam said, waving at him.

Adam walked up the steps to the inn with Silver perched loyally on his shoulder. He knocked thrice on the door, and the kindly face of Madam Gliddela appeared in the window.

"Oh, my! Hold on one moment," she said quickly, as she hastened to open the door.

When the door flew open, Adam thanked her and asked her where the others were.

"Oh, they're in your room. Waiting, I think."

Adam ascended the stairs in a hurry and headed down the long corridor until he found Room 318. Slowly, he reached out and clutched the handle. With a little push, the door creaked open, and the sight that met Adam's eyes was overwhelming.

In a cluster of chairs, Leon, Seth, Leira, Tyrule, and Balian sat with welcoming smiles. Adam hurried into the room excitedly to meet his friends.

"Well, took you long enough," Tyrule said teasingly.

Adam laughed.

"We were so worried!" Leira exclaimed.

"It takes more than a Shadowlord to stop me. I thought for sure you'd know that."

"From what I understand, you really gave him what he deserved," Balian remarked.

The others snorted with laughter.

"Well, Adam. I just have one question," Seth piped up.

"Sure."

"How come you never told us you were the Razorwolf?"

"Er—well, I never really gave it much thought, to be honest." Adam shrugged.

Seth chuckled at this remark.

"Tell us what happened! We could all use a good story!" Leon laughed.

"All right then. I'll try to keep to the truth," Adam said jokingly.

He took a seat next to Leon and began to deliver his story. His audience was brilliant because they gasped in all the right places. Adam told them about the visit from Rowtag, their entry into the fortress, and how Rowtag had suddenly turned on him. They listened intently as Adam described the battle that ensued and how Acacius, the Master of the Tower, came and rescued him. He closed the story with a detailed account of his one-on-one visit with Acacius; however, he neglected to mention Rowtag's death.

When Adam was through, everyone in the room remained silent for a moment. Finally, it was Leon who spoke.

"Well then. I suggest you get some real clothes on because we are going to celebrate!" he exclaimed.

In a flash, he and Seth darted out of the room to get ready. Adam laughed at the humorous sight of the small twins hurrying to leave. Tyrule, Leira, and Balian remained in their chairs.

"Where are we going?" Adam asked them.

"Oh, Seth says he knows of this great place to eat. After what we've been through, anything sounds great," Leira said.

"Yes, I agree, but Adam?" Tyrule asked.

"Yes?"

"What's this Acacius fellow like?" he asked.

"I dunno, really. He seems wise, but at the same time, it's easy talking to a younger kid. We'll have to wait and see," Adam answered.

CHAPTER NINETEEN

"What about Mustafo? Did you tell Acacius about him?" Tyrule pressed.

Adam looked at him with a hint of remorse. "We were wrong about Mustafo this whole time. It seems that all he wanted to do was to help me."

"Oh," Leira and Tyrule said sheepishly.

"Well, one day, when I learn to master this power, I will return to Roddington and apologize," Adam said firmly.

"That day is a long way off. In the meantime, we're going to leave you to change into suitable clothes." Tyrule stood up.

Leira followed suit, but she stole a quick glance at the bird on Adam's shoulder. "Adam, what is that?"

He looked down at his shoulder. "Oh, this? His name is Silver. He's a gift."

"Charming!" Leira twittered excitedly before leaving the room with Tyrule.

When everyone had left, Adam quickly changed his clothes and allowed Silver to fly about the room for a few minutes. When he was ready to leave, he called the bird back, and Silver landed squarely on his shoulder.

Adam met the others at the entrance. They bid farewell to Madam Gliddela and headed outside. Seth led them to a nice-looking restaurant, and they all filed in. They sat at a freshly cleaned table and all discussed what they were to order. Adam did not really care. He was just happy to be safe and with his friends.

He let his eyes wander all about the clean restaurant. When his eyes finally rested on a window, he saw something very peculiar. He squinted at the tiny outline on the windowsill. When the object came into focus, Adam smiled at what he saw.

On the windowsill sat a butterfly. It was not any old butterfly, but one of the magical butterflies that Flaugherty had shown him many years ago. The butterfly's wings, it appeared, were colored azure and violet.

When a woman came and delivered their food, Adam looked to his friends. They all raised their glasses, which were filled with water, and clinked them together.

"To Adam," Leon said.

The others echoed his words. "To Adam!"

They all took a swig and placed their glasses down. Adam bashfully lowered his head and felt his ears turn red. At last, all of them began to eat a terrific meal. They laughed and told many stories about their lives, and it seemed that the great fun would never end. Adam sat back with a wide grin extending from ear to ear. For now, nothing could shake his elation. He was among friends, and he thought to himself, *That's the best place to be.*

* * *

Far away in a lofty tower, Prince Nicolas peered out of an archaic window, his spiderlike fingers wrapped around the edge. There was a knock from behind, but he remained still, his hungry eyes fixated upon the horizon.

"My liege?" came a voice from the other side.

"Come in."

A portly man slipped inside the prince's personal chambers noisily. Prince Nicolas continued staring out into the vast world, a world where the darkest of secrets were beginning to come to light. The messenger held a tightly wrapped scroll and stood awkwardly as he waited for a response. When none came, he cleared his throat noisily. A barely noticeable wave of irritation flitted across the prince's young face.

"What news do you have for me?" he asked in a drawling voice.

"Not good news, sir," the man answered timidly.

CHAPTER NINETEEN

Prince Nicolas turned to face the messenger. "Do not speak to me in riddles. I asked you a question, so I expect an answer. Instead, you delay me. Now, I will ask you again. What news do you have for me?"

The messenger quivered and wiped a stray bead of sweat from his furrowed brow. Hastily, he held the scroll out in front of him and unrolled its contents. He gulped before opening his mouth to speak.

"Do not read to me. Tell me only what I need to know."

Nodding anxiously, the messenger moved the parchment behind his back and cleared his throat once more. "I'm afraid the boy, the Crescent boy, has evaded our man."

"You think I know nothing of this?" the prince asked scathingly.

"I should have known, but I only wanted to deliver any messages, just as you have asked of me."

"Very well. His blunder may have cost us some more time, but Zenia was just the beginning. As for the boy, he has created greater trouble for himself. Do not be so naïve to assume ineptitude on many decades of careful planning."

"I would never do such a thing," the man answered nervously.

Nicolas smirked in amusement. "You don't sound so sure of this. But it matters not. I will have my way."

The messenger nodded and turned quickly to leave. Before his hand made contact with the door handle, the prince's voice stopped him.

"I have a question for you."

Hesitating for only a fraction of a second, the messenger turned around and faced his master with wide eyes. "You have a question to ask of me?" he asked incredulously.

The prince took his place by the window and watched as the sun began to disappear beneath the ocean. "You sound surprised. That amuses me. In any event, I do have a question for you."

"Yes, my liege?"

"Do you know how to defeat a hero?"

The man's features went blank. "No, my lord, I can't say that I know."

"I wouldn't expect you to, anyway. I'll tell you. You destroy his heart."

The messenger eyed him curiously. "How do you expect to do that?"

"Let's just say there's a storm coming, and when it hits, nothing will be the same. Fear is a powerful weapon," the prince answered cryptically.

Prince Nicolas looked down at his hands, which clasped a smooth, mahogany box, worn by many years of possession. The messenger regarded the prince with a quizzical expression. The evil prince sensed the growing confusion and stared back to the sky. As the sun dipped below the horizon completely, a dark smirk curled along his sinister features as he reflected over the shadows that were to fall.

And now for a sneak peek at the next part of the epic tale,

ADAM CRESCENT
AND THE FALL OF AGES

THE DARKNESS RISING

*T*he corridor extended far into the darkness. Lighting flashed erratically in the skies outside of the broken windows. Under the rumble of the thunder, the sound of crunching glass was barely audible. The howling wind whipped along the interior, and the rain pelted the icy, stone floor. At the very end of the hallway was a dim light, a contradiction to this peculiar evening. The footsteps were slow, but cautious. Little by little, the distance to the glow shrank. An exceptionally powerful blink of lighting illuminated a lone silhouette at the very end. A stranger was watching, beckoning him to come. The figure stepped towards him, the two of them working together now to close the space between them. The heavens above were unnaturally silent as they drew closer, neither recognizing the other. As the stranger drew closer, another flicker of lighting revealed a face. Suddenly, the ground beneath them rumbled, and the world spun into the abyss.

CRRRRACK!

CHAPTER ONE

Far away, in a land unlike any other, a boy sat bolt upright in his four-poster bed. His brown hair resembled a bird's wiry nest, but his enticing blue eyes widened with alarming vigilance. Breathing quickly, he surveyed his surroundings carefully. There was no sign of movement, and the boy looked to his window, which depicted the ferocious artistry of a great storm looming overhead. The rain pelted the glass like a tiny drum, and the great gray clouds swallowed the moonlight. To the untrained eye, it was a storm, and nothing more. The boy, however, did not possess an untrained eye because he knew exactly what this storm meant.

The curse was unraveling.

Fourteen-year-old Adam Crescent examined the skies carefully. Months ago, it was he who broke the keyhole between lands, the perpetual storm that existed between the sisterlands. Once the weather breached the unremarkable land of Roddington, people would begin to question the world around them. As he looked through the water-encrusted window, Adam could not help but wonder what his dark foe, King Nicolas, was up to. Leader of the nefarious warriors known as the Shadowlords, Nicolas ruled Roddington with an iron fist. It was he who placed the potent curse upon the sleepy land that caused all of its inhabitants to forget the existence of magic. Now that Adam had escaped to Fallador, the curse was quickly coming undone. It would not be long, he realized, before the evil king reappeared to destroy the only obstacle to his infinite power.

The figure in the dream haunted him like a shadowy specter. The scene, the narrow corridor, was one he had visited many times during his stay at Reximen Heights. Even the ominous flashes of lighting mirrored the storm outside. Could it be that someone really waited for him? Master Acacius had assured him that danger could not reach him inside of the stronghold, but something still felt out of place.

Taking a deep breath, Adam lowered himself down again and let his head rest upon his warm pillow. Behind closed eyelids, the bright flashes branded his vision. Try as he might, the roaring thunder prevented him from nearing slumber. His mind echoed with the sounds from the dream. The crunching glass alone was enough to give him goosebumps.

Sighing, he sat upright once more and rubbed his eyes. There would be no rest until the perplexing dream was demystified. Adam pulled away the soft, linen covers and shifted his feet over the edge of the bed. A pair of sandals lay lifeless on the floor. Most of the people in Reximen Heights owned a pair of slippers, but not Adam. He found them impractical and absurd. The very thought of being seen in the soft footwear was enough to make him cringe.

Adam slipped his feet into the straps quietly, and bent over to fasten them to his feet. Once they fit snugly, he yawned and rose from the bed. He did not bother to search for a candle, for his keen eyes could operate in complete darkness. This and other special traits he possessed were attributed to his remarkable gift. Adam Crescent was the Razorwolf, a being of great power. Although he was unable to control it, the Razorwolf power saved him many times during his quest to Reximen Heights. All of the instances had been accidents, and he remained conscious for only one episode. Despite the great power, Adam knew that his status as the Razorwolf was precisely why King Nicolas was so keen on destroying him. A being that strong, with acute senses and amazing strength, would be a near-perfect match for the darkest of the Shadowlords.

Slipping through the door was easy business. The hallway outside remained perfectly still. He already knew that everyone planned to shut themselves up in their rooms until the storm had passed. The weather concealed his quiet footsteps as he crept down the walkway to avoid waking the other residents. Both sides of the hall were lined with identical doors, and Adam assumed they could only be dormitories like his own. The corridor bent at a corner, and before it was a wide staircase.

Looking over his shoulder, Adam found that he still traveled alone. With brisk strides, he hurried to the mouth of the stairs. The location of the dream was easily recognizable as the second floor observatory, a place that was set far apart from the rooms. Logically, the observatory was a sound meeting place at this time of night. But just who waited for him?

The question seared within his mind as he reached out to the stone railing and guided himself down below. Descending three floors proved to be an easy task under the cover of the raging storm overhead. Hopefully, no one would be out and about during these turbulent hours, but many a strange character dwelled within these halls. For instance, Adam once heard rumors of a girl whose tears turned to ice when she cried. There were even worse accounts, such as the boy who turned everything he touched into dust. Adam shuddered at the thought of bumping into such a calamity.

As he expected, the second floor landing was left unattended. *The cautions still must be observed*, he thought as he leaned his head out of the archway. The second floor corridor was devoid of any sign of life. Exhaling deeply, he stepped outside and walked briskly into the open, his eyes scanning for the wide double-doors that led to the observatory. The mystery as to why the observatory was on the second floor and not the top eluded Adam, but he shoved the absurdity aside and kept moving.

Suddenly, the sound of creaking wood shattered the sleepy atmosphere. An icy jolt of terror coursed through Adam's spine, and he stopped dead in his tracks. No noise, not even a gasp or a breath, left his lips as he stood rooted to the spot. He listened intently for the sound of footsteps, but none could be heard, not even by his powerful ears. There came a small groan from a nearby room, followed by another creak and snoring. Adam allowed himself a sigh of relief and quickened his step.

After rounding a corner, he spotted the familiar mahogany doors immediately to his left. Pressing his ear to the door, Adam heard the sound of rain collecting on the floor, just like his dream. He silently clutched the handle and eased the door open. A sudden blast of thunder muffled the sound of creaking hinges as Adam quickly slipped inside.

The doors closed of their own accord and sealed him within the vacant observatory. The scene that met his eyes resembled the dream exactly. The large, glass windows lay upon the floor in pieces, probably due to the severe weather. Many stray raindrops found their way into the room, making the floor a slippery mess. Lighting and thunder followed one another in a bizarre cycle.

Adam turned and spotted the other wing, which was filled with a clutter of telescopes and other astronomical objects. He gulped and faced the wreckage once more and placed one foot in front of the other. The way the glass crunched beneath his soles sent a shiver through his entire body. The whole scene reminded him of a ghostly apparition, an eerie encounter with déjà vu. Adam suddenly remembered the figure in his dreams. Looking braver than he actually felt, he marched forward.

He gasped sharply when he spotted the dark stranger walking towards him. Even in real life, the figure seemed airy and spectral. For a moment, Adam considered running back the way he came, but he knew the specter would continue to haunt the dark corners of his mind. Compelled only by his wavering courage, Adam continued towards the stranger.

As the distance between them grew shorter, the thunder and lighting seemed to grew louder, and each terrible roar caused Adam's heart to race even faster. A strong flash of lightning revealed the stranger's face for a split second, but Adam could tell that his visitor was a woman. A mighty blast of thunder echoed across the heavens, and he fell still.

"Who are you?" his voice cracked from disuse.

The woman drew closer to him. "I could ask you the same question."
Her voice was unnaturally smooth.

"You mean you don't already know?"

Even in the shadows, Adam could spot the grin that formed over her lips. "You amuse me. How did you come to find this place?"

Adam paused for a moment. "I had a dream," he finally answered.

The grin disappeared quickly. "As did I. What did you see?"

"I was in this place, and I saw you, only I didn't know anything of what you looked like."

"Indeed. I saw you, too, Razorwolf."

"How did you—" he began.

"My dreams are much more informative than yours. Belle Ismerdle," the woman said when she stood before him. She extended a bony hand, and Adam reluctantly accepted the gesture.

"Adam Crescent."

"You're the new one they've been talking of, aren't you?" she asked.

"I hope not."

"Well, Adam Crescent, if not now, then I fear you will become a subject of numerous discussions sooner than you think."

This ominous statement did not bode well with Adam. "It's the curse, isn't it?"

Belle removed ruby hair from her face. "I know nothing of curses."

"It's not about the curse?" he asked in a tone of surprise.

"Oh, it very well could be, but like you, I am not privy to such information. I can only tell you what I know based on what we have shared."

"The dream. You had it too."

She nodded. "Yes. The people at Reximen Heights have unusual...*powers*, I suppose you might say. Mine is unusual, even for people like us. I share dreams with others. It does not happen frequently."

"How many times has it happened before?"

"Once. My mother. Our dreams coincided one night, not nearly as stormy as this one. One day later, she died."

Neither one of them said anything for a while. Belle stood quietly in reflection as all the color drained from Adam's face.

"How...how did she die?"

Belle looked at him through black eyes. "Not naturally, if that's what you're asking."

He gulped. "Do you think that I'm going to die?"

"It's difficult to say, Razorwolf. Your fate is young. I wouldn't ignore the possibility, but I don't think death is close at your heels. No, a greater danger looms overhead. Of this I am certain."

"How much do you know?"

"Very little. I know who you are, but I can sense powerful forces. They surround you. I suspect you are aware of this."

Adam blinked. "Yes, I've had *suspicions*. How do I avert these forces?"

"I fear it may already be too late. Be careful that you do not become a pawn in this shadowy game. I've told you what I know. Perhaps if you revealed more to me, we could make light of the situation together," Belle advised.

Hesitating for a moment, Adam shuffled his feet. "How do I know that you can be trusted?"

Belle smiled thinly. "I could have easily not shown up tonight."

"Hmmm, fair point."

"So, Razorwolf, are we going to do this or not?"

"Your powers of persuasion could use refining," Adam remarked.

She scoffed in reply.

"Very well. A couple of months ago, I lived in the other land, Roddington. Now, as I understand, neither of the two sisterlands have known of each other's existence. Until now. That is because I have begun to break King Nicolas's horrible curse. I did that by sailing through a rough storm. From there on out, my friends and I went through the Forest of Belliteth, destroyed the bridge over the River of Thanatos, scaled the great mountain, and found ourselves here. As you can see, I've been out and about for quite some time," he explained.

"Rough sounds like a gentler way of putting things, and I guess that explains the curious weather patterns. Your story's a bit patchy, but I've got the gist of things. There's someone out to get you. You and I both know, naturally, that he wants revenge."

"Sounds like his type."

"The question is, how does he exact it?"

"He's tried to kill me in the past," Adam answered.

"And by the looks of it, he hasn't been too successful."

Adam shrugged.

"How powerful would you say this king is?" Belle asked.

"I'd say his powers are severely limited. Every curse has its price," he said, remembering the words of Mustafo.

"Then I'd be willing to bet that he's making arrangements to fix his minor handicap, wouldn't you say?"

"Minor's an understatement."

"Wordplay. It reeks of inexperience. We both know you're here tonight for a reason. The game's afoot. Do you make the first move, or does he?" Belle retorted.

"What would you have me do? I can't even control my own powers, much less manage someone else's."

Belle brought her face uncomfortably close to his. She did not flinch as the rain fell upon her white cheek. "That is no excuse. These forces won't take your ineptitude into consideration. The danger is real, can't you see?"

"I-I-I know there's danger, but look where we are. They wouldn't dare to come here," Adam stammered.

A cold smirk formed on her face. "You think numbers alone will stop them? How foolish."

Adam narrowed his eyes in irritation. "No, we have superior leadership. If anything, Acacius can easily trip up anyone who tries anything."

"Yet even Acacius's power has its limits."

"And mine don't?"

"You have power that many would kill for. Don't underestimate yourself, kid."

"But I can't control it," he insisted.

"Look. An evil has followed you into Fallador, an evil that will twist the very fabric of our world. They're after you. They want nothing with Acacius. They want you, Razorwolf. Only you can end this darkness," she said hotly.

"I need more time!"

"We need lots of things. You can either accept the inevitable and start preparing, or you can sit here and wait for them to find you. Your choice."

Adam balled his hands into fists. "How can I prepare for the unknown?"

"Like I said, you have more power than you realize. You and I, we're not so different. But if you think that a couple of sparks and a transformation is your limit, then you're sorely mistaken. You think this ends with Rowtag? This is only the beginning."

"How do you know about Rowtag?" Adam asked.

Belle grinned darkly. "Our time here has reached its end."

"What if I need to find you again?"

"Do not look for me. You won't find me. I don't normally associate with others. Of course, I hear things now and then, but I keep to myself," Belle said.

"I understand."

CHAPTER ONE

"Good night, Adam Crescent, Razorwolf. I wish you the best of luck in mastering your abilities. Speak of our encounter to no one, unless you wish them to join in your great plight," she warned.

Adam opened his mouth to speak, but she ignored him and turned around quickly. Her heavy black garments dragged along the floor, causing the glass fragments to rattle. When at last she rounded the corner and disappeared from view, Adam became aware that he had not yet moved. With haste, he turned and hurried through the double doors, and through the corridor. He heard the familiar snoring as he dashed towards the tall archway at the end of the hall. The trip up the stairs was a blur, all three floors, and before he knew it, he was back inside of his room safe and sound, yet wet.

Regardless of how soaked he was, Adam jumped into his bed and pulled the covers up to his nose. The lighting and the thunder were as aggressive as before, but somehow the heavenly forces did not appear as dangerous. The greater threat of impending doom made even the brightest lightning bolt seem tame.

Belle's words haunted him. He had already seen so much, especially the terrible powers of the Shadowlords. After barely surviving a murder attempt, what could be even more terrible? The thought of King Nicolas's gaunt face was enough to make his insides churn with fear.

He could not afford to keep this secret completely hidden. Acacius, he decided, would be the best person to inform. He could help Adam gain mastery over his powers before the oncoming threat of the Shadowlords tainted Fallador. Even though Belle had instructed him otherwise, Adam had full confidence in Acacius's skill as protector. For the first time, he also planned to keep this from his two best friends, Tyrule and Leira.

Sleep did not come easy. Adam spent the remainder of the evening tossing and turning as the thunder droned on and on. Words, fragments, dreams, and memories floated around in his mind, making him restless. At last, when he did finally settle in a cozy slumber, the forces of nature began to soften. The storm was not nearly as fierce as it had been in earlier hours.

At last, he finally nodded off to sleep. No one else stirred in the great halls of Reximen Heights, but there certainly were darker forces at work in other parts. For now, he slept quietly and innocently, just like any other teenager would. Unfortunately, Adam was no ordinary teenager. The very fact that he lived posed great dangers, dangers that no one could ever hope to imagine, least of all a teenage boy. On that night, a terrible darkness was rising. It remained a matter of time until Adam Crescent would be forced to take a stand against one of the deadliest forces ever to threaten the world, or both worlds, for that matter. For now, he continued his soft slumber, unaware of his powerful enemies and the forces they had yet to unleash.

ABOUT THE AUTHOR

Before Adam Crescent, there was Adrian Eves. Born in the sprightly town of Norfolk, Virginia, Adrian learned to love stories at a very early age. At the age of seventeen, he penned the first pages of the book you now hold in your hands. Today, Adrian attends Auburn University, where he eagerly anticipates whatever the future holds in store for him and the colorful worlds he has created.

ABOUT THE ARTIST

Lisa Johnston Hancock's artistic practice is informed by observations of the world around her, more specifically, as humans, our ever-changing connection to the natural world and our need to control it. Hancock is inspired by art history including the 19th century Hudson River School of Painters, who constructed environments from sketches and memory where human beings and nature coexisted peacefully. Like the Hudson River School of Painters, her compositions are layers of multiple scenes and memory, incorporating techniques of collage and expressionism while appealing to the senses through texture, color and light. Hancock has participated in numerous group and solo shows on the southeast coast, including Generation X at the Mobile Museum of Art in Mobile, AL. Hancock lives and works as an Adjunct Professor in Richmond, VA.

ACKNOWLEDGEMENTS

The path I've taken to get this first book out has been a great adventure, and it has changed my life forever. Like Adam, I've been fortunate enough to have several friends join me along the path, and to let them go unmentioned would be a terrible injustice.

Firstly, I would like to express my thanks to my amazing family,

Mama, Papa, Paulette, David, Bradley, and Macy. Even before this book became a reality, you helped me realize that I can be someone who could set a good example, and for this, I am extremely thankful.

Kendal and Casey, you two have been listening patiently to my stories since day one, and I hope this one lives up to your expectations. And BeBe, I hope this one lives up to your honorable expectations as well.

I owe a special thanks to a select group of people for editing a wide assortment of drafts. Abbe, Caroline, and J.T., I hope you know just how thankful I am for your advice. I'm sure the readership would too if they knew the truth about certain tumbling individuals that shall remain unnamed for the sake of inside jokes.

As much as I'd really like to name each and every one of you, I'd have to write another book to fit in the names of the wonderful McGill-Toolen family. Rest assured that each and every one of you hold a special place in my heart, and I could never forget you.

And where would I be without the gang at Camp Beckwith? You've all been great friends to me, and you've helped me in so many ways. For that, I will always be thankful.

We all know it would come sooner or later, but I just have to extend a mighty *War Eagle!* to my friends and family here at Auburn University. If you root for another team, no hard feelings.

And speaking of college, some adjustments can be hard. Luckily, mine weren't because I had great friends there for me. Trent, Tyler, Wesley, Zacc, Patrick, Ashley, Josh, Mason, Kevin, Cole, Alex, Courtney, Alexann, Shelby, Paulina, Melrose, Sarah, Jordan, Katie, and Blake, this one's for you!

To Benjamin, Joseph, the Pelhams, the Dekles, and the Eves: know that I remembered each and every one of you during the creation of this tale. Just in case you were wondering, some of Adam's powers were inspired by the Lightning Room!

To the real Nick, you are by far a better hero than a villain. And Jeriel, you've been just amazing.

And hey Mary! We did it!

And last but not least, thank you, friend, for picking up this
book and giving magic a chance.